DOOMSDAY: Apocalypse

The Doomsday Series

Book One

by

Bobby Akart

Copyright Information

Other Works by Amazon Top 100 Author Bobby Akart

The Doomsday Series
Apocalypse
Haven

The Yellowstone Series
Hellfire
Inferno
Fallout
Survival

The Lone Star Series
Axis of Evil
Beyond Borders
Lines in the Sand
Texas Strong
Fifth Column
Suicide Six

The Pandemic Series
Beginnings
The Innocents
Level 6
Quietus

The Blackout Series

36 Hours

Zero Hour

Turning Point

Shiloh Ranch

Hornet's Nest

Devil's Homecoming

The Boston Brahmin Series

The Loyal Nine

Cyber Attack

Martial Law

False Flag

The Mechanics

Choose Freedom

Patriot's Farewell

Seeds of Liberty (Companion Guide)

The Prepping for Tomorrow Series

Cyber Warfare

EMP: Electromagnetic Pulse

Economic Collapse

DEDICATIONS

For many years, I have lived by the following premise:

*Because you never know when the day before
is the day before, prepare for tomorrow.*

My friends, I study and write about the threats we face, not only to both entertain and inform you, but because I am constantly learning how to prepare for the benefit of my family as well. There is nothing more important on this planet than my darling wife, Dani, and our two girls, Bullie and Boom. One day, Doomsday will come, and I'll be damned if I'm gonna let it stand in the way of our life together.

The Doomsday series is dedicated to the love and support of my family. I will always protect you from anything that threatens us.

ACKNOWLEDGEMENTS

Writing a book that is both informative and entertaining requires a tremendous team effort. Writing is the easy part. For their efforts in making the Doomsday series a reality, I would like to thank Hristo Argirov Kovatliev for his incredible cover art, Pauline Nolet for her editorial prowess, Stef Mcdaid for making this manuscript decipherable in so many formats, Chris Abernathy for his memorable performance in narrating this novel, and the Team—Denise, Joe, Jim, and Shirley—whose advice, friendship and attention to detail is priceless.

In addition, my loyal readers who interact with me on social media know that Dani and I have been fans of the television reality show, Big Brother, since it began broadcasting on CBS in the summer of 2000. The program was one of the greatest social experiments ever imagined. Each season, more than a dozen contestants compete for a half-million-dollar cash prize.

During the months-long airing of the program, the houseguests are isolated from the outside world, but we, the viewers, get to watch their every move via more than a hundred cameras and microphones. The opportunity to study how people interact under these unusual stressful circumstances has allowed me to create diverse and interesting characters for you, dear readers.

Over the years, we've been fortunate to meet several of the past Big Brother contestants and this year, for the second time (the first being our friend, Judd Daugherty, who was a doctor in The Boston Brahmin series), I've actually written four of them into the characters through the use of their first name and unique character attributes.

During the airing of season twenty during the summer of 2018, early on in the show, an alliance formed between a group of six who controlled the game from start-to-finish. You can imagine the high-fives Dani and I exchanged when they named their alliance—*Level 6*, the name as the title of book three in my *Pandemic Series* released in the summer of 2017.

To season twenty winner, Kaycee Clark; our favorite *showmance* of all time, Angela Rummans and Tyler Crispen; and to one of the funniest, most real people I've ever seen on television, "JC" Mounduix—thank you for inspiring the Rankin family in the Doomsday series!

Thank you all!
Choose Freedom and Godspeed, Patriots!

ABOUT THE AUTHOR

Bobby Akart

Author Bobby Akart has been ranked by Amazon as #55 in its Top 100 list of most popular, bestselling authors. He achieved #2 bestselling Horror Author, #2 bestselling Science Fiction Author, #3 bestselling Religion & Spirituality Author, #7 bestselling Historical Author and #8 bestselling Action & Adventure Author.

He has written over twenty international bestsellers, in nearly fifty fiction and nonfiction genres, including the chart-busting Yellowstone series, the reader-favorite Lone Star series, the critically acclaimed Boston Brahmin series, the bestselling Blackout series, the frighteningly realistic Pandemic series, his highly cited nonfiction Prepping for Tomorrow series, and his latest project—the Doomsday series, seen by many as the horrifying future of our nation if we can't find a way to come together.

His novel *Yellowstone: Fallout* reached #50 on the Amazon bestsellers list and earned him two Kindle All-Star awards for most pages read in a month and most pages read as an author.

Bobby has provided his readers a diverse range of topics that are both informative and entertaining. His attention to detail and impeccable research has allowed him to capture the imaginations of his readers through his fictional works and bring them valuable knowledge through his nonfiction books.

SIGN UP for Bobby Akart's mailing list to receive special offers, bonus content, and you'll be the first to receive news about new releases in the Doomsday series.

VISIT Amazon.com/BobbyAkart, a dedicated feature page created by Amazon for his work, to view more information on his thriller fiction novels and post-apocalyptic book series, as well as his nonfiction Prepping for Tomorrow series. Visit Bobby Akart's website for informative blog entries on preparedness, writing, and a behind-the-scenes look into his novels.

BobbyAkart.com

Author's Introduction to the Doomsday Series

November 8, 2018
Are we on the brink of destroying ourselves?

Some argue that our nation is deeply divided, with each side condemning the other as the enemy of America. By way of example, one can point to the events leading up to the Civil War in the latter part of the 1850s, right up until the first cannon fire rained upon Fort Sumter in Charleston, South Carolina. It's happened before, and it could happen again.

The war of words has intensified over the last several decades, and now deranged people on the fringe of society have taken matters into their own hands. Ranging from pipe bomb packages mailed to political leaders and supporters, to a gunman shooting congressmen at a softball practice, words are being replaced with deadly, violent acts.

To be sure, we've experienced violence and intense social strife in this country as a result of political differences. The Civil War was one example. The assassination of Martin Luther King, Jr., followed by the raging street battles over civil rights and the Vietnam War, is another.

This moment in America's history feels worse because we are growing much more divisive. Our shared values are being forgotten and a breakdown is occurring between us and our government, and between us and the office of the presidency.

Our ability to find common ground is gradually disappearing. We shout at the television or quit watching altogether. Social media has become anything but *social*. We unfollow friends or write things in a post that we'd never dream of saying to someone's face.

Friends and family avoid one another at gatherings because they fear political discussions will result in an uncomfortable, even hostile, exchange. Many in our nation no longer look at their fellow Americans as being from a different race or religion, but rather, as supporting one political party or another.

This is where America is today, and it is far different from the months leading up to the Civil War. Liberal historians label the conflict as a battle over slavery, while conservative historians tend to argue the issue was over state's rights. At the time, the only thing agreed upon was the field of battle—farms and open country from Pennsylvania to Georgia.

Today, there are many battle fronts. Media—news, entertainment, and social, is a major battlefield. The halls of Congress and within the inner workings of governments at all levels, is another. Between Americans based upon class warfare, cultural differences, and race-religion-gender, pervades every aspect of our lives.

Make no mistake, on both sides of the political spectrum, a new generation of leaders has emerged who've made fueling our divisions their political modus operandi. I remember the bipartisan efforts of Ronald Reagan and Tip O'Neill in the eighties. Also, Bill Clinton and Newt Gingrich in the mid-nineties. The turn of the century hasn't provided us the types of bipartisan working relationships that those leaders of the recent past have generated.

So, here we are at each other's throats. What stops the political rancor and division? The answer to this question results in even more partisan arguments and finger-pointing.

Which leads me to the purpose of the Doomsday series. The term doomsday evokes images of the end of times, the day the world ends, or a time when something terrible or dangerous will happen. Sounds dramatic, but everything is relative.

I've repeated this often, and I will again for those who haven't heard it.

All empires collapse eventually. Their reign ends when they are either defeated by a larger and more powerful enemy, or when their financing runs out. America will be no exception.

Now, couple this theory with the words often attributed to President Abraham Lincoln in an 1838 speech interpreted as follows:

America will never be destroyed from the outside. If we falter and lose our freedoms, it will be because we destroyed ourselves.

The Doomsday series depicts an America hell-bent upon destroying itself. It is a dystopian look at what will happen if we don't find a way to deescalate the attacks upon one another. Both sides will shoulder the blame for what will happen when the war of words becomes increasingly more violent to the point where one side brings out the *big guns.*

That's when an ideological battle will result in bloodshed of innocent Americans caught in the crossfire. Truly, for the future of our nation, doomsday would be upon us.

Thank you for reading with an open mind and not through the lens of political glasses. I hope we can come together for the sake of our families and our nation. God bless America.

EPIGRAPH

To argue with a person who renounced the use of reason
is like administering medicine to the dead.
~ Thomas Paine
*****

I never considered a difference in opinion in politics, religion,
or philosophy as cause for withdrawing from a friend.
~ Thomas Jefferson
*****

"I'm right!" "No, you're not, I am right!"
"Yes, I am!" "You're stupid."
"No, I'm not, take it back!" "I won't, you stupid idiot!"
"Shut up!" "No, you shut up!"
~ Two seven-year-old friends on a school playground
*****

America will never be destroyed from the outside. If we falter
and lose our freedoms, it will be because we destroyed ourselves.
~ paraphrased from a speech by Abraham Lincoln, 1838
*****

All empires collapse eventually.
Their reign ends when they are either defeated
by a larger and more powerful enemy,
or when their financing runs out.
America will be no exception.
~ Author Bobby Akart, 2015

PROLOGUE

Monocacy Farm
South of Frederick, Maryland
October 31

Any two of them rarely met in person, and only on one other occasion had they congregated as a group. Their backgrounds and ideologies were as diverse as the country in which they lived. Matters of race, gender, religion, and culture were irrelevant. Commonality of purpose was tantamount in their minds.

If the meeting were known to the public, one day it would be deemed historic. The gathering, located at a hundred-acre farm twenty miles south of Frederick, Maryland, was not called hastily. Hushed conversations and encrypted messages, starting several months earlier, preceded the clandestine meeting.

As fall set upon the Northeastern United States and the first Tuesday in November rapidly approached, the men and women began to feel a sense of urgency. The whispers grew louder—*a meeting must be convened posthaste*. October 31 was agreed upon.

The location sitting on the banks of the Monocacy River was a given, especially in light of its historic significance. One by one, they arrived at the mansion, a beautiful antebellum structure that had been in their host's family for generations dating back to its construction in the early nineteenth century. Sitting nearly a mile off the road, the stately home and adjacent barns were enveloped with sugar maple trees, whose leaves had mostly changed to golden yellow and brown. Interspersed around the property to maintain its privacy were enormous eastern hemlocks that managed to avoid a plague caused by the infestation of the hemlock woolly aphid, a blight upon the beautiful tree, which resulted in its slow deterioration and death.

The heir to the farm, who concealed his ownership through a blind trust, stood on the front porch despite the cool autumn air, and greeted his guests one by one. Although it was not intended to be a festive occasion, the attendees took the rare opportunity to socialize with their comrades by enjoying hors d'oeuvres and cocktails.

The staff who waited upon them were well trained and sworn to secrecy by more than a nondisclosure agreement that had become a worthless legal document in this day and age. No, they feared for their lives, for they presumed the tentacles of their powerful employer reached far and wide.

For the next several hours until midnight approached, they commiserated and debated. A consensus was reached, and then arguments began about things like moral high ground and sacrifice.

A plan was set forth to advance their goals, and countermeasures were adopted in anticipation of their enemies' reaction. All of them envisioned a high-stakes game of chess that history would prove to be unparalleled in the modern age of geopolitical stratagems and tactics.

As the evening drew to a conclusion, their host proposed a toast.

"I was once confronted by a man of great political power who stood in my face and said, 'You're not strong enough to withstand the storm.' Today, my friends, drawing from our collective strength and love of country, we have taken our stand. I would say to those who will condemn our actions—*we are the storm!*"

"Hear, hear!"

The group raised their glasses and drained them. Then their acknowledged leader stepped forward into the spacious living room that had hosted gala affairs and events over the centuries. He positioned himself in front of a massive stone fireplace containing a blaze that shot flames well up the chimney flue.

Before he spoke, he glanced up at the emblem carved out of granite that was inset into the stone. The skull and crossbones were fitting for their Halloween gathering. The numbers three-two-two carved beneath, were shrouded in mystery just as those who attended on this cold evening.

He slowly turned and looked around the room. "Messenger, are you ready?"

"I am," replied a younger, bespectacled man, who apologetically pushed his way through the group.

Their host addressed him authoritatively. "Read it before it's disseminated to your usual platforms."

The Messenger already had the screen open on the secured, data-encrypted application designed by him for this specific purpose. As the Messenger, he was responsible for communicating with other like-minded individuals around the world. He pressed the enter button, and the message was sent.

Their demeanor solemn, the guests quietly exited and returned to their homes and families, the weight of their decision hanging over them. Their host allowed himself another drink and poured two fingers of Glenlivet single malt scotch whisky into a glass. He dismissed the staff and walked out on the veranda overlooking the Monocacy River to be alone with his thoughts.

He gazed up at the full moon, that had taken on a somewhat bluish tint, befitting its significance. Historically, the first full moon of autumn, known as the harvest moon, allowed farmers extra time in their fields to bring in their crops. That had occurred earlier in the month of October.

On this Halloween night, this second full moon of the month, much to the consternation of soothsayers and zealots, represented the proverbial blue moon, the second full moon in a calendar month, which rarely occurred. The unusual astronomical event was coupled with the second moon of that October being designated the hunter's moon, so named as the next full moon following the harvest moon. The confluence of the three designations in the same month caused the cable news media outlets to take notice.

Throughout the month of October, psychics, clairvoyants, and prophecy pundits filled the airwaves. The media countered with scientists and historians, who roundly mocked the prognosticators as crackpots. Even so, many said the rare occurrence of the harvest, hunter's and blue moons occurring in the same month portended doom and that the apocalypse was upon us all.

They were right.

As if to confirm that the evening's events were real, he pulled out his phone and read the message appearing on the screen.

On the day of the feast of Saint Sylvester,
Tear down locked,
Green light burning.
Love, MM

And so it begins …

4

NEW YEAR'S EVE

CHAPTER 1

One World Trade Center
New York City

It was cold in Manhattan as darkness overtook the city on New Year's Eve. A light snow had just begun to fall on the concrete jungle, which spread out one hundred four stories below them. The rebuilt One World Trade Center boasted the tallest building in the western hemisphere and the sixth tallest on the planet. It was America's way of giving the middle finger to the terrorists who had attacked the nation on 9/11. On this evening, a terror of a different nature was going to be unleashed on the world's superpower. One that would lead to an upheaval not seen in more than a century.

The SkyPod elevators carried them one hundred two stories to the One World Observatory in just forty-seven seconds. It was a remarkable ride to the top of the building that transformed the landscape with a herculean endeavor. Also known as Freedom Tower, the new World Trade Center stood proud at the heart of a forest of skyscrapers dotting the center of the world's financial markets.

The view from the observatory was nothing short of spectacular. As the snow fluttered from the blue-black winter sky, the visitors to the One World Observatory didn't seem to mind their view being obscured slightly. Many pressed their faces as close to the glass as they could, longing to reach out and touch the frozen snowflakes as they fluttered past.

The excitement of New Year's Eve added to the jovial mood of the visitors. This was the legendary city in which the ball drops in Times Square, to the delight of millions in attendance and many millions more watching around the world. On New Year's Eve, New York was more than a place of power for the world's financial elite, it was a preeminent city against which all others were measured.

Admired by most, envied and despised by others for what it represents, the Big Apple was more than a collection of tall buildings and financial brokerage houses. It was a cosmopolitan gathering of cultures, races, and ideologies—constantly in motion.

New York City was alive as people made their way to elaborate dinners or to find a place in New York's Times Square, four miles from the World Trade Center, in Midtown. From the observation deck, visitors could feel the surging energy throughout the island. Multitudes of office towers and apartment buildings were lit up as parties were in full swing, or revelers were readying themselves for the big night.

Many of the visitors focused on the beautiful panoramic views. They looked intently through the telescopes located around the perimeter of the observation deck. Their focus was on what was happening outside and not the two men who leaned quietly against a wall on the inside.

A gaunt-faced man in his fifties wore a black woolen trench coat with the collar turned up around his neck. His old, wire-rimmed spectacles contained lenses that made his eyes look larger than life. His flat cap hat resembled those worn by newsboys in the 1940s, those young street-corner newspaper sellers who helped their families make ends meet during World War II. The man was a throwback to the last century in more ways than one.

His associate, a much younger man built like the Incredible Hulk, was more out of place than the older man. Unlike his partner and the majority of the visitors, he wore khaki pants and a short-sleeve, black polo shirt. His chest and arms bulged, threatening to tear the shirt apart at the seams. The skull and bones tattoo on his right bicep seemed to come alive as his muscles flexed. The number 322 underneath fluttered like a flag atop a ship's mast.

The older man made casual conversation, not attempting to hide his native Irish accent. "I watched them tear it down, only to build it back up again, stronger and more powerful than before."

"Yeah," the young man replied. To the casual observer who might be eavesdropping on the conversation, his method of speaking didn't fit his stereotype. He didn't grunt his words or puff out his chest. His words were carefully chosen and articulate, befitting his Yale education. "It's a testament to American ingenuity and perseverance. When the new design was revealed, the architects proudly stated the structure would top off at one thousand seven hundred seventy-six feet—1776. Ironic, wouldn't you agree?"

"It is," replied the older man, pausing as a strong gust of snow enveloped the windows, to the delight of the tower's visitors. He removed a gloved hand from his coat and waved it toward the windows. "I assume you've checked the weather for this precipitation. Will it alter your plans?"

"The moisture is heading our way from the south, while the jet stream is pulling down cold air from Canada. There's already snow predicted from Washington to Philly to Boston for this evening. We'll get our share, but it doesn't materially impact our operation. The wind is a factor, but we've made the necessary adjustments in our calculations."

"Good." The man, who'd made a career out of killing, allowed himself a slight smile. He enjoyed the exhilaration of battle. As a young warrior, the dangers associated with combat never frightened him. He'd never admitted to anyone that war aroused him more than any woman had. The closer he got to taking another's life, the more enthralled he became.

In just a few hours, he would launch the biggest and most complex attack on the United States of America since 9/11, or even Pearl Harbor. It would not necessarily be the most violent, but it would certainly be the most memorable in American history, ranking alongside the *shot heard around the world* at Lexington and Concord, or the firing of cannon upon Fort Sumter in South Carolina.

A young boy interrupted his thoughts as he walked by with his mother. He pulled on her sweater sleeve and looked up to her. "Mom, is a storm coming?"

The older man managed a chuckle as he mumbled to himself, "It sure is, young man. A storm is coming."

Chapter 2

The Florida Panhandle

The incessant ringing of the phone had awakened him from a deep sleep that New Year's Eve. He'd had a crazy night of partying and carousing with other members of his team, blowing off steam from an operation they'd just completed in Venezuela. The handlers who employed him had plans for the Caracas regime, which had driven a once-thriving economy into the ditch. After their successes, the people of Venezuela would have a new slate of candidates to choose from while they mourned the old set.

After he cleared the fog from his brain, he digested the orders he'd been given. On the surface it was a simple op. Two-man team, plus one man with advanced training in a specific weapon to be deployed. He recalled the conversation with his handler.

"I'm not going to repeat this for you, so pay attention. You're tasked with delivering the shooter from point A to point B. Nothing else. Once the mission is accomplished, you extract and leave no trace behind."

It had sounded simple enough, although a thousand questions swirled in the operator's head such as when, where, who, and how. He'd learned years ago the *why* didn't matter. Somebody smarter than he was made those decisions. Besides, it didn't matter. He just wanted to get paid.

He'd also learned to check his emotions and morals at the door. When you worked in the dark shadows of the world's geopolitical underbelly, everybody was a target. Nothing, and no one, was immune from their manipulation of world events.

The four-hour drive from Atlanta to a desolate farm located in Florida's Panhandle was uneventful. He tuned in to the Liberty Bowl game being played in Nashville between Tennessee and Oklahoma State. He'd become a fan of American football, although it didn't compare to his beloved soccer matches. It was the emotion of the fans that first grabbed his attention.

The Vols were trying to recover from years of substandard play, while Oklahoma State was just coming off a probation by the NCAA for introducing potential recruits to *hostesses*, as they were called. When the sex-filled parties leaked to the media, *Sports Illustrated* in particular, the Cowboys' football program was almost given the death penalty.

The operator had a real name, but few people knew it. His travel documents and government identification would change periodically, printed to suit the clandestine mission. There were only a handful of operatives like him stationed on American soil. They were ghosts, living a secretive life, and only interacted with one another.

He followed the coordinates given to him on his GPS device. He was located in the middle of the Apalachicola National Forest outside a small town called Carrabelle. Dusk was approaching as he drove down a single-lane gravel and dirt road through stands of pine trees mixed with saw palmettos.

He checked the GPS again to be sure, and then suddenly a clearing appeared in front of him. He was surprised to see an Airbus UH-72 Lakota helicopter sitting alone. The chopper had been painted black, a divergence from its typical olive drab. In the past, the UH-72 was a light-utility helicopter utilized by Army National Guard units. As the U.S. Army moved toward the Black Hawk fleet, the UH-72s were sold to state and local law enforcement for police activities. The complete lack of markings told him this was privately operated, most likely by one shell corporation that was owned by another and so on. That was the modus operandi in his world.

He parked his car and walked toward several vehicles and a box truck, where he was greeted by another member of his team whom he'd worked with in Venezuela.

"Long time no see, mate," his partner said with a smile. The two didn't shake hands, a slight to the customary greeting in America.

"We could've come from Atlanta together," the operator lamented.

"Nah, mate. I'd already left for Miami when the call came through. I've been here for hours."

A third man, small and unremarkable, was seated inside the helicopter. Joining him in the cargo compartment was a long black case, the kind that was designed to carry a MANPADS. Man-portable air-defense systems were shoulder-launched surface-to-air missiles designed specifically to take down helicopters and punch holes in the sides of ships. The operator had used them in the Balkans years ago and was impressed with their effectiveness.

He turned to the member of his team who had proven to be a consistent and reliable partner on their past missions together. "Any idea of where we're going?"

"Don't be a drongo, mate. They haven't said a word," he replied in his thick Australian accent. He pointed in the direction of two men dressed in black pants, dark jackets, and navy-blue shirts. If they had not been so mysterious in their appearance, they might have been laughable. "And the men in black over there have been real tight-lipped. You wanna give 'em a try?"

He nodded and replied, "Sure. Who's the guy in the chopper? Is he wearing a wet suit?"

"No idea. He's cool as the proverbial cucumber. I tried to make conversation with him. You know, like, *what's in the case?* I got nothing out of him. And yeah, he's in a wet suit."

"I hate this crap," the operator mumbled as he pulled his shoulders back, hoping to relieve some of the stress from the drive.

Two pilots emerged from behind the chopper, with their helmets attached as if they were ready to go. He gave the pilots the once-over and then looked past them to a group of four mechanics who emerged from the back of the box truck. They were carrying a Zodiac MilPro rigid inflatable boat. A fifth man carried two duffle bags with black combat vests and headed toward him.

One of the men in black approached. "Gentlemen, we'll need you to get out of your civvies and into the wet suits. The combat vests will be supplemented with weapons inside the chopper. They've been cleaned, checked, and are ready for you."

"Got it, but we like to check our own weapons before we go into an op."

"You'll have an hour while in flight." The handler turned to walk away.

"Wait, what's with the Zodiac?"

Without turning, the man responded, "It's going to be strapped under the chopper."

The operator paused as the men approached the helicopter with the inflatable. The military-spec boat measured approximately sixteen feet long and six feet wide. From his experience, with the fuel bladders and the outboard motor in place, the weight exceeded four hundred pounds. They slowly positioned the Zodiac behind the helicopter and spoke briefly with the pilot.

"Hey," the operator shouted to the handler, "I'm not riding outside the chopper. You can forget that!"

The handler ignored him and approached the helicopter to give instructions to his team. As he did, the operator and his partner changed into their gear. Within minutes, they were loaded into the chopper next to the third member of their squad and the mysterious case.

The pilot joined them and gave them more information on their task. While the operators reviewed the packet of materials, the pilot explained the transportation apparatus.

"Your Zodiac will be strapped to the skids of the chopper using these harnesses," he began, showing them the heavy-duty straps similar to those utilized on a flatbed trailer of an eighteen-wheeler. "When we reach the drop-off point, there is a single latch release that will be located in the center of this compartment. Then you'll all fast-rope into the boat." *Fast-roping* was a technique using a thick rope to rappel from a helicopter onto the ground or, in this case, into a boat.

The operator turned to the smallish man, who hovered over the large case like it was filled with gold. "What about speechless here? I take it he's coming with us. What's in the case?"

"It is none of your affair," he responded with a French accent.

"Whoa, he does talk!" the operator exclaimed. "And he's a Frenchy. This is a true international op. Now, you wanna tell me what the hell is going on?"

CHAPTER 3

Undisclosed Military Installation

Human nature hadn't changed since the time of Cain and Abel. The act of war, however, had. In the minds of the world's military powers, drone warfare was considered to be *proximate war*. The notion was related to the concept of *proximate justice*. Proximate justice theory posited that something was better than nothing. It allowed us to make peace with the realization that some justice meted out was better than none at all. It allowed a victim's family to accept a life sentence as opposed to the death penalty for their loved one's murder.

Proximate war allowed those who wanted to inflict true bodily harm and death upon their adversaries to find some satisfaction in a lesser, albeit subdued, victory. Drone warfare accomplished that purpose. Modern military leaders fashioned themselves to be moral warriors. After World War II, after the atomic bombs were dropped onto Nagasaki and Hiroshima in Japan, the world collectively gasped, then paused to view the end result.

To be sure, the attacks hastened the end of the massive global war, but the civilian death toll was enormous. In America, after the dust settled and the country resumed its routines, conversations began among its leaders as to whether the use of atomic weaponry was overkill, pardon the tone-death pun. Talks began with the U.S.S.R. and agreements were reached. The concept of *mutually assured destruction* was born.

Those accords did not, however, prevent the world's preeminent military powers, which now included China, to develop modern, advanced weaponry capable of annihilating one another. Further, with new technologies, weapons of mass destruction were created that didn't necessarily take lives upon detonation like the atomic bombs of 1945, but the human toll was catastrophic nonetheless.

The rampant nuclear testing of the 1950s opened scientists' eyes to a byproduct, for lack of a better term, that, if harnessed, could be a valuable weapon in battle. An electromagnetic pulse, or EMP, was a burst of electromagnetic energy that occurred naturally during intense geomagnetic storms from the sun. As the atomic testing showed, the same result could be generated by both a nuclear detonation or a nonnuclear EMP weapon using nuclear technology.

The highly charged gamma rays, a form of light generated by the EMP weapon, slammed into air molecules, displacing electrons. Upon impact, the negatively charged particles circulated through the atmosphere at nearly ninety percent of the speed of light. It only took a fraction of a microsecond for the targeted area to be filled with the surge of energy.

The higher the detonation occurred above the earth's surface, the broader the area of impact. A low-altitude EMP could be more targeted, specifically intended to impact a smaller area.

The electromagnetic pulse could have a variety of devastating effects depending upon the type of weapon used. Today's modern electronics and computer devices are made up of tiny circuits that cannot withstand the powerful burst of energy. The power grid, phone and internet lines, and anything interconnected to electronics melts under the abrupt pulse of energy.

The United States, China, and Russia led the way in developing EMP technology. Once the capability was realized, then different and varied delivery mechanisms were sought. A nuclear-tipped intercontinental ballistic missile was the first, most logical means of delivery.

In the past decade, great advances had been made that allowed EMPs to be deployed by satellite, via directed energy weapons similar to ray guns in popular culture, and now launched from underwater, submarine drones.

Russia, with its Kanyon project, led the way, quickly followed by the United States and China. Soon, all three nations sought to expand their underwater drone capabilities, controlled from remote destinations around the world that could launch nuclear missiles of all sizes and payloads.

With the advent of drone warfare, nation-states could wage wars in places far from their own borders, all designed toward securing an advantage in small-scale skirmishes and counterinsurgency fights abroad.

In the U.S., the Pentagon refers to it as drone warfare. In the U.K., military strategists call it remote warfare, which includes both drones and cyber attacks. This was considered the means to wage wars of the future. For military leaders, it was an opportunity to accomplish a strategic military objective with no loss of life to their troops. Further, it meant less public oversight and internal analysis as to whether the missions themselves were achieving their objectives. Nothing raises public scrutiny more than body bags arriving at Dover Air Force Base, especially if the mission was deemed a failure.

As a result of this lack of oversight, in the U.S. and abroad, only those with direct involvement and knowledge of the operations would report back to the people who ordered the mission. In essence, a feedback loop of secrecy could be created, detached from criticism and accountability. The lack of transparency made independent verification of a nation's actions near impossible.

Plausible deniability ruled the day in a proximate war using drones.

CHAPTER 4

CityCenter Apartments
Atlanta, Georgia

"All right, gentlemen, let's make one thing real clear about this op." The former captain in the British Office for Security and Counter-Terrorism looked into the eyes of his three comrades as they prepared their gear. "We get in, place and activate our respective devices, and get out. There'll be no radio contact, so we're on our own inside. If you're caught, you're on your own too. We've all learned that the words *plausible deniability* have meaning, correct?"

"Yeah, roger that," mumbled one of the two Americans on his team.

"Use the commotion and mayhem to make your exits when the time comes. Don't leave early, because you're sure to be caught on camera. The rally point will be at Cleopas Johnson Park to our south. Avoid walking down Northside Drive; use the neighborhood side streets instead. The feds will react quickly once the call is made to the stadium offices, and the place will be crawling once we implement the plan."

"Chief, we've never worked with our man on the inside. I don't like trusting a mission to an unknown quantity," commented the other American operative.

"Yeah, I hate surprises, too." The first man echoed his concern.

"Our inside man is rock solid. He's been employed here for a couple of years and is fully aware of the ramifications of the mission. Now, remember, we have a limited window of opportunity to be at the Magnum Street loading dock. Your uniforms and credentials are in these duffle bags. They're designed to fit easily over your existing clothing, so you can discard them once inside."

After opening his assigned duffle, the Australian member of the team spoke up for the first time. "Very official looking. They've got the Mercedes logo on the sleeves and maintenance stitched across the pocket."

The team leader nodded. "They're actual uniforms. Like your credentials, they'll give us the cover we need to get in. Once you're in position, drop the uniforms and mind your watches. We've got this perfectly choreographed, so don't lose track of time."

The team leader checked his own watch. They still had over an hour to make the short walk from the CityCenter Apartments on the west side of Mercedes-Benz Stadium to the loading dock. The men would walk in pairs as if they were co-workers reporting for duty at the concert.

He looked at his hardened operatives, who'd performed so well under pressure for him in all corners of the planet. "We've got plenty of time. Any questions?"

One of the Americans spoke up. "Yeah, chief, I've got one. Listen, I'm a country music guy, and I've got no use for Beyoncé or her husband, Jay-Z. So don't get me wrong, I'd take issue with us screwin' up a Kenny Chesney concert. Why do you think this is the target?"

The leader walked away and ran his fingers through his hair. He was only able to speculate, but based upon the text message instructions he'd received, and the source, he suspected he knew the reason.

"Listen, you guys know the drill. It's like your old Budweiser commercial—*why ask why?* Our employers pay us well. They give us the latest in high-tech gear. In fact, it's stuff Her Majesty's Armed Forces know nothing about."

One of the American men began to chuckle. "I bet the chi-comms know all about it. Those hackers have all of our secrets."

"Well, maybe so," the team leader continued. "Regardless, I wasn't provided a reason, and anything else is speculation on my part."

The American shrugged and appeared indifferent. "I'm just curious, that's all. Regardless of the motivation, it's gonna fit a pattern of concert attacks in recent years. They'll be chasing their tails, pointing the fingers of blame."

The Australian spoke up. "You're right on that, mate. They never figured out the reasoning behind the Mandalay Bar shooting in Vegas. The Rascal Flatts concert in Indy was evacuated due to an anonymous security threat."

The Brit added, "And in Manchester, the Ariana Grande concert suicide bomber was identified as a bloody Islamist. For our purposes, there will be no discernible reason for the attack, so it can't be tied to us or our employer."

The men sat in silence for a moment as they contemplated his words. Then one of the Americans asked, "And do you have any idea who our employer is on this job?"

"I do, and no, I won't tell you. Trust me, you don't want to know."

The men shrugged and went about their preparations. They studied a printed map of the arena and confirmed their assignments. After a final sweep of the apartment that had been rented for them a month earlier, they gathered any trace of their personal effects and made their way through the parking lot of the apartment complex, systematically dropping trash bags of clothing, leftover food, and the map of the stadium into the dumpsters. Despite it being the New Year's holiday, it was a Thursday night, and the waste management trucks would be through to empty the dumpsters around ten o'clock. Any trace evidence of their presence would be incinerated just before midnight, when the fun began.

21

CHAPTER 5

Undisclosed Residential Location

The messages were always cryptic. Coded in such a way that certain sets of eyes could understand them all, while others were more compartmentalized based upon their sphere of influence. Everyone had a job to do. Some required physicality and military training. Others simply used the powers afforded them by way of their position. And then some, like the lonely young man sitting in the dimly lit basement of his home and surrounded by computer monitors, used their expertise. The common thread between them all? A sense of duty and the ability to respond on a moment's notice.

The message was short, but its words had a profound meaning.

!!!mG4VJxZNCI 12/31 19:34:28
As the snow cascaded downward,
The wild rides halted immediately.
One instance among many more,
As we seek Justitia Omnibus.
Fare thee well.
MM

He set his phone aside with the message on the 4chan chat board still in plain view. He reached to his side to pull open the desk drawer. At first, he hesitated, not sure if he was ready to fulfill his handler's wishes. He'd been paid well and given everything he needed.

But he'd contemplated his exit strategy on many occasions. He'd begun to stockpile supplies and cash. He had a vehicle that would go anywhere, under any circumstances. Although he was not an outdoorsman, he'd studied how to survive in the woods.

Not on these computers, of course. He was sure he was watched. His keystrokes monitored. Prying eyes were everywhere, and not just through camera lenses. His handlers were capable of anything.

The small black book had been given to him after he'd proven his loyalty. To be sure, he was once a rising star within the ranks at INSCOM, the United States Army Intelligence and Security Command garrisoned at Fort Belvoir, Virginia.

He had come out of high school as a broken teen. Constantly bullied as a nerd, and due to his being undersized compared to his classmates, the seventeen-year-old was not ready for adulthood. He worked on the Geek Squad at Best Buy for a while, but his real passion was not repairing computers. He preferred hacking them instead.

Just to be clear, he never engaged in criminal enterprise, at least not in his mind. Yes, he was guilty of accessing unsuspecting coeds' wireless cams on their laptops and watching them from time to time. Later, he decided to try his hand at cyber intrusions upon small businesses' computer networks. He was more of a gremlin than a full-blown hacker up to nefarious activities.

None of this paid the bills, however, and he soon became bored. With little going for him, he walked into the Army Recruiting Office in Tampa, Florida, and enlisted. It was a decision that changed his life.

He entered basic training and found himself overwhelmed by the rigors of the Army. In need of warm bodies due to attrition in recent years, the Army kept him in the program. One fateful day, he was having a conversation with another following their successful completion of the third and final field-training exercise known as the Forge, when he brought up his computer acumen as it related to hacking.

A senior drill sergeant pulled him aside and began to quiz him about his statements and expertise. A day later, he was sitting in the offices at INSCOM in Fort Belvoir, speaking with two of their technology personnel. The rest was history.

He moved on from basic training and took a position in the electronic and information warfare areas of responsibility at INSCOM. There, he was groomed under the careful, watchful eyes of the Military Intelligence Corps.

Four years later, he was at the top of his game, assisting Army Intelligence in their never-ending challenge to keep track of Chinese and Russian military assets. At one point he was brought on board to conduct *pen testing*, a term used by hackers for penetration testing of a computer's network, looking for vulnerabilities and security weaknesses.

He was in his element. He had a process, which he developed, that was ultimately adopted by others within his unit. He spent an inordinate amount of time conducting reconnaissance by gathering information about the targeted system. He would identify possible entry points, conduct several penetration tests, and record his findings for his superiors.

Using comparison models of other systems, he would eventually create a map, so to speak, of the target computer system. To look for weaknesses, he'd systematically test an organization's security policy compliance, the computer operator's security awareness, and finally, the target's ability to identify and respond to his intrusions.

The current administration turned the nation's cyber-warfare capabilities from a defensive posturing to being placed within its weapons arsenal. For decades, the Russians had used cyber attacks on critical infrastructure as a precursor to war. The Chinese preferred to steal military secrets with their efforts. INSCOM was tasked with following the Russians' method of military tactics.

He became an expert in accessing and potentially shutting down critical infrastructure on Russian targets, whether it be utilities, communications, financial markets, or transportation systems. In order to gain advantage in a military conflict, crippling one of these major components in a nation's critical infrastructure became a primary strategy in war planning.

He was becoming the best in his field, respected by his co-workers and appreciated by his superiors.

Then he was kidnapped.

It was never the intention of the kidnappers to cause him bodily injury. His life certainly wasn't worth ransoming. He was, as his kidnappers assured him, a potentially valuable asset. During the twelve hours he remained tied to a chair and blindfolded, he was assured that he wasn't going to be killed. They only sought two things from him, and he needed to understand their request was serious.

Cooperation and loyalty.

He asked if they expected him to betray his government. He insisted that he was a soldier and would never turn on the United States of America. He was assured that the plans they had in store for him would not require such a betrayal. He was simply told *trust the plan.*

So he did, and for the last nine months, he'd followed instructions and was paid handsomely for it. He still reported to duty at INSCOM, but he fulfilled his obligations to his nameless, faceless handlers. The ones who watched him.

And although he'd grown comfortable with the arrangement, he knew someday his time clock might be punched, or he'd have to disappear, hopefully on his terms.

CHAPTER 6

Undisclosed Residential Location

He opened his *little black book*, as he unimaginatively called it, and studied the initial sequence of codes and numbers. The first three exclamation marks indicated a level of priority, with one being the lowest and three the highest. The date and time stamp was generated by the chat board.

The message was encrypted as always, and he looked into his book to decode the string of characters and numbers. He underlined the ones of significance based upon the code sequence and key provided to him.

!!!mG<u>4</u>VJ<u>x</u>ZN<u>CI</u> 12/31 19:34:28

As the snow <u>cascaded</u> downward,

The wild *rides* <u>halted</u> immediately.

One instance among <u>many</u> more,

As we seek *<u>Justitia Omnibus</u>*.

<u>Fare</u> thee well.

MM

The number 4 represented the mode of delivery, in this case, the 4chan website, a social media site that allowed users to post anonymously. It was split into various chat boards discussing such topics as sports, entertainment, and politics. A similar site known as 8chan was also used from time to time. It differed slightly in that 4chan was moderated by administrators, and 8chan generally was not.

He thumbed through the sequence of letters and studied the sentences. Only certain words were considered important and part of a potential directive. To the casual conspiracy-minded observer, reading the post as a whole, they might point out the phrase *Justitia Omnibus*. This was translated from Latin to read *justice for all* in English. He also knew it by another meaning.

The Seal of the District of Columbia depicted Lady Justice hanging a wreath on a statue of George Washington. The motto of the District was Justitia Omnibus, justice for all. Others might arrive at this conclusion on their own, but only he knew it made the District the designated target of his activities.

He finished decoding the rest of the statement and set his glasses on his desk. He rolled his neck around his shoulders to relieve some stress and flexed his fingers. To his left was an undercounter refrigerator. He retrieved a miniature bottle of Tropicana orange juice and took a sip.

He spoke to himself aloud. "Last chance, pal. Whatcha gonna do, boy?" He could've shouted at the top of his lungs and not a soul on earth could hear him unless, of course, his watchers had their own form of listening device within his basement, which he affectionately dubbed the *Cave*.

After another moment consumed with conflict and introspection, he scooted his chair up to the modular desk and ran his fingers across his keyboard. He'd reached a decision.

This was a victimless hack in his mind. He wasn't directly killing anyone. In fact, in his mind, it was slightly humorous to derail the plans of the partygoers who were out carousing and enjoying adult beverages on New Year's Eve. He wasn't going to any parties, nor was he invited to any. There was no local pub nearby to ring in the New Year with a hearty chorus of "Auld Lang Syne." *Why shouldn't some other people be miserable like I am?*

His desk resembled the cockpit of a modern airliner with eight flat-panel monitors at the ready. He pulled up different sets of notes on his upper-level computer monitors, which were mounted directly to the wall.

One was labeled *AIRPORTS*—Reagan and Dulles. Another was labeled *AMTRAK*. The next screen was marked *BUS*

TRANSPORT—MegaBus, Battle's and Vamoose. The final screen was marked *WMATA*—DC Metro.

He studied his notes. He'd been tasked early on with pen testing of each of the major infrastructures of a dozen of the nation's largest cities plus Washington. Transportation, communication, utilities, and financial markets were all potential targets. Once he'd established a particular methodology for entering the computer systems of each of the subcomponents, like Reagan National Airport, he would conduct pen testing periodically to make sure countermeasures hadn't been adopted.

This was how he filled the extra hours of his day when he was away from INSCOM, in addition to monitoring chat boards and social media for instructions. Now he had work to do.

He set about his task. The keyword *Fare* in the post indicated he was to target transportation infrastructure that was ordinarily paid for with a fare.

The bus transport companies were the easiest to deal with. They were small companies with an unsophisticated firewall. It was easy for him to access their servers individually and schedule a DoS for the precise time indicated in his instructions.

He thought of the ramifications of his cyber attacks and others like them. The message had read *One instance among many more.* He was not the only one participating in this plan, which he was admonished to trust.

A DoS, or denial of service attack, was used to temporarily interrupt a web server's ability to connect to the internet. The common method of attack saturated the target network with external communications requests to the point the computer system was unable to respond to legitimate web traffic. The result was server overload and a shutdown of the entire system, creating chaos within the bus transportation network.

The servers at Washington Dulles and Reagan National airports would be attacked in a similar fashion, except the intrusion would involve the airlines as well. In this case, he would use a DDoS, or distributed denial of service attack, to completely weigh down the computer systems of the airports and the airlines that service them.

He would employ multiple servers around the world to remotely access the computer systems of the two airports and the three major airlines that service them—American, United, and Delta. Each of the remote servers controlled multiple computers, both public and private, around the world. All of them would simultaneously attack the servers at the two DC airports, bringing air travel to a standstill.

Amtrak would receive treatment similar to the airlines. The Washington Metropolitan Area Transit Authority, or WMATA, consisted of both bus and rail transportation. The bus transportation could be halted by a DoS attack easily enough.

The DC rail system was a little more complicated. Because the rail system encompassed such a wide area, he thought it best to take down the dedicated power grid for its lines. He was instructed to undertake a cascading failure of the entire rail system without creating widespread power outages throughout the District. It could be done, but he hadn't war-planned it.

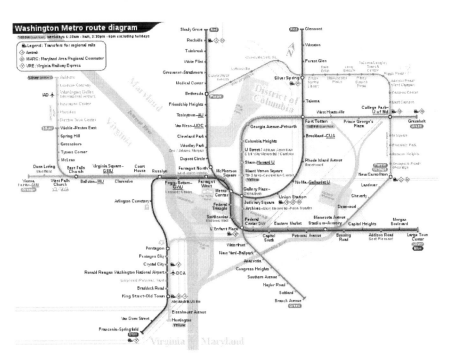

The trains would be brought to a halt, and the power would be taken down in the stations and tunnels, adding an extra layer of chaos. He smiled as he added his own demented twist to the instructions he'd been given. He planned on creating a cascading failure by penetrating DC Metro's antiquated Windows-based servers.

He logged on to his VPN, a virtual private network, which prevented his identity being tracked by cyber investigators. His earlier pen tests had allowed him to sneak a peek without prematurely alerting the IT department at WMATA of his presence.

"Now that I'm in," he mumbled, "let's find their schematics and see what kind of software they're using."

He raced through the internal servers of the WMATA, his fingers clicking faster than the screen could keep up. After several minutes, he found what he was looking for. The WMATA used an Automatic Train Control software, which dealt with all aspects of train operations from routes, scheduling, operations, and communications. Most importantly, it provided safety and protection by monitoring life-critical functions of the trains.

"Hello, SCADA, old and out-of-date friend," he said with a smile as he dug deeper into the network.

SCADA, which is an acronym for supervisory control and data acquisition, was used by industrial utilities to provide interconnectivity across various platforms and networks throughout the utilities' network.

Many energy and transportation utilities around the world used SCADA despite the widely reported weaknesses and vulnerabilities the system was subject to. He reached for a USB drive and inserted it into a laptop that sat on the desk to his left. The portable computer went everywhere with him, you know, just in case he had to make a quick exit from public life.

His adrenaline was pumping as he navigated through the laptop in search of the perfect worm to insert in the SCADA system. Do-gooder companies like Symantec always professed to be one step ahead of hackers, but, of course, they were wrong. If they were one step ahead, there would never be a cyber intrusion, right?

The hacker community had a network, which he was part of. He rarely contributed anything of value, although he did post things from time to time to disrupt Russia's activities in Syria. On one such occasion, it got a Russian Sukhoi Su-24 shot down near the Syrian-Turkey border by a Turkish F-16.

The Turks swore the Sukhoi violated its airspace. What they were unaware of was the hack performed on their air defense radars that had temporarily moved the positioning of their border vis-à-vis the Russian aircraft. They thoroughly convinced the Russians that their military fighter had deviated into Turkish airspace, when it had not.

The hack, and the subsequent downing of the aircraft, created an international incident, with Moscow blaming Washington for not informing them of the aircraft's deviation. Washington never admitted that their data differed from Turkey's. Eventually, the matter went away.

He was applauded by the hacker community for providing the tools necessary to disrupt geopolitical affairs, and as a result, complex hacks were shared with him on a regular basis. He would deploy one of them that New Year's Eve to bring the DC Metrorail system, along with the entirety of Washington's transportation apparatus, to a screeching halt.

CHAPTER 7

Undisclosed Military Installation
The Philippines

The naval lieutenant eased back in a wooden office chair that was barely capable of remaining on its swivel base. The old facility in which he operated with the two junior members of his unit had been thrown together last summer. In the five months they'd been stationed there, they had done absolutely nothing except train on their simulators. They had minimal voice contact with their superior officers, instead relying upon daily directives and briefings via internal military communications.

The room the trio occupied stank of body odor and Thai food. The drab, vanilla walls surrounded three desks with computer stations enabling them to conduct training sessions and, if called upon, deploy the drone submarines that fell under their purview.

The lieutenant reviewed the newly received orders before he verbally passed them along to his team. The chain of command he'd been accustomed to had changed, but that was not unusual since their arrival. The new program was in the middle of an internal political struggle within the military that he wanted no part of.

He read the new orders again, which were marked *Top Secret Mission Sensitive*. From his experiences, when a mission was marked *sensitive*, it meant there were certain operational aspects of a task that were eyes only for the commander of a unit, albeit a small one like his. Since their arrival, every set of orders received fell under a classification that required no level of secretiveness.

He pushed his chair back from his work console and stood. He paced back and forth before speaking.

"What's the situation, sir?" one of his men asked.

"We need to clean up this room, now!" The lieutenant's demand was out of character for his normal demeanor. Ordinarily, he was able to joke with his team and even spend after-hours time in local bars, chasing available women.

"Okay, I'm almost—" one of his men protested, hurriedly finishing his meal.

"Now. I have orders and we need to get prepared. There's very little time before implementation."

The men scurried about, pulling a plastic trash can out of the restroom and shoving the take-out dinnerware into it.

One of his men began to question his lieutenant. "Is this a drill, sir? Are we about to get a visit from someone?"

The officer walked back and forth as sweat poured profusely from his brow. "No. At least I don't think so. The suddenness of the orders puzzled me, but they are authenticated, and that leaves us a job to do."

"What is it?" one of the men asked.

"Obviously, this is classified, but I'm going to tell you more than you should know. We're a team and our actions may have an effect on a global level."

"Tell us."

"It's labeled *Operation Ocean Aero*."

"Are we at war?"

"Listen, I know as much as you do, but we need to focus. We only have a limited amount of time to position our AUV to hit a very defined target."

An AUV, or autonomous underwater vehicle, was commonly known as an unmanned submersible designed for survey missions like mapping the ocean floor, searching for sunken ships, or clearing possible obstructions to navigation for other vessels. Unlike an ROV, a remotely operated vehicle that is connected to another vessel by cables, AUVs had advanced technology to be controlled from locations on the other side of the planet via computer and satellite relay transmissions.

The proliferation of these underwater drones allowed nations that possessed them to park the AUV on the ocean floor, sometimes miles beneath the surface, awaiting orders from its controller.

Until now, no underwater drone in their fleet had been tested to fire an actual missile. The lieutenant and his crew conducted simulated war games daily, in part by orders from their superiors, but also out of sheer boredom. It was not unusual for them to pick locations to target all over the world, with varying degrees of difficulty and weaponry options.

If they chose to obliterate Israel, for example, they'd maneuver one of their drones into the Mediterranean Sea undetected and run a simulation of detonating a nuclear warhead over Tel Aviv.

Likewise, their AUVs were capable of attacking a ship or an airline with less destructive weapons. The arsenal at their disposal was as varied as the targets that they could be tasked to strike.

"Sir, what is our objective?"

"And what payload are we delivering?" asked the other man in the small unit.

The lieutenant continued to study their mission orders. He began to mumble as he read them. "One-megaton, EMP-tipped warhead. Just above the visual horizon," he summarized the orders. Then he paused, rubbed his temples, and considered the instructions. "Why is it so low? Targeted? None of this makes sense."

"Sir? Maybe this is just a drill."

The lieutenant shook his head and grimaced. "I don't think so, unless they removed the payload without our knowledge, which is impossible. Let's do our duty, gentlemen. Here are your coordinates."

He paused, and then he read them slowly to his team. "40° 0' 34" north latitude and 75° 8' 0" west longitude."

After several keystrokes were made at the terminal of one of the men, he took a deep breath and stated the physical location.

Philadelphia.

CHAPTER 8

Hyatt Centric Times Square
New York City

From Central Park to Carnegie Hall to the Metropolitan Museum of Art, Midtown Manhattan and the Times Square Theater District was the epitome of New York's world-renowned persona. Once a year, on New Year's Eve, Times Square becomes the center of the universe as revelers ring in the new year.

The time ball itself was located on the roof of One Times Square, a twenty-five-story skyscraper located at Forty-Second Street and Broadway. Beginning at one minute until midnight, the ball descends one hundred forty-one feet in precisely sixty seconds until it rests to signal the start of the new year.

This year, the special guest to activate the ball drop was former Secretary of State and presidential candidate Hillary Clinton, who'd just been defeated in the previous spring in the Democratic primary for the nomination. She and her husband, the former president, were residents of Long Island and were being honored by New York's mayor for their service.

Her entourage was staying at the Hyatt Centric, a luxury high-rise property overlooking Times Square. Security was tight and intentionally visible at the hotel. In fact, security was beefed up at all the buildings overlooking Times Square, as the memories of the Mandalay Bay shooting in Las Vegas were fresh in the minds of law enforcement. Rooftops were closely monitored for sniper activity, and several of the hotels employed temporary luggage scanners to detect for weapons.

All of this didn't dampen the spirits of Tom and Donna Shelton, who'd come to the city for the first time. In fact, they liked the added comfort and peace of mind afforded by the enhanced security measures.

The Sheltons were celebrating their fortieth wedding anniversary, although the actual event had taken place back in October. Donna had always wanted to come to New York to experience the shopping, dining, and overall excitement the city exuded. When Tom promised her the trip as part of their anniversary celebration, Donna upped the ante to set a specific weekend—New Year's.

Tom couldn't deny his bride her request. He loved her with all his heart. During his tenure as the commanding officer of the Naval Weapons Station at Joint Base Charleston in Goose Creek, South Carolina, he'd spent an exorbitant amount of time doting over his ordnance cache of more than sixty million pounds of conventional explosives.

For thirty-five years, he'd given his life to the United States Navy, oftentimes to the detriment of his wife and family. Since his retirement three years ago, he'd vowed to make it up to them. After Donna was diagnosed with breast cancer shortly thereafter, Tom's outlook on life changed, and his love for Donna grew deeper.

Donna was on a FaceTime call with their oldest daughter, Willa, and their three grandchildren. As she talked with the grandkids about the Christmas presents they'd received, Tom was deep in thought as he looked out the ceiling-to-floor plate-glass windows overlooking Times Square. It was only seven that evening, but people were packed shoulder to shoulder as they started their New Year's Eve celebration.

Erupting like tantrums, another strong gust of wind struck the building, pelting the glass with icy crystals of snow. Their view of the ball drop would be incredible that night. The room cost them over a thousand dollars a night for the weekend, but Tom didn't hesitate to pay it. For one, he owed his wife this vacation and many more for the years when he couldn't leave the base. Secondly, not that he was afraid, he preferred to stay in the safe confines of the hotel on a night when crazy was spelled with a capital *C*.

As it was, parties were ongoing throughout the hotel, especially in Bar 54, where he and Donna had dinner reservations at eight. He'd tried to make them for later, hoping to view the ball drop from the outdoor balconies, but the restaurant closed at nine for an expensive, black-tie soiree, which involved four-hundred-dollar bottles of champagne and table reservations requiring a minimum purchase of a five-hundred-dollar bottle of Belvedere vodka. Tom was not frugal, but he wasn't wasteful either.

"Tom, do you wanna say good night to Willa and the kids?"

Tom shook off the chill he'd received standing near the window and joined Donna, who was sitting on the edge of the bed. The king-size bed was in a separate room from a small living area that made up their suite. The modern design and the art deco paintings that adorned the walls were a far cry from the traditional Southern style found throughout their home in downtown Charleston.

"Of course, my darling," said Tom as he walked through the doorway and joined her side. With the curtains drawn, the bedroom was much warmer, so he removed his jacket while Donna held the phone for him.

"Hi again, Grandpa!" one of the youngsters exclaimed as he came into view on the FaceTime app.

"Hi, munchkins!"

They squealed in delight. He enjoyed his relationship with Willa and his grandchildren despite the distance between them. She and her husband lived in North Las Vegas near Creech Air Force Base, where Willa, a captain, served as a drone pilot. Her days were spent staring at glowing video screens and toggling a joystick that controlled armed drones flying throughout the world. At any given moment, hundreds of Predator and Reaper drones were aloft, most of which were controlled from the sun-scorched desert outpost north of Las Vegas.

Donna handed Tom the phone. "Dear, I'm going to finish putting on my face before we go upstairs. Will you call our other daughter after you sign off?"

"Of course," replied Tom as he bent over to kiss Donna on the cheek. He managed a smile as she left and entered the bathroom suite in the thick sherpa bathrobe he'd purchased for her at Macy's. Even though her cancer was in remission, her body tended to chill easily, even in the warmer confines of Charleston.

He turned his attention back to the phone. "Are you guys gonna stay awake for the ball drop later?"

The oldest of the three granddaughters replied, "We sure are, Grandpa, but only for the New York ball. It will be too late for the Vegas ball."

"That's okay," he said with a laugh. He adored his grandchildren every bit as much as he loved his wife and two daughters. He was surrounded by women and that suited him just fine. As the only man in the Shelton family, he was taken care of like no other grandfather. "After midnight here, you guys can close your peepers, and when you wake up, it will be a brand-new year at your house too!"

"Okay, Dad." Willa stepped in because she'd overheard her mother say that Tom had another call to make. "You may not be able to get right through to sis, so we'll let you go. We love you very much, right, girls?"

Their youthful cheerfulness came through the phone loud and clear.

"Yes, we do!"

"Happy New Year, Grandpa!"

"We love you!"

Tears came to Tom's eyes. He quickly turned the phone's camera lens toward the bathroom to bring Donna into view while he wiped them away. He truly loved his family and regretted the years he'd missed with them all because of his sense of duty.

"Your grandmother and I miss you and love y'all very much. Happy New Year!"

Donna walked out of the bathroom with a blush brush in her hand. "I love you and happy New Year!"

Tom returned the camera to his face and smiled. "Good night, munchkins. Good night, Willa. Happy New Year." And then he disconnected the FaceTime chat.

Tom sighed and looked at the phone as he scrolled through the contacts list. The next call would be a little less cheery. It always was.

CHAPTER 9

Hyatt Centric Times Square
New York City

Tommie Shelton, Tom and Donna's youngest daughter, served in the Military Sealift Command, a branch of the U.S. Navy. The MSC was dedicated to replenishing supplies and transporting service personnel to naval vessels deployed around the world. This sealift operation, however, was in many respects a façade for the MSC's real purpose—intelligence gathering.

Tommie was stationed on the USNS *Invincible*, one of two tracking ships operated by the MSC. The Stalwart-class surveillance ship was initially dedicated to patrolling the oceans for submarines utilizing its large passive sonar array. The *Invincible* was later refitted with advanced radar capability and mobile surveillance. Now it looked like a spy ship and performed like one too.

Officially a naval intelligence officer, Tommie never married and, like her father, became dedicated in her service to her country. She'd advanced through the ranks to lieutenant commander of the intelligence operation aboard the *Invincible*.

Tom knew this was one of the busiest days of the year for Tommie and those within her charge. Large events in the United States were always the potential targets of terrorists. Tommie would have her hands full sorting through radio and internet chatter, but he wanted to fulfill his wife's request to wish her a happy New Year.

His relationship with Tommie was excellent. They talked as often as possible, but the conversations never dwelled on the usual small talk, such as the weather, health, and planned get-togethers that never materialized. They invariably revolved around more serious subjects like the threats to the nation they both served with distinction.

"Commander Shelton speaking." Tommie answered the phone exactly the way her father had when he was in the service, perhaps a little more brusquely.

"Good evening, Commander. This is the other Commander Shelton calling to wish you a happy New Year."

After a short delay, Tommie laughed heartily on the other end of the line. The phone call was relayed through secured lines, which resulted in a two-second gap of dead air. "Hi, Dad. I figured it was you. Happy New Year to you and Mom."

"Thanks. Your mom is getting ready for dinner, but she wants to say hello before we go upstairs."

"Good. Say, where are you staying again?"

"The Hyatt Centric hotel, overlooking Times Square."

"Dad, promise me you'll stay in the hotel to watch the festivities. You know that I've been against this trip, especially at New Year's. At your age, you're not ready to deal with the madness that New York can generate."

Tom laughed, which drew Donna out of the bathroom to see what was going on. He waved at her and gave her a thumbs-up.

"Tommie, it's not like your mother and I have one foot in the grave, you know. We're barely sixty."

"Still, Dad," she continued her admonition, but Tom was having none of it as he continued.

"I think we should start referring to age as *levels*. You know, when you turn seventy, it's referred to as *level seventy*. It sounds more badass than just being an old person."

Tommie started laughing and her protests stopped. She, above all, knew that Tom Shelton could hold his own at any age. He was never a man to tangle with.

"Aye-aye, Commander. You win this round. Listen, Dad, before Mom comes on the phone, I need to mention something."

As expected, Tom braced himself for the serious part of their conversation. Tommie, like her father, wanted to shield Donna from the realities of the world. Some people were prepared to hear about the terrorist threats or the beating of war drums; others were not. Tom and his daughter, the naval intelligence officer, were not afraid of the geopolitical chest-pounding or terroristic threats. They prepared for the worst and hoped for the best.

"Talk to me, Goose," said Tom, channeling *Top Gun*, their favorite movie.

Tommie began. "The locals have New York City on lockdown in light of recent events. They've doubled their rapid-response teams and have created dedicated sniper patrols on the rooftops of every building in the vicinity of Times Square. I'm pretty confident every available resource is being used to beef up security."

"Good to hear," interjected Tom. "I sense a *but* coming."

Tommie paused longer than the dead air typically required as she gathered her thoughts. "Dad, there's something else."

Tom sighed. He wanted this weekend to go smoothly. "What is it? Something from the Middle East?"

"Our monitoring has revealed nothing out of the ordinary in the region. In the last couple of years, as you know, the military has shut down al-Qaeda and ISIS. They execute local insurgency operations but not much more. The information I'm receiving is stateside."

"Are you referring to the Islamist terrorist cells inside the country? I thought they were contained."

"Dad, my counterparts are focusing on domestic sources, chat boards, text messages, and phone calls. I've been told that numerous FISA warrants were issued this afternoon."

Pursuant to the Foreign Intelligence Surveillance Act, the FBI, under the direction of the Department of Justice, was allowed to conduct surveillance on both international and domestic terror suspects. Over time, the FISA court's authority was extended to all manner of criminal activity, whether terror related or not.

"Do you know any details?" asked Tom.

"No, other than the fact that this is strictly a domestic investigation and the level of scrutiny indicates the threat is credible."

Tom glanced over at his wife, who'd slipped on her dress purchased for this special occasion. She was just as beautiful as they day they'd met. His eyes took her in as his attention turned back to his daughter.

"Tommie, are we in the crosshairs?"

She hesitated. "Dad, I honestly don't know. I will say this—New York City is always somebody's target."

CHAPTER 10

Mercedes-Benz Stadium
Atlanta, Georgia

The teams entered Mercedes-Benz Stadium in pairs, spaced just a minute apart so they could mix in with other arriving workers. The security guard manning the rear entrance at the loading dock glanced at their security passes and quickly waved them through without question. Once inside, they dispersed in all directions, wearing the dark blue utility coveralls they were assigned, which were bulky enough to cover their street clothes underneath, and carrying a variety of bags ranging from soft-sided lunch totes to small backpacks. Even if they'd been stopped, their devices would've passed scrutiny. They possessed some of the best covert weapons developed in many years.

The stadium was considered a modern wonder of architecture, designed to be a multipurpose venue for the NFL's Atlanta Falcons and the major league soccer team Atlanta United. The extraordinary roof design featured sliding panels. The design firm HOK-USA had studied the way sunlight passed through the oculus in the roof of the Pantheon in Rome. Using their observations as inspiration, they designed eight petal-shaped roof panels that moved together along individual tracks so that the roof closed and opened like the aperture of a camera.

Wrapping the entire perimeter of the oval-shaped roofline was a high-definition, wraparound video monitor system that created a one-of-a-kind theater-like experience. For football games, seventy-one thousand fans could sit in comfort and watch the game. For a two-and-a-half-hour concert like the one that evening, a similar number would be attending, many thousands of whom would be standing at ground level in front of the stage.

The Australian operator broke away from the group first and made his way into the bowels of the stadium that housed the mechanical rooms. Around the lower levels, several rooms contained communications equipment and the hub for the nearly four thousand miles of fiber-optic cable woven throughout the stadium. He'd taken a considerable amount of time to review the schematics available online through the Atlanta City Planning Department's website. Based upon his analysis, he'd found the central location of the entire fiber-optic system.

The two Americans were tasked with accessing the primary control rooms for the ventilation system of the complex. Once they located the maintenance panels for the massive ductwork, they'd strategically place their devices to perform to their maximum potential.

Lastly, the team leader from the UK was tasked with lighting the fuse. Police departments in major cities received dozens of bomb threats every day. They rarely turned out to be real, and as a result, due to reduced budgets and manpower shortages, first responders had begun to scale back their initial responses.

The City of Atlanta had the largest division of the Counter-Terrorism Task Force, designated CTTF, in the state of Georgia. Led by the Georgia Emergency Management Agency in conjunction with the FBI's Atlanta Field Office, the CTTF devoted much of its time to surveillance and prevention of attacks.

In a recent interview for the *Atlanta Journal-Constitution*, the head of the CTTF responded to a question regarding the number of false alarms this way: "Bombers make bombs, and people who make bomb threats make bomb threats, and they don't cross paths."

He cited recent examples around the country, such as the Hampton Roads Navy installation in Virginia Beach, where seven credible bomb threats were made in a forty-eight-hour span. Fortunately, none of the threats materialized.

He also went on to explain how Cesar Altieri Sayoc, the delusional former male stripper who had sent package bombs to more than a dozen democrat politicians and financial supporters, avoided law enforcement's notice despite having a 2002 arrest for a bomb threat. When he sent bombs through the mail in October 2018, which were later discovered to be incapable of exploding, he didn't make any specific bomb threats, only the now-typical vile, hateful things spewed on social media by a lot of political partisans.

The head of the CTTF went on to disclose the agency's philosophy when a bomb threat comes in. He said local authorities should hold off on any kind of evacuation until something beyond the threat was actually identified, like a suspicious package. His philosophy was simple. By eliminating knee-jerk responses to threats, the frequency of false calls would diminish and, hopefully, copycat threat makers would be discouraged because they didn't get the results they'd hoped for.

When the Brit watched the interview, he'd shaken his head in disbelief. It wasn't that he disagreed with the CTTF's approach. He thought it stupid that they would disclose it to the public through the media. Did the head of the CTTF not think terrorists would hear his words and plan accordingly? His team certainly did.

The mission that evening was unusual in that their employers wanted the CTTF and first responders to react. His instructions, although cryptic, once decoded were crystal clear.

Terrorism was different from murder. In any battle, collateral damage in the form of innocent lives lost was to be expected. But the overall objective of a terrorist, in the broadest sense, was to use a person's fear against them. Acts of terrorism had proven to be extremely successful since 9/11 in achieving recognition for the cause of radical Islamic terrorists. Since then, terrorist acts around the world have effectively allowed bad actors to level the playing field with their adversaries in furtherance of their political, religious, and ideological aims.

His financial benefactors were not interested in murdering the attendees of the Beyoncé concert. He surmised this operation was part of a much larger overall plan that would reveal itself in due time.

The head of the team was in place and checked his watch. Precisely at 9:00 p.m., two local Atlantans who'd made a name for themselves in the hip-hop scene began their thirty-minute set as the crowd began to file in. Following their performance, the stage would be cleared and reconstructed for the feature performance that would last until midnight.

Reports indicated that Beyoncé and Jay-Z would perform their own special rendition of the poem written by a Scotsman, Robert Burns, in 1788. The poem was eventually adopted by countries throughout the English-speaking world to be sung at the stroke of midnight as a new year was rung in.

The lyrics to "Auld Lang Syne" began with a rhetorical question, one the team leader of the operation considered to be apropos.

Should auld acquaintance be forgot, and never brought to mind?

He chuckled to himself as he thought of the literal meaning. Is it right that old times be forgotten? Or should we remember the old times and forget the ones in between then and now?

"I guess we're about to find out," he muttered with a smile.

CHAPTER 11

Six Flags Great Adventure
Jackson, New Jersey

"Guys, welcome to the world's scariest theme park!" exclaimed Dr. Angela Rankin to her two kids and man-child of a husband, Tyler. Angela was an intensivist, oftentimes referred to as a critical care physician, at Virginia Commonwealth Medical Center in Richmond, a renowned critical care hospital. Her primary field of study was emergency medicine.

"Let's go!" Kaycee, their oldest, exclaimed, banging her hands on the back of the seat as if she were playing the bongos. The eleven-year-old had a zest for life that was unparalleled. Perhaps it was her adventurous parents who taught her the thrill of the outdoors and pushing their bodies to the limits, or maybe it was her own brush with death as a child that gave her a new lease on life coupled with an outlook that she was invincible. "Right, J.C.? We've got this!"

"I'm not scared, Peanut," replied her younger brother of eight. J.C. had been overshadowed during his childhood by the trauma the family had been through when Kaycee almost lost her life five years prior in a freak accident.

The family had been vacationing at the beach in their hometown of Hilton Head, South Carolina, when a tour helicopter flying overhead suddenly lost power. The pilot attempted a crash landing in the shallow waters off the shoreline, but the unpredictable nature of the chopper's glide path brought it toward the sandy shore, catching the Rankin family in an untenable position.

J.C. was still a toddler at the time, and when the helicopter started to crash, his parents scrambled to carry him out of harm's way. They

48

managed to miss the spinning rotor blades of the helicopter, but the fuselage bounced across the sand and landed on top of Kaycee, who had been separated from the group during the chaos.

She was being crushed under the weight of the chopper as her parents frantically dug the sand out from under her. For several minutes, her parents thrashed in the sand, trying to dig under the wreckage so Kaycee could be freed. However, they couldn't move her due to the extensive injuries she'd received. Helpless, they waited for an ambulance.

For several weeks thereafter, Kaycee was in intensive care and went through a significant amount of physical rehabilitation before she was released from medical supervision. To the young girl's credit, she came through the trauma as if she'd won the lottery of life.

"Of course you're not, buddy," said Tyler Rankin. Tyler had grown up on the beaches of Hilton Head, spending his days as a lifeguard and his nights on the town. After meeting Angela while at a house party in Los Angeles during spring break one year, he got serious about life and became a firefighter. He then obtained his certification as an emergency medical technician.

The two married after Angela got her undergraduate degree, and Tyler helped support the young family while she attended medical school. The four of them were inseparable, despite the long hours Angela had to spend at the hospital. When available, they hiked throughout the southeastern United States and visited places of interest to help further their kids' education.

Angela was given a rare two-week vacation between Christmas Eve and into the first of the new year. The family decided to take a road trip to Boston, Philadelphia, and Washington to see historic sites related to America's founding.

After Christmas, they drove up to Boston and saw several historic sites around the area. There next planned stop was a day in Philadelphia for a walking tour and finally two days in DC. But first, they were going to celebrate New Year's Eve at Six Flags Great Adventure in Jackson, New Jersey, about thirty minutes east of Trenton near Fort Dix.

"Dad, I've been studying our options ever since we planned the trip," said Kaycee, who clearly was taking over the tour guide duties from her mother, at least for today. "There's a reason they call this place the world's scariest theme park. They've got the fastest, tallest, wildest, gut-wrenchingest roller coasters on the entire planet!"

"They do?" Angela asked with a smile.

Kaycee was serious. She sat a little taller in the back seat of Tyler's 1974 Bronco, a truck he'd driven since he turned sixteen when his father passed away. It was in pristine condition and painted orange and white. Most importantly, it was a constant reminder of the close relationship he'd had with his dad.

Kaycee continued. "Yep. They've even got record breakers."

"What kind of record breakers, Peanut?" asked J.C. His eyes grew wider at the thought of the roller coasters breaking records mid-ride.

"Well, the newest ride is called the Cyborg Cyber Spin. It's seven stories high and it makes you feel like you're floating in space."

J.C.'s tone turned apprehensive. "Do you sit in a chair? How do you hold on?"

"You're strapped in, J.C.," replied Kaycee condescendingly. "They don't let you float in the air. People can't float or fly. Don't you know anything."

"I know things!" J.C. shot back.

Angela quickly intervened. "All right, you two. What else do they have, Peanut?"

"The Dare Devil Dive will be pretty cool too. You go up fifteen stories through the air at sixty miles per hour like you're skydiving. Um, we have to pay a little extra for that one."

Tyler laughed as he reached over for Angela's hand. He whispered to her as he followed the parking lot attendant's instructions, "Naturally, I have to pay extra to crap my pants."

Angela burst out laughing and kissed her husband on the cheek. The two had been in love since the day they met, and their affection for one another never waned.

"Peanut, which one breaks the records?" asked J.C.

"That, my little brother, would be Kingda Ka," said Kaycee authoritatively. "Now, listen to this."

Kaycee paused for dramatic effect to make sure she had everyone's attention. She lowered her voice and adopted a golf announcer's hushed, serious tone. "Once we're strapped in and ready, Kingda Ka throws into warp speed at one hundred twenty-eight miles per hour. In just three seconds, we're shot up a four-hundred-fifty-six-foot track until we reach the top, where we're suspended for a moment, and then, *WHOOSH*, we sail down the other side, screaming at the top of our lungs. Isn't that awesome?"

The family was quiet as they soaked in Kaycee's words until Tyler started laughing. "Angela, I'm gonna need to bring an extra pair of pants inside."

CHAPTER 12

Atlanta Hartsfield Airport
Atlanta, Georgia

Will Hightower nervously milled about the baggage-claim area in the South Terminal at Atlanta Hartsfield Airport. His kids were technically unaccompanied minors. Although underage, they certainly had the ability to travel without adult supervision. On the one prior occasion he had been allowed to visit with them alone, their mother, his ex-wife Karen, insisted upon Will paying for her round-trip ticket to escort them to and from Philadelphia. It was an unnecessary expense he could ill afford at the time, but it was worth it to visit with his children on his own terms. This New Year's weekend visitation marked their first trip to Atlanta without his ex-wife's interference.

He caught a glimpse of himself in a full-length mirror affixed to a wall near the restrooms. He looked out of place in a security guard uniform. Will studied himself and frowned. He hadn't worn the uniform to impress his kids. If anything, he preferred not to publicly wear the drab brown matching shirt and pants with the Mercedes-Benz logo emblazoned across the left chest and on both sleeves. He looked more like a mechanic than he did a security officer.

There were other security personnel around him. Atlanta's airport was one of the busiest in the world, but the security officers here consisted of local law enforcement, many of whom wore SWAT team gear or at least tactical body armor and protection. They also carried AR-15 rifles, a far cry from the boxy stun gun he had holstered in his utility belt.

Watching the two SWAT officers casually walking along the

baggage conveyer belts made him long for his days on the Philadelphia Police Department when he was part of the one-hundred-man special weapons and tactical squad. He'd started with Philly SWAT at Philadelphia's East Division, initially handling high-risk warrants, hostage situations, barricaded shooters, and hazardous materials response.

Over time, as the political climate in the country shifted, Philadelphia became front and center as societal unrest gripped the inner cities. His job duties began to shift from tactical response to crowd control. He was one of fifty officers assigned to cover the entire city of one and a half million people on a moment's notice, twenty-four seven. Philly SWAT prided itself on its quick reaction time and enormous successes in maintaining the peace. Then one dark day descended upon the City of Brotherly Love that tarnished the reputation of Philly SWAT and cost Will Hightower his job, and his family.

"Daddy!" The voice of his young daughter, Skylar, could be heard over the casual hustle and bustle of arriving passengers greeting their loved ones. Will pulled himself out of the nostalgic doldrums, which overcame him frequently, and turned to the sound of her voice.

"Sky! Look at you. You're blue, just the way I like it!"

His daughter, wearing a light blue track suit, ran and jumped into his arms.

"I've missed you, Daddy." Tears poured out of her eyes. It had been six months since Will had seen his kids, and the last visit to Philadelphia hadn't ended well.

"You have no idea how much I've missed you, baby girl," said Will as he lifted her up to squeeze her tight. He looked toward the entrance to the baggage-claim area. "Where's your brother?"

"He's back there, Daddy. He didn't want to run to find you like I did."

Will frowned. His relationship with eleven-year-old Skylar hadn't changed in the last two years since he left Philadelphia for Atlanta in a move he felt was for the betterment of everyone. As for fifteen-year-old Ethan, he never got over the life-changing event that precipitated Will's involuntary retirement from the Philadelphia Police Department and the subsequent breakup of his family. He laid the blame squarely on Will's shoulders, and since then, their relationship had been icy at best.

"There he is," said Will as he lowered Skylar and took her by the hand. She had a small backpack, and both kids had a suitcase they'd checked. Will and Skylar walked to meet Ethan, who was standing in front of Delta 322's baggage carousel.

Ethan's hair had grown considerably since Will saw him last, and the matching set of earrings was certainly a new addition to his appearance. Will, who was not authoritarian by any means, immediately frowned at his son's new look and dour demeanor.

"Hey, Dad," Ethan offered unemotionally.

Will put his arm around his son's shoulder and tried to hug him, but Ethan recoiled slightly.

"Happy New Year, son." Will tried to appear cheerful.

"Yeah, right," mumbled Ethan in response. "Couldn't be any worse than the last two."

Ouch.

Will had learned to push aside Ethan's snide comments, but he couldn't ignore them. Each time they saw one another, Will inwardly hoped this would be the time his son set aside the past, glad to see the father who loved him and had been his hero before the incident that changed their lives.

"I see ours coming, Daddy!" exclaimed Skylar in her usually chipper way. "Frankie bought me the pink one with the pastel flowers. Isn't it awesome?"

Will couldn't help but roll his eyes at the name synonymous with *Judas Iscariot*, the world's most famous betrayer. Frankie Scallone had been a member of Will's unit on Philly SWAT. He later became outed as the man Will's wife was having an affair with during the height of the scandal.

"Yeah, baby girl, it sure is," replied Will. Once again, he had to shake off the natural repercussions of a nasty divorce. He couldn't fight every small skirmish in an attempt to change the past. He had to rise above it and be glad he got to spend time with his children, something that had been a challenge in the past due to his financial situation.

His ex-wife had no compunction to withhold his visitation rights over his periodic underpayments of child support. His inability to pay fully, or perform his end of the bargain, as she put it, resulted in contact with the children being limited. Her own selective enforcement of the final divorce decree was not sanctioned by the judge.

Most likely, if Will hired a lawyer, the court would set her straight. But if he didn't have the resources to pay child support in full every month, together with extra medical and school expenses that frequently arose, how could he afford to hire an attorney to protect his rights?

So the formerly happy family tried to find a way to coexist from afar. Will took a new job at Mercedes-Benz Stadium as a member of their enhanced security team. Karen moved on with his former partner, happily cruising to the Caribbean on this New Year's Eve. And his two kids, one loving and the other not so much, were going to see Beyoncé and Jay-Z in concert while their dad worked.

CHAPTER 13

McPherson Building
Washington, DC

Gone were the days when you had to hustle down to the courthouse and file a pleading or brief before the clerk's office closed at four o'clock. With the advent of modern, sophisticated computers systems and the internet, *end of the day* meant having your document filed electronically before midnight.

The clock was ticking toward the proverbial witching hour, and Hayden Blount, the newest partner in the prestigious Washington law firm of Stein, Mitchell, was putting the final touches on the most important legal document she'd created in her career.

She read it on her computer for the fourth time, constantly tweaking a word here and there, editing the supplemental brief requested by the United States Supreme Court in the matter of *The Removal of the President of the United States*.

A chill came over Hayden's body despite the cozy seventy-two-degree temperature in her office. It was the gravity of the pleading that she was drafting, both for the occupant of the Oval Office and the benefit of future presidents as well.

Politics was in her blood, although not enough to encourage her to seek public office. She was the descendent of a long lineage of American statesmen dating back to North Carolinian William Blount, a signer of the Constitution and the man who played a leading role in helping Tennessee become a state. The children of William Blount and Mary Grainger went on to become congressmen, judges, and military heroes.

For Hayden, the Blount family history was something to be proud of, but not necessarily judged by. She planned to make her own way in life. With a drive and passion unparalleled in her peers, she strived for excellence.

Strikingly attractive and in her mid-thirties, Hayden had been anointed one of DC's top forty most eligible women on Hinge's Most Eligible annual list. Driven, powerful, and aloof, she didn't care anything about being eligible or attractive. She cared about winning, especially when it came to defending those under attack.

Hayden had been brought on board at Stein, Mitchell for many reasons, including her stellar clerkship for Supreme Court Justice Samuel Alito. Justice Alito, a Yale grad and Bush appointee, had been on the Court since 2006. After Hayden graduated from Duke Law School with high honors, she chose to join the group of clerks under Justice Alito's tutelage. She was glad she did.

The prestige of clerking for a Supreme Court justice could only be surpassed by being appointed to the Court itself. She'd learned the inner workings of the Court and thought processes of the justices, which served her well in preparation of this brief.

Nothing like this particular issue had been in front of the Court in its history. It came as the result of politics at its worst on all sides of the issue. From the moment this president was declared the victor in his first bid for public office, he came under considerable scrutiny from the media and the half of the country who opposed him. Even some within his party were having buyer's remorse.

As a result, his first two years in office swirled in turmoil and rancor. The political divide in America, which had begun decades prior and grew wider during the prior administration, developed into a full-blown chasm over the president's first term.

Day after day, with every twenty-four-hour news cycle, a new crisis or accusation beset his presidency. Some questioned the ability of the president to continue under the never-ending barrage he suffered, some of which was deserved, much of which was not.

As the midterm elections approached in the president's first term, the Democratic party was poised to make huge gains in Congress. A blue wave was predicted in the House and Senate. However, the wave election never materialized. The president's party gained seats in the Senate to widen its majority, and the number of losses in the House were far below expectations.

The confirmation battle surrounding the appointment of Justice Kavanaugh to the Supreme Court, considered by most pundits to be a winning argument for the minority party, backfired. It served to rally supporters of the president, and the record turnout resulted in an evenly divided House of Representatives.

The divided Congress served to stymie much of the president's agenda, and like others before him, he chose to govern through executive orders, directives issued by the president that managed the affairs of government and had the force of law.

The number of executive orders issued by the president during the second half of his first term troubled members of his own party because of the precedent it was setting, and caused the democrats to scream bloody murder.

While the battles fought in his first two years in office were largely related to his personal activities and his inarticulate expressions, which were often deemed offensive, in his second two years in office, he was attacked for circumventing Congress. As a result, the federal court system was inundated with litigation in an attempt to curtail the powers of the presidency.

Despite all of the inside-the-beltway drama that the average American cared little about, the president succeeded in implementing his policies, and he was easily his party's nominee to seek a second term. On the opposite side of the aisle, a crowded field of thirty-eight vied for the party's nomination to take on the president in the next election.

Heavily funded and widely popular among young adults, an obscure Texas congressman, Robert "Beto" O'Rourke, won the democratic nomination. Young, energetic, and seen as the second coming of John F. Kennedy, O'Rourke took on the president, who was nearly thirty years his senior.

The battle was hard-fought, but thanks to an unusual boost from union workers and African-Americans, the president won a narrow electoral victory, but lost the popular vote for the second time.

As had been the case in the 2000 and 2004 elections, the final state to announce its results was Florida. Voting machine failures and allegations of absentee-ballot abuse marred the results. Assertions of voter fraud in Nevada placed those election results into the hands of the newly constituted Ninth Circuit Court of Appeals, which now included Arizona, Nevada, Montana, Idaho, and Alaska. The states of Hawaii, California, Oregon, and Washington were merged into a newly created Twelfth Circuit. The case was still moving its way through the courts as the investigation into the alleged voter fraud continued. It was not expected to alter the outcome of Nevada's six electoral votes that went to O'Rourke.

Over the last four years, the president had grown increasingly distrustful of his cabinet and many of his advisors. Repeated leaks to the media were a problem he'd battled since he was first elected. Staffers were known to undermine his authority. Some members of the cabinet openly defied his authority and refused to act upon his executive orders.

Within those early days after his reelection, there were the whispers. The hushed insinuations that the president was increasingly mentally unstable. That the rigors of office were beginning to cloud his judgment. That he'd circled the wagons so tight around him that only his immediate family was able to provide him counsel. In essence, he'd walled himself in.

All of the drama surrounding the White House reached a crescendo seven days after the election when Florida certified its vote in favor of the president. The media led the outrage at the methodology followed by the state. Democrats rallied their legal machinery and flooded the Sixth Circuit Federal Courts with legal proceedings using several angles. Even the vice president decried the decision because of the questionable means by which it had been reached.

The president was fed up with his elections being challenged as illegitimate. When the vice president made his feelings known, he found several allies within the president's cabinet. The democrats vowed to initiate impeachment proceedings in the House, which they retained, and now those on the fence two years ago were willing to join in. The never-ending string of controversies didn't end with the election; they were renewed with a new robustness.

On Veteran's Day following the election, a letter was delivered to Congress by the vice president, which was signed by a majority of the cabinet. The letter was succinct and to the point.

To the President pro tempore of the Senate and the Speaker of the House of Representatives:

We, the majority of the cabinet of the United States, duly established in Article II, Section 2 of the Constitution, hereby declare pursuant to the Twenty-Fifth Amendment to the Constitution, that the president is unable to discharge the powers and duties of his office and should be removed from office accordingly.

If the president hadn't lost his mind prior to the invocation of the Twenty-Fifth Amendment, he certainly did after receiving delivery of the letter to Congress. After his head exploded, figuratively speaking, his first call was to his lead outside counsel at Stein, Mitchell—Pat Cipollone.

CHAPTER 14

McPherson Building
Washington, DC

Cipollone called the partners into an emergency meeting to lay out the facts. They created a legal strategy, and then Cipollone, along with Hayden, met at the White House with the president, his chief of staff, and his oldest daughter.

Since the enactment of the Twenty-Fifth Amendment following the death of President John F. Kennedy, the amendment was only invoked three times. In 1985, President Ronald Reagan sent a letter to then Vice President George H. W. Bush to perform his duties while he underwent surgery to remove cancerous polyps from his colon.

President George W. Bush invoked the Twenty-Fifth Amendment twice during his presidency as a result of colon-related procedures. In both cases, Vice President Dick Cheney acted as president during those brief colonoscopies.

There had never been a discussion of using the Twenty-Fifth Amendment to remove a sitting president as a means of changing the occupant of the White House, until now.

Cipollone was personally outraged at the thought of removing the president for the publicly stated reason that the cabinet disapproved of his leadership style, which was deemed impetuous, adversarial, petty, and ineffective. To the senior partner and head of the president's legal team, such action could precipitate a constitutional crisis. Yet this issue was what the legal minds at Stein, Mitchell faced.

The firm quickly drafted a letter in response and it was delivered to Congress. Rather than litigating the matter in the court of public opinion or provide details of their legal position in the letter, they simply denied the charge with three simple words—*no inability exists.*

The procedural move would result in the matter being sent to Congress for a series of hearings and votes, during which time the vice president and the cabinet members would state their case. They never got the chance.

What happened next would go down in American history. The day after the president's response letter was acknowledged as received, he called an emergency meeting of his cabinet at the White House. Some refused to attend, but twelve members, plus the vice president, were in attendance.

The president, flanked by Cipollone and his chief of staff, calmly said the words that had made him famous during his long-running reality television show, *The Apprentice.* One by one, he said, *"You're fired!"*

It was labeled in the media as the *bloodletting,* a word that typically was used in conjunction with the surgical removal of a patient's blood to prevent or cure illnesses and disease. In this case, the patient, the president's administration, was bitterly divided and in need of change. When the brief, eight-minute meeting was over, only four loyal members of his cabinet remained, and the rest were escorted out of the White House by the Secret Service.

That was when the legal battle began.

The matter was now before the Supreme Court to determine whether the president had the authority to fire most of his cabinet and, as a result, circumvent the Twenty-Fifth Amendment as invoked by the prior members of the cabinet.

Hayden was tasked with writing the supplemental brief requested by the Court. She drew upon her knowledge of the justices and their individual points of view. Case precedent didn't help one side or the other, as this was clearly a matter of first impression.

After the president appointed new members to his cabinet and submitted the name of a new vice president to replace the one who had led the charge against him, the dynamics changed. Hayden argued that the proceedings should be stopped because the fired cabinet members no longer fit the Twenty-Fifth Amendment's requirements for *principal officers* who could discharge the president. Only the new cabinet members and the vice president had standing to bring such a declaration, and they were handpicked loyalists to the president.

It was an interesting legal maneuver that had not been anticipated by the fired group, but it still would require litigation. The president's goal was to make it to Inauguration Day without the matter being resolved, at which time he felt cooler heads would prevail.

Hayden and her firm believed the president had an absolute right to clean house, as it were. This narrow issue would be litigated first, and the briefs were to be filed by New Year's Eve. Next Friday, the Court, while in conference, would take up the writs of certiorari filed on both sides, to take up the rulings of the DC Circuit. While the Court was not under an obligation to hear those cases, it usually did if it was necessary to harmonize conflicting opinions within the Circuits, or if it was a matter of national significance, which this naturally was.

The Court had requested a supplemental brief on the matter dealing with the specifics of Hayden's argument that the president had unfettered authority to remove any member of his cabinet, with or without cause. Her opponents argued that the president was effectively deemed incapacitated at the time the cabinet invoked the Twenty-Fifth Amendment, thereby rendering his powers limited until a full hearing in Congress.

Against that backdrop, while the rest of her firm shared New Year's Eve libations in the large conference room, Hayden toiled over the fate of a president.

CHAPTER 15

Atlanta International Airport
Delta Flight 322

Either you control destiny, or destiny controls you. His father-in-law's deep, gravelly voice echoed in his ears as he gazed at the holiday passengers scurrying back and forth in front of him. Cort was in a trance, one that had overtaken him several hours ago in Washington and left him realizing he had very little recollection of departing a snowy Reagan National Airport only to arrive at Hartsfield-Jackson in Atlanta a couple of hours later.

A continuous barrage of announcements from airport personnel tried to invade his head as he recalled his father-in-law's words, which consumed him by the power of their meaning—if he only knew what they meant.

"If you are in the gate area and an originating passenger of Delta Flight 322 connecting from Philadelphia to Mobile, we ask that you retake your original seats on board the aircraft now. We apologize for the delay, but we are going to begin boarding the flight to make a determination on our standby passengers. Thank you."

Cort leaned back in his seat to narrowly avoid a teenage boy who was engaging in horseplay with a younger girl, most likely his sister. They'd joined a number of passengers who'd departed the Delta flight from Philadelphia, and he hoped that provided a seat for him.

His mind drifted back to the old man's bedside. His condition had unexpectedly deteriorated in the last sixty days. It was if the life was being sucked out of him. Yet he was completely lucid, if not philosophical, as he prepared to die.

To his right, two men were talking loudly in the nearby bar, obviously enjoying their New Year's Eve libations and relishing the upcoming demise of the President of the United States. A young couple carried their children just in front of him, rushing past in a frantic attempt to meet a flight connection. The airport was a sea of bodies on the night most people should be celebrating an upcoming new year. Even though many were not.

"Paging the following Mobile passengers—Disney, party of two, Cortland, and Hamilton. Please see the Delta agent at gate D29."

He closed his eyes and fought to remove the words from his head, but they grew louder and more ominous with every attempt. Like a bad song that played over and over, begging to be displaced by a catchier tune, his father-in-law's words rang inside, growing larger until he could visualize them pulsating in his mind.

Either you control your destiny, or destiny controls you.

The old man was usually more direct. He was not one to mince words, sugarcoat bad situations, or speak in cryptic phrases. What did he mean?

The two men in the bar continued their ribbing of one another over the politic story of the day, or the new century, for that matter. They brushed past, smelling of alcohol and reeking of BS.

"Final call for Mobile standby passenger Cortland, Michael Cortland. Please see the Delta agent at gate D29."

Oh, crap!

Cort awakened from his daze. Hearing his name repeated brought him back to the present. He shot out of the padded seat, bumped into another business traveler, who barely noticed, and pushed his way through other standby passengers crowded around the gate agent with hopeful faces.

"Excuse me. Excuse me," he said politely as he wedged his way through two broad-shouldered men in suits. He reached the gate agent and introduced himself. "Sorry, I didn't, um, I'm Michael Cortland. Here's my identification."

Out of habit, Cort, who had been given the nickname by his father at an early age, produced his Alabama driver's license and his Capitol Hill credentials identifying him as the chief of staff to

Alabama Senator Hugh McNeil.

The gate agent smiled and entered some information into the computer terminal. As she did, she hummed the tune to "Auld Lang Syne" and then added the only words most people knew.

For auld lang syne, my dear, for auld lang syne. We'll take a cup of kindness yet, for auld lang syne.

Within seconds, she was reaching below the counter, and the sound of the printer spitting out his boarding pass could be heard. With a weary smile, she stamped the boarding pass, handed him his two IDs, and wished him a good flight.

Cort paused for a moment and then said, "You know, I think I will take a cup of kindness. We all should. Happy New Year to you!"

The puzzled gate agent returned the good wishes, and Cort was off to take Delta Flight 322 home to his family.

He walked down the jet bridge as the last passenger to be boarded. A slightly irritated, but attractive gate agent stood with her arms crossed, awaiting his arrival. A couple of ground personnel chatted by the jet bridge instruments, wrapped in scarves and knit hats as they endured the cold front that had swept across the eastern part of the country, bringing snow and freezing temps into parts of the south.

Cort glanced out the small jet bridge window before he stepped on board, noticing deicing trucks stationed next to the wing of the McDonnell Douglas MD-88 aircraft. He shrugged. He expected to see deicing taking place in the northeast, but not in Atlanta.

He ducked to avoid bumping the top of his six-foot-five frame, a height he had reached in high school that enabled him to go to Yale on a basketball scholarship. Cort was extremely intelligent and had maintained a near-perfect GPA throughout high school. Ordinarily, he wouldn't have the pedigree to make his way into a prestigious Ivy League school like Yale, but his basketball talents caught the eye of their recruiters. His personality and boy-next-door charm made him a perfect fit for their program.

He walked through first class, where the passengers were scrolling through their phones and sipping on cocktails in real glasses. Cort managed a chuckle when he thought of the plastic cup of Coke and one-ounce bag of peanuts that was in store for him.

In the last row of first class sat a man who was famous in Alabama and now throughout America. Johnson Pratt, incoming chairman of the House Judiciary Committee, lived on a farm just north of Mobile. His name and face were in the news on a daily, if not hourly, basis over the last eight weeks since the election was held. If there was ever a *big man on campus* in Washington, the nearly three-hundred-pound Pratt was the one.

Cort paused to wish Pratt a happy New Year, and the congressman cordially responded. The two men had worked with one another on a recent budget battle to prevent the closure of the Redstone Arsenal in Huntsville. Redstone Arsenal housed several government agencies at the sprawling Huntsville base, including the Department of Defense, the ARMY, NASA, and Department of Justice facilities.

Although Pratt was on opposite ends of the political divide from Cort and his boss, one that had grown into a contentious chasm in recent years, the two legislators were able to find common ground for the good of their state.

He made his way to his seat and turned sideways to avoid contact with a buxom flight attendant who came up the aisle toward him. She paused and leaned dangerously close to Cort. In a heavy Southern accent, not unlike his wife's, she advised that because he was the last passenger to board, he could take the first open seat. He smiled and nodded, choosing to run rather than converse with the attractive woman.

An aisle seat was the first available opportunity for Cort to get settled. As he slid in, he noticed the two men sitting in the exit row in front of him. They were the same two guys from the bar who were boozing it up and talking loudly. They brought the smell of the bar with them.

Cort pushed his soft-sided leather briefcase under the seat and adjusted his long legs to fit into the tight space that was customary on domestic flights in recent years as the big carriers tried to compete with low-cost, budget airlines. Cort furrowed his brow and mumbled to himself. Flying sucked anyway but was much worse when you were seven inches taller than the average American male.

Two elderly women sat in the seats to his left, both of whom appeared to be uncomfortable with the prospect of flying. Or perhaps something was weighing heavily on their minds.

"Good evening, ladies," greeted Cort, attempting to break the ice and let them know he was nothing like the men sitting in front of them.

The woman closest to the window smiled and turned away, placing her fingers under her nose to mask the smell of the passengers in front of them. The other woman replied politely with a simple hello.

The airplane shook slightly as the Jetway pushed away from the door. The final bags were loaded beneath the plane, and the deicing trucks drove to another job. Delta 322 began to roll backwards as the flight attendants began their duties.

The lead attendant cued the microphone and spoke to the passengers. "On behalf of the flight crew, I'd like to welcome you aboard Delta flight three-two-two, nonstop service from Atlanta to Mobile, Alabama. If you were expecting to fly to New York for the New Year's activities, well, I'm sorry for your luck. You can enjoy it on TV in Mobile."

The joke drew a smattering of laughter from the passengers but drew a snide remark from one of the men in front of them.

"Yeah, you know what Delta stands for, right?" He slurred his words as he answered his question, which was his intention anyway. "Don't even leave the airport. Get it?"

His buddy laughed uproariously as if it was the funniest thing he'd ever heard, although the acronym joke had been around for many decades. Cort was sure most everyone was familiar with the saying and ignored its meaning.

He was wrong.

CHAPTER 16

Atlanta Hartsfield Airport
Atlanta, Georgia

Will gathered the kids' luggage and made small talk as they exited the south terminal of the airport. Will reminded them that he had to work tonight, but he had a real treat in store for them at the concert. Beyoncé and Jay-Z were two of the most successful performers in music, although Beyoncé was not one of his personal favorites due to her continued attacks on law enforcement in the wake of the Black Lives Matter movement.

Will would love to challenge her to put on a beat cop's uniform for the evening and deal with the violent crime and drug-related offenses in Fairhill, Tioga/Nicetown, and the Hunting Park neighborhoods of Philadelphia. Nobody understood the challenges cops faced until they wore that uniform. Monday morning quarterbacking was unfair to the officers who risked their lives on every tour of duty. Nonetheless, she was a great talent, and he hoped the kids would enjoy seeing her perform live.

All of these thoughts pervaded his mind as the three of them came upon an unruly group of black teens who were horsing around near the narrow entrance to the parking garage. Will subconsciously squeezed Skylar's hand and tugged her back somewhat as he slowed his pace.

Ethan, who kept walking before noticing Will's abrupt change in speed, stopped and addressed his father sarcastically. "Whadya gonna do, Dad? Say *time to go, savages*?"

Ethan's words stung Will to the core, immediately conjuring up that fateful night at Fairhill Square in North Philadelphia. Philly SWAT had received a call of a large disturbance at the inner-city park, with shots fired.

On a Monday night in Fairhill, the city's most violent neighborhood, a barrage of bullets rang out within the park. The shooting occurred just as darkness set in, but the park was still full of children enjoying the last week of their summer break before school started.

Recently, the Philadelphia Police Department had seen a spike in homicides and rapes in Fairhill, and the *Philadelphia Inquirer* had led the charge in pressuring the force to be more responsive to violent criminal activity.

Philly SWAT arrived in force to the call amid reports that three dozen shots had been fired in the melee. Two men were reported dead, and several others, including children, had been wounded. Tensions were high when the teams arrived to get control of the situation.

Will and his team were the first to appear on the scene and were attempting to take charge when several local residents began scolding them for their slow response time, which had been close to fifteen minutes after the first call had come into 9-1-1.

The team began to forcibly push the young black men out of the park and away from the active-shooter scene for their own protection, and to preserve the crime scene for investigators. Tensions flared as some accused Philly SWAT of using excessive force in their efforts to control the crowd.

Vulgarities were hurled in their direction, in addition to rocks and bottles. At one point during the melee, out of frustration, Will yelled, *"Come on! It's time to go. Quit acting like a bunch of savages. You need to get to safety and go home!"*

Twenty-two words. One of which caused a firestorm for the department, and Will's family.

Savages.

Will didn't consider himself to be a racist. Three members of his unit were black. They were brothers-in-arms who unquestionably had each other's backs in all manner of dangerous situations. Within Philly SWAT, nobody looked at one another through the prism of race. They were a team. Will prided himself on being color-blind.

However, when his words were heard by the youths, they became angry and began misquoting Will to others gathered around. They quickly changed the word *savages* to the *n-word*, a hateful term that wasn't even in his vocabulary. During the intense investigation, his body-cam footage later proved Will's account as being accurate, but it didn't matter. *Savages* was good enough for the mob, which quickly undertook to destroy his life.

In the coming weeks, Will learned a lot about perceptions and political correctness in America. He was unfamiliar with the political use of the word *trigger*, a word he'd always associated with a part of his weapon. In today's social climate, a *trigger*, or *trigger warning*, included a word that might offend someone's political sensibilities, as in matters of sex or race.

Likewise, the newly defined term *dog-whistle* was applied to Will's statement. According to some in America, a dog-whistle involved the use of a term that might mean one thing to the general population, but would have an offensive, different meaning for a targeted subgroup based upon race or sex.

Will's intent didn't matter as the forty-year-old white male, in a pressure-packed environment, likened the out-of-control, unruly youths to acting like primitive, uncivilized humans. The term was immediately assumed to be used in a racist manner, and the lives of the Hightower family were turned upside down.

The media headlines in Philadelphia and certain cable news networks made little mention of the reason Philly SWAT was called to the scene that night. They said nothing about the fact the unruly crowd refused to heed the officer's warnings or obey their orders to disperse from the violent, active-shooter scene.

The entire conversation centered around Will's use of the word *savages*, and it was declared to be indicative of the way law enforcement throughout the nation treated the black community.

Will was placed on administrative leave during the investigation.

The paid leave worked out to the family's benefit, as he was needed at home to deal with the repercussions of the media firestorm.

His kids were physically attacked at school. His home and car were vandalized on several occasions. Police protection was refused to them, under the circumstances. But his wife found police protection from another source, Will's ex-partner, Frankie.

The affair started during the constant media scrums, which occurred outside their home. Anytime a glimpse of a family member was seen by the reporters, they rushed toward the house with cameras rolling and microphones at the ready.

For a time, Karen was the only member of the Hightower family who left the house to ostensibly run errands and do grocery shopping. One evening, as the family gathered to eat dinner in front of the television and watch the nightly news, a report came on that shook everyone to their core.

Earlier that day, a reporter had followed Karen, who had discreetly entered a nearby hotel room with Frankie. They filmed her exiting later, adjusting and buttoning her blouse as she gave a long kiss to a shirtless Frankie.

Karen scrambled for the remote to turn off the news report, but it was too late. Skylar began crying and ran into her room and slammed the door. Ethan ran out the back door and didn't return the entire night. Will lost his mind.

He and Karen screamed at one another for an hour. She blamed his actions on that evening in Fairhill for forcing her into the arms of another man. He defended himself on the basis that how could his utterance of one word lead her to Frankie, his partner, and an illicit affair.

The argument became so heated that the prying media called the police to report a domestic dispute. When the patrol cars arrived, the cameras were rolling when Will was walked out of the house and taken away, not under arrest, but as a way to diffuse the situation.

The resulting divorce was very public, and an emotionally defeated Will gave his wife and kids everything he could to begin the healing process. His wife healed in the arms of her new boyfriend. His son never healed and obviously continued to hold a strong resentment against his father, whom he blamed for the family falling apart. His daughter was the most forgiving of the Hightower family, as Will would never forgive himself for the inartful use of a single word—*savages*.

"Daddy?" Skylar pulled down his arm to bring him back into the present. "Are we gonna go to the car?"

Will snapped out of it, looked down at his daughter, and smiled. "Yeah, baby girl. You guys have a concert to see."

Will led the way toward the group, who just now noticed the three of them.

"Excuse us," said Will as he pulled Skylar a little closer to him. He wanted to avoid confrontation.

"There ain't no excuse!" shouted one of the teens, drawing laughter from his friends.

Will managed a smile, then reminded himself that this was Atlanta and these kids didn't know who he was or what had happened up East. Without saying another word, he stood a little taller so his security uniform could be seen. With his right arm, he eased his hand over the stun gun that, when holstered, resembled a Glock firearm in the diminished light. The subtle move was immediately noticed by two of the teens.

"Hey, dude's packin'!"

"Dayum, look at Clint Eastwood!"

"Good evening, gentlemen," said Will in his most polite voice, but through gritted teeth. "Thanks for letting us through."

Like Moses parting the Red Sea, the boys spread apart and stood against the concrete railing of the walkway, allowing the Hightowers to pass without incident. Once in the parking garage, Will exhaled, letting out a sigh of relief. That evening at Fairhill Square would forever live in his mind.

Proud of himself, Will unlocked his truck and loaded the kids inside. As he was about to close the passenger-side door where Ethan sat, his son couldn't help but get in one last dig.

"See, Dad, that wasn't so bad, was it?" he asked sarcastically.

Will hesitated, allowing his son's words to hang in the air for a moment. He sighed and gently shut the door without answering—heartbroken.

CHAPTER 17

Mercedes-Benz Stadium
Atlanta, Georgia

During the ride to the stadium, Will turned the conversation toward school. The kids had been kept out of school for the first four months during the media uproar, hoping the unwanted attention would die down by the Christmas break. The media finally left them alone, but now Skylar, who was in fifth grade, and Ethan, who was in high school, had to face the taunts of their fellow classmates and the harsh scrutiny of their teachers.

For the remainder of the school year, the challenge of making up schoolwork coupled with the emotional attacks took their toll. By the next summer, Skylar had become withdrawn and Ethan started to act out. He began hanging out with high-school-age kids and frequently came home after school smelling of alcohol.

Meanwhile, Will had moved to Atlanta to draw the media attention away from the family at a time when the kids really needed a father figure in their lives. Karen, to her credit, didn't rush into marriage with his ex-partner, but she certainly didn't hesitate to flaunt their relationship, including at home. Frequent sleepovers confirmed to the kids that their father was out of their lives and that any hope of reconciliation with their mother was out of the question.

Will tried to convince Karen to let the kids live with him in Atlanta. He knew he never had a chance in front of a judge. He hoped to play on her newfound freedom and offered to relieve her of the burden of raising kids. For Skylar and Ethan, a change of scenery and a new school, far away from the media-driven drama, was Will's best solution to save them from the emotional agony.

75

It didn't work, and instead, Karen doubled down on her pressure to make Will pay higher child support and on time. The postdivorce battles continued between them, as they often do, to the detriment of their children. A once loving family was now torn apart as the parents were at war with one another. Will hoped to reverse the trend this weekend by showing an extraordinary amount of love and attention to his daughter to reinforce their bond, and to indicate to Ethan that he respected him as a young man.

They pulled into the top level of the employee parking lot at the stadium and found one of the last available spots. Will had notified the head of stadium security that he'd be arriving late with his kids. Because he wasn't originally on the schedule for that evening, they allowed it. In addition, Will received tickets and all-access passes for Ethan and Skylar, giving them premium seats and the ability to enjoy all of the interactive features of the stadium.

For his part, Will was hired for his expertise attained during training and working for Philly SWAT. Anytime there was a large gathering at the stadium, coupled with alcohol being served, it was a recipe for trouble. The security team was able to set aside his past and hire Will for his ability to help them keep their facility safe for visitors during the myriad of events held at the stadium.

To assist them further, he'd undergone additional training in counterterrorism activities. He was to keep a watchful eye out for anything out of the ordinary and be prepared to work with Atlanta SWAT personnel to diffuse any potential mass-casualty event. With over seventy thousand New Year's revelers descending upon the stadium for a high-energy concert, Will expected to have his hands full.

After they entered through the employee entrance, Will pulled Ethan and Skylar aside and gave them instructions. He placed lanyards over their heads that contained laminated tickets and displayed their all-access pass to any ushers or security personnel.

"I've got you guys club-level seats at the top of section C111. This gives you easy access to the restrooms and food services. With this pass, you can visit some of the specialty areas where you can watch different camera angles of the concert, but I'd prefer you stay in your seats where I can find you."

"Okay, Daddy," said Skylar. "Where will you be?"

Will bent over slightly and patted his daughter on the head. "Baby girl, I'll be all over this place, making sure people behave. But I have my cell phone, of course, and if you need something, send me a text. Don't try to call because, as you can hear, this place gets really loud when the performers are onstage." The opening act for Beyoncé and Jay-Z was onstage, and the music reverberated throughout the stadium.

"Um, Dad, can we have some money?" asked Ethan.

Will smiled and reached into his pocket to retrieve all of his cash, a little over eighty dollars. "This should get you both something to eat and a souvenir tee shirt or something."

"Yeah, thanks," said Ethan, a young man of few words unless something was on his mind.

Will turned to his son and placed his hands on his shoulders. "Son, I'm counting on you to take care of your sister. There's a lot of people here and it's New Year's Eve. You know what that means. It's the one night of the year when people get stupid drunk and do stupid things. I don't want you guys to get caught up in the madness, okay?"

"Sure, Dad."

Will smiled and nodded. "Now, I want you two to stick together, stay in your seats for the concert, and text me if you need anything. When the concert is over, I'll make my way to your seats and find you."

"Okay, Dad, we've got it," said Ethan.

Ethan wrapped his hand under Skylar's arm and began to lead her away when Will shouted after them, "No matter what, stay off the concert floor!"

Neither child acknowledged his admonition.

CHAPTER 18

Hyatt Centric Times Square
Bar 54
New York City

New York City was known as a culinary adventure with cuisines from around the world to tempt a visitor's palette. On the top floor of the Hyatt Centric at Times Square was one of the trendiest restaurants on Broadway—Bar 54. Known for its handcrafted cocktails, gourmet appetizer-style meals, and breathtaking river-to-river views stretching from the Chrysler Building to lower Manhattan, the tallest rooftop bar in Times Square was an especially difficult reservation to obtain on New Year's Eve, but the Sheltons had theirs.

Tom and Donna enjoyed a glass of champagne with their dinner of Chateaubriand-for-two. The king of steaks was wonderfully complimented with smoked mushrooms, fingerling potatoes, and a sauce made with smoked peppercorns, something Tom was sure would aggravate his hiatal hernia at some point.

Dinner was enjoyable and lasted well into the nine o'clock hour when the party guests began to arrive. After their table was cleared, Tom paid the bill, and the couple was about to leave when their server encouraged them to take a look at Times Square from Bar 54's observation deck.

The server warned them it would be cold, especially with the increased wind on the fifty-fourth floor, but he assured them they'd never forget it. To top off their fantastic meal, he also brought each of them a glass of Cristal champagne. Tom and Donna thanked him and braved the elements as they moseyed into the outdoor lounge.

A cold breeze immediately blew across the platform, causing some of the partiers to shriek and then giggle. Donna took Tom by the hand and led him past the early arrivals to the gala affair and scooted behind the outdoor seating so they could look over the railing. Just a few blocks away, the famous ball sat atop One Times Square, glistening with its combination of lights and crystals, awaiting its sixty-second moment of being the center of attention.

"Tom, this is incredible!" Donna had to raise her voice slightly to overcome the wind and the noisy group of four women who were standing nearby. They were clearly drunk, and she doubted they'd make it to midnight in their condition. She leaned in to Tom's ear and whispered, "That bunch is four fingers into a jug of wine."

Tom chuckled and smiled. "This is the one day of the year everybody seems to let their hair down, right?"

"I guess so," she replied sarcastically. Donna glanced back at them and frowned. They were her daughters' age but were completely different people. Her girls proudly wore the uniforms of the United States military. These partygoers wore fancy dresses beneath equally fancy coats, living in the moment.

The women were waiting to be seated inside one of the two giant *bubbles*, as they were called by Bar 54. Created especially for cold-weather dining, the bubble-like igloos were inflatable plastic domes, which provided seating for eight. From inside, a guest's view was somewhat distorted, but it was a way to withstand the elements on a night that was becoming increasingly colder.

Donna turned her attention back to the scene below. Live music was playing on the stages, which dotted the streets around Times Square. Nivea had provided large hats and foam wands in their signature color to most of the revelers, who repeatedly waved them, to the delight of some Madison Avenue advertising firm and their clients.

She took photos and videos, which she'd promised to send to the girls. She also asked one of the nearby servers to take a picture of the two of them with the ball in the background. The loving couple hugged and kissed as they took in the moment. Then Donna took one more look at the New Year's Eve party that was unfolding in Times Square.

"Tom, you've done so much to make this trip happen. You know, it's fulfilled one of my lifelong dreams."

"I know, dear, and it's long overdue. These types of things are not my usual thing, but I'm glad we came."

Donna leaned in to Tom and hugged him. Then she stood on her toes and whispered in his ear, "Would you consider indulging your wife with one more favor?"

Tom began to laugh. "Donna, I may be too old for that."

She swatted him. "I know for a fact that you're not too old for that, Tom Shelton, but that's not what I'm referring to."

"Okay, what can I do for you, Mrs. Shelton? I am at your service."

Donna hesitated; then she popped the question. "Take me down there. You know, into the crowd. I want to feel the energy and excitement of experiencing the ball drop."

Tom thought for a moment and scowled. He'd do anything to make his wife happy. "Honey, I don't know. I mean, there are so many—"

Donna pouted and looked into her husband's eyes. "Come on, Tom, please. I know it will be a hassle until we get used to it. But, listen, if you want the rainbow, you gotta put up with the rain, right?"

Tom looked skyward, and a big, fat flake landed on the bridge of his nose. The Sheltons burst out into laughter, drawing looks from the rooftop crowd at Bar 54. *How could he say no?*

CHAPTER 19

Union Oil Company of California
Offshore Oil Platform, Lease Block 916
The Gulf of Mexico

"Deliver this gentleman to the destination. Once the mission is complete, leave no trace behind and head to the extraction point. Understand?"

"Yeah, but what's the target?" asked his partner.

"Need to know, gentlemen. Get strapped in. We've got a fifty-minute flight, and then you're on your own. Prepare your weapons, inspect the contents of your dossiers, and do your jobs."

For the next forty-five minutes, the operatives studied the maps provided and the location where the operation was to take place. Neither of them had been on an oil rig before, so they took time to study the images and discuss potential hazards. Even though the limited intelligence they'd been provided indicated the offshore platform was unmanned, their instructions were clear. Eliminate any threats, or witnesses, as the situation required.

"Five minutes out. Prepare for deployment."

He and his partner were ready. They'd checked their weapons and adjusted the chest rigs they were supplied. Attempts to engage the third man on the team proved to be fruitless. He was intense and rarely made eye contact. Efforts to inquire about the nature of the target or the type of weapon to be used were rebuffed with silence.

The Lakota helicopter hovered over the water and the copilot turned to the operatives. He gave them the signal to release the Zodiac, and with the quick flip of a latch, the straps loosened. The helicopter gained a few feet in altitude as it was freed of the additional weight. The Zodiac spun slightly as it floated to the turbulent waters below.

The two operators didn't bother speaking with the pilots before they descended toward the dark waters of the Gulf. Using battery-operated headlamps attached to their foreheads with straps, they swung toward the Zodiac and landed inside with a hard thud.

One of the operators immediately fired up the outboard engine to gain control of the boat, making it easier for the third member of their party to rappel on board. Once he was safely in place, they looked upward as the edge of the large hard plastic case emerged from the compartment.

"Give it room to drop," the Frenchman ordered, prompting the operative to steer clear of the helicopter. The case came sailing down, nose first, until it struck the gulf waters and plunged under the surface. Seconds later, it emerged into view and bobbed in the choppy waters created by the helicopter's rotors.

Using an aluminum boat hook found inside the Zodiac, the Frenchman retrieved his case, and the helicopter disappeared toward the twinkling lights of Florida's Forgotten Coast.

With the outboard motor idling, the operators set their course using waterproof GPS devices strapped to their wrists next to their watches. The trio took seats and set out for one of thousands of offshore oil platforms that dotted the Gulf of Mexico along the coasts of Texas, Louisiana, Mississippi, and Alabama.

Lease Block 916, as this particular rig was known, was owned and operated by Union Oil Company of California. Like other rigs of its kind, it had been built by connecting a series of modules together. In addition to the derrick, which pumped the oil from the mineral-rich floor of the Gulf, the facility consisted of a central well-bay structure, a power module, and administrative quarters used by the employees during the construction and drilling phases of the operation.

The operators were tasked with clearing the rig first, and then the third member of the team was to be left alone to perform his, still unknown, contribution to the mission.

After an hour ride, the three men found themselves at the base of the well-bay module, where they tied the Zodiac off and disembarked. First, the operators moved throughout the rig, checking every room and equipment space. As the intelligence had suggested, the rig was unmanned.

The Frenchman, who knew the layout of the offshore rig without referencing the materials provided to them, waited for them by the Zodiac. Once they regrouped, he led the way up a series of steel stairwells.

The operators easily carried the case as they made their way up the steel steps. Fifteen minutes later, slightly crisp air greeted them as they emerged on the top of the rig. The skies were clear, and the flickering lights of other wells in the vicinity could be seen in the distance.

Several miles away, the bright lights of a city were visible to their right, followed by a dark void in the middle, and then more lights to their left. The Frenchman caught his breath, looked at his watch, and turned to the operators.

"Thank you, gentlemen. You are no longer needed up here."

"Wait, what do you mean? You're not going to show us what's inside the box?"

The Frenchman folded his arms and stood a little taller. "All will be revealed soon enough. Please, I have work to do, and time is of the essence. Please leave me alone. Thank you."

The operators sheepishly retreated and bounded down the steel stairs to the bowels of the offshore rig. Satisfied they were gone, the Frenchman opened his case.

The molded foam inside the MANPADS case was specially designed for a mission like this one. A laptop computer and a small collapsible satellite receiver provided him internet access. He set up the computer and logged on to several websites to observe his target.

Then he removed the parts to his weapon and began the assembly process. Not quite as simple to assemble as the shoulder-fired rocket, the device was far more powerful in its use and capability.

Rockets with detonating warheads were the weapons of the past. Futuristic weapons were now being developed and tested by nations like China, Russia, and the United States. Included in this advanced weaponry were DEWs.

Directed-energy weapons were developed initially by DARPA, the Defense Advanced Research Projects Agency within the Department of Defense. A DEW inflicted damage on a target by emitting highly focused energy, including microwaves, particle beams, and lasers, depending upon the intended result.

Despite a decade of research and development, the directed-energy weapons were still considered experimental by DARPA and considered unfit for deployment until several more years of testing. However, with the advent of cyber warfare, no technology was kept secret for long, and eventually the conceptual drawings were stolen by China and Russia.

All three nations ramped up their programs, hoping to be the first to claim directed-energy weapons as part of their arsenal. Only one, however, had perfected its use during experimental trials.

Tonight, a single French scientist, hired to be the first to deploy the weapon on the battlefield, made his preparations. He studied the laptop and reconfirmed his calculations. The clear sky assisted his visibility. He checked, and rechecked, his tracking devices. He adjusted the DEW's internal hunting capabilities. There was little margin for error in order to achieve the desired result.

It was almost time.

CHAPTER 20

McPherson Building
Washington, DC

Hayden stood to stretch her legs and relax her tense body. She was confident in her brief, and it had already been reviewed by the senior partners working on the president's defense with her. She picked up the remote of the television monitor nestled in a ceiling-to-floor bookcase on the wall to the right of her desk. She navigated to the DVR and sought a press gaggle that had occurred earlier in the day as the president was departing the White House en route to Mar-a-Lago in Palm Beach, Florida, for the New Year's weekend.

The president approached *Marine One* with his wife and son in tow as the questions were fired at him.

"Mr. President, you're leaving the White House at a time when many thousands of protestors have gathered outside the fence. Do you fear for your family's safety?"

The president paused and then turned to the reporters. "Naturally, I fear for the safety of my family when you have an angry mob surrounding your home. I do, however, have every confidence in the Capitol Police and the Secret Service, who've done an admirable job of protecting us and the people's house."

"Sir, Senator Booker has stated that the protestors have every right to be heard, and that the extraordinary action of calling in the National Guard to quell dissent is an affront to Americans' First Amendment rights of free speech. How do you respond?"

"I understand the passions of the moment. But I would say to the senator, and others from my own cabinet who've stoked the flames of division in our great country, your words have meaning. Millions of Americans listen carefully to you. Given the rhetoric, would it be any surprise that some are willing to do anything, including making physical threats against my family and sending threatening messages to my son at school?"

The president paused, and then his face was overcome with anger. "They've insinuated threats against all of my children and even my closest friends. They've threatened to blow me up and take me down."

The reporter interrupted the president. "But, sir, surely you don't mean to imply that the senator's comments and those of your own party are respons—"

The president closed on the reporter, causing the press gaggle to back up a step. "Let's get something straight. The coordinated strategy to destroy my presidency was soundly rebuked at the polls. Their further attempts to undermine the will of the people will have long-lasting effects on our republic." He looked directly into the camera of one of the cable news networks.

"You've sown the seeds of discord into the wind. I fear our great country will reap the whirlwind for decades to come."

The president had summarized a proverb from the Old Testament that meant one will suffer the consequences of his own actions.

"Mr. President, another question, please?"

The president took a deep breath and calmed his nerves. He'd just given the press a rare glimpse into a temper he normally reserved for behind-closed-doors meetings. It showed a crack in his demeanor that needed to be kept private until these hearings were completed.

"Go ahead," said the president.

"Mr. President, going into the New Year, how confident are you that you will prevail?"

He chuckled and smiled. "What they did a few weeks ago, in an attempt to overturn the will of the people, was nothing short of a coup d'état. I'm very disappointed in those members of the cabinet and my former vice president for the choices they made. That said, let me remind you that their efforts didn't work. They worked overtime to undermine my presidency and have me defeated at the ballot box.

"They failed, so a new tactic was needed. They were lying in wait, ready to use the so-called nuclear option of invoking the Twenty-Fifth Amendment. I believe their letter to Congress was waiting to be submitted long before the election, but these Washington swamp creatures couldn't afford to lose the White House, so they waited. Once the election was certified, they fired this salvo.

"Well, I'm a fighter. When you punch me, I'll block it and then throw my counterpunch. This fight is just beginning, and so is the storm. Thank you."

The president walked away, and despite the barrage of additional questions, he simply waved his arm as if to say goodbye.

Hayden exhaled, realizing for the first time that she'd been holding her breath during the entire exchange. They'd implored the president to stay off Twitter and avoid controversial statements to the media with the important Supreme Court arguments upcoming. She felt like today's remarks were appropriate considering the righteous indignation the president was entitled to under the circumstances.

Hayden powered off the television and turned when she became startled at the sudden appearance of Cipollone in her office. He was gazing out her office windows down upon Lafayette Square and the fully illuminated White House just beyond it.

"I apologize for startling you, Blount," he said, referring to her by her last name, as was his practice. He spoke in his typically calm voice. She'd never seen him angry or excited. He was like a robot with nerves of steel and a brain wired by artificial intelligence.

"That's fine, sir. It's been a long day and I became engrossed in the president's remarks to the press. I've been trying to monitor his public statements and social media posts in order to address any new issues that might arise."

Cipollone chuckled and removed his wire-rimmed glasses. He was wearing his signature charcoal gray suit and a red power tie. He was a complex man who exuded a strikingly consistent exterior.

"He needs our help. Storm clouds have been brewing over the president for years, but it's more than that. Much larger than this president, in fact. This is a challenge to the office of the presidency itself and the ability of future presidents to govern."

Hayden joined his side. She shook her head as she observed the throngs of protestors that encircled the White House grounds. Lafayette Square had become a tent city and an outdoor restroom for the protestors to relieve themselves.

"He said as much during his responses to the media," she added.

"I heard, and I have to say he has been remarkably restrained. But you know, the reporting of this press gaggle will be far different from the words the man said."

"Naturally, sir."

"Blount, mob rule cannot win out. Political partisanship cannot hamstring the occupant of the White House, regardless of party, with constant threats of impeachment and endless congressional investigations hanging like a thundercloud over an administration's head. America will lose respect internationally, and confidence in the office of the presidency will be eroded among the American people."

Hayden pressed her index finger against the tall plate-glass window. "Look at the protestors. Their numbers have been increasing for weeks despite the holidays and the inclement weather. Now that the president has left for Florida, I doubt they'll disperse."

Cipollone shrugged. "You see protestors; I see an angry lynch mob who, if it wasn't for the Capitol Police and the National Guard, would storm across the White House grounds and ravage the place like it was the presidential palace of some banana republic."

"It's never been this bad," remarked Hayden. "During the sixties and early seventies, the Civil Rights Movement and the Vietnam War protests generated passion, but the public discourse was largely civil. Even prior to the Civil War, the so-called gentlemen spoke to one another in archaic, but civil tones."

"The president is trying to take a stand, although many don't like his approach. But that's what the ballot box is for, and our Constitution was designed to deal with situations like this. To some the Constitution is a tired, worn-out document that needs to be replaced, but until it is, we have to respect its meaning. Removing a duly elected, sitting president because you disagree with his rhetoric, or even his policies, by some means other than an election is simply unconstitutional."

Hayden nodded in agreement. "In response to actions he was taking while in office, the president's predecessor once stated that elections have consequences. If that maxim is applied to one president, it should be applied to all, regardless of their political leanings."

Cipollone adjusted his jacket and turned toward Hayden's desk. "Which brings us to your brief. I take it you're satisfied and ready to let it fly?"

Hayden checked her watch. It was almost ten o'clock. She'd planned on waiting until the last minute, but she wasn't all that interested in riding the DC Metrorail to her home after midnight on New Year's Eve.

She replied, "It is, sir. I'll affix the appropriate signatures and file it before I leave. Hopefully, at least in the next seven days prior to the justices' conference, there won't be any bombs dropped in the media that might derail our arguments."

Cipollone rapped his knuckles on the edge of her desk and headed for the door. As he did, he added, "Your former boss, Justice Alito, once said, *I think the legitimacy of the Court would be undermined in any case if the Court made a decision based on its perception of public opinion.*"

"I remember that, sir."

"Let's trust that his opinion hasn't changed and the other justices agree with him."

"I agree, sir."

An outburst of laughter made its way down the hallway so that it could be overheard by them. Meanwhile, above them, a financial-planning firm was having a more high-spirited affair with loud music and what sounded like a herd of buffalo thundering past but was most likely dancing.

Cipollone looked up and laughed. "I'm not much for these things, but it's good for the troops. Our firm is entering a new era in Washington. We've emerged from a boutique law firm to a powerhouse, and you're an integral part of it."

Hayden blushed slightly, clearly appreciating the accolades heaped upon her by the boss. "Thank you, sir."

"Blount, after you file the supplemental, why don't you join us for a celebratory drink in the conference room. It's been a great year for this firm, and the future looks bright for us all. As our firm has been thrown into the spotlight, we face an interesting year of complications and challenges."

"To be sure," Hayden interjected.

Cipollone glanced out the window toward the White House one last time. The snowflakes had become thicker and were sticking to the glass momentarily before melting. Then he added, "Challenges not unlike the ones our client faces."

CHAPTER 21

McPherson Building
Washington, DC

Despite wanting to leave, Hayden did the right thing from an office-politics perspective and made an appearance at the party. She was not much of a drinker in public settings. Instead, she opted for a can of strawberry Perrier that she kept stocked in the small refrigerator located in her office. She quickly made the rounds, speaking with everyone and exchanging the obligatory New Year's wishes before she left.

Donning her Burberry cashmere trench coat, she loaded her briefcase and waited for the elevator. The noise from the boisterous party above her floor was amplified through the elevator shaft, causing Hayden to grimace and shake her head. Sometimes, she missed the comfort and serenity of the Blount farm in East Tennessee. After her parents had passed, she sold the property in order to live full-time in the DC metroplex.

With a ding, the elevator announced its arrival, and without looking up, Hayden made her way into the cab. She glanced at the only other passengers in the elevator, a couple making out in the corner. The man was kissing the woman aggressively and had pulled her short dress above her waist as he pressed his body against her. Hayden forcibly cleared her throat to announce her arrival.

"Oh, hey there," the man said provocatively. He backed away from the younger woman, taking his time about allowing the woman's dress to fall into place. "I didn't know we'd have company."

Hayden nodded and pressed the L-lobby button without speaking.

"She's a party pooper," the young woman slurred, pulling the man closer to her. "Let's pretend she's not there, you wanna?"

"Hey, I like it," he said, and the two resumed their sloppy, drunken make-out session.

The elevator began its descent under the watchful eye of Hayden as she begged for the illuminated numbers above the door to continue dropping. Seven, six, five.

The elevator suddenly stopped, jerking to a halt. The lights dimmed, then flickered, and eventually all power went out. At first, the cab remained still, as did its passengers. But when the elevator mechanism shook, causing the cab to move up and down slightly, the young woman shrieked.

"What the hell?" said the man from the dark corner of the elevator.

"John, what's going on?" asked his oversexed friend.

"I don't know. Do I look like an elevator expert?" he responded rudely. He turned his attention to Hayden. "Hey, lady, push some buttons or something. Or better yet, use the phone to call somebody downstairs. It's hot as hell in here."

Quit blowing hot air, and it might get better.

Hayden smirked and fumbled through her coat for her cell phone. She had the McPherson Building's security desk as one of her contacts. She scrolled through her phone and then dialed the number. The phone rang repeatedly.

"No answer," Hayden mumbled.

"Did you call the police?" asked the young woman.

"No, building security. I'm sure they're working on it."

The man turned back to his conquest and resumed pawing her. "Come on, why waste time? Besides, maybe with a little encouragement, our new friend will join us."

The girl giggled and the two resumed kissing. Hayden tried the desk security again but didn't get a response. Using her phone's display as a light source, Hayden looked around the small elevator, wishing for an escape from the two inconsiderate gropers.

She was comfortable knowing that safety measures were in place to prevent the cab from crashing to the bottom of the elevator shaft.

What concerned her the most was the lack of oxygen and the fact there wasn't an emergency generator system in place to provide some type of lighting and airflow.

Hayden had experienced claustrophobia in the past. She thought she'd left the form of panic disorder behind as a child, but it began to rear its ugly head again. She began experiencing shortness of breath, and her pulse quickened as anxiety took over.

Hayden tried to block out of her mind the cause of her phobia, a frightening day as a child when she went into a cave on the family farm and got stuck. Her playmates couldn't help her and left to find an adult. None of them thought to stay with Hayden during the ordeal. For thirty minutes, she remained alone in the semidarkness, where she was visited by bugs and mice.

As an eight-year-old's mind is prone to do, fears of abandonment and even death at the hand of the critters that crawled around dark spaces overcame her. As a result, she battled her fear of confined spaces for years until, as an adult, she was able to function despite the potential of a reoccurrence.

Her cell phone was still illuminated, which helped her define the space around her, but it also resulted in her catching an unfortunate glimpse of the progress the man was making with his conquest. Hayden was not a prude, but she was not a selfish exhibitionist either.

She tried the security desk again and began to grow frustrated that nobody was answering. Then her mind began to race. Was the power out in the city? Had the security team been attacked as part of some elaborate robbery or takeover of the building?

She considered the masses of people outside the White House, which was only four blocks away. Had they broken through the front entrance security and mobbed the building? Maybe they'd vandalized it as well?

Hayden's mind went to all of these outlandish scenarios because she'd become consumed with the news of discord sewn throughout the country. A simple thing like a power outage suddenly became something much larger.

Then the lights flickered to life and the air fan came back on.

The couple scampered to rearrange their clothing amidst nervous giggles. Hayden tried to ignore them and instead pressed the L button to take them to the lobby. Relief washed over her as the elevator started its descent once again.

When it opened, she burst through the doors first and stormed across the marble floor of the lobby as fast as her Bruno Magli heels could carry her. She saw the security personnel emerge from the building's maintenance office, but she didn't care to wait for an explanation.

She just wanted to get home.

CHAPTER 22

Mercedes-Benz Stadium
Atlanta, Georgia

Will began his patrols and building security checks after touching base with the main security office located on the field level. He'd never seen the stadium this loud and chaotic. During football games, a big play might bring the fans to their feet, screaming and cheering for their team. In a concert setting, the dancing, singing, and loud music could be overwhelming.

Tonight, Will was assigned to the 200 Concourse, the outermost reaches of the galaxy, as the security team referred to it. In addition to being the seats closest to the retractable opening roof, the restricted areas of the uppermost concourse included utility and maintenance rooms, which housed the operations nerve center of the facility.

He walked along the public access part of the 200 Concourse, scanning the concertgoers for suspicious activities and constantly checking for unexpected bags or packages lying around unattended. He watched for unusual spills and tried to detect any out-of-the-ordinary odors, which would indicate a bioterror attack, a task that became increasingly difficult as the night went on due to the pungent smell of marijuana, which permeated the upper levels of the stadium.

Early on during his rounds, he slipped down to the lower levels and checked on the kids. He was relieved to see they were sitting in their assigned seats, watching the concert. He didn't hover, as he wanted to avoid being busted double-checking on them. He wanted to establish a level of trust with Ethan and hoped his son would notice the gesture.

Satisfied the kids were safe, Will returned to the top level and made his way into the back hallways of the 200 Concourse to inspect the facility maintenance rooms.

*****

"Hey, Sky, this place is cray-cray!" Ethan shouted over the music.

"What?" came her response.

Ethan laughed and gave his sister a playful shove. "You know, crazy. Amped. Awesome."

"Oh, yeah. Pretty noisy too." She still appeared confused at the street language Ethan had picked up in high school, which hadn't quite reached the fifth grade.

Ethan pointed down to the concertgoers who were standing on the floor, dancing and waving their arms in unison. "Look down there. That's where the real party is!"

Skylar stood slightly to see over the adults' heads in front of her. She shrugged and sat back in her seat, apparently uninterested. She was enduring the concert because her father brought her there, and because this was the happiest she'd seen Ethan in a long time.

Ethan was rocking back and forth in his seat when he leaned over to his sister so he could speak into her ear. "Hey, you know our passes let us go anywhere we want, right?"

Skylar nodded.

"I've got an idea. Come with me."

"Where?" asked Skylar.

"You'll see. Come on." Ethan stood and grabbed his sister by the hand. She set down her Coke and scrambled to keep up as he led her down the pedestrian ramps leading to the lower level. They made their way through the throngs of people crowded around the field-level entrances, and they joined the massive party going on in front of the stage.

"Ethan, I don't like this. Let's go back to our seats." Skylar was overwhelmed and uncomfortable by the size and closeness of the crowd. A drunk girl staggered into her and spilled some of her beer on Skylar's shoe, which added to her feelings of concern.

"It'll be fun, trust me. Let's get closer to the stage." Ethan grabbed his sister by the hand and wove his way through the mostly inebriated crowd, who were oblivious to the two making their way closer.

They were now close enough to see Beyoncé, clad in a white beaded leotard, strolling the stage in her customary sensual manner. While Jay-Z rapped, Beyoncé added the lyrics, both adoringly looking into each other's eyes.

Ethan had reached the front corner of the stage, and they got settled in for the up-close-and-personal performance of "'03 Bonnie & Clyde," the couple's first collaborative duet from years ago. As the heart-pounding music slowed for the more sensual tune, Ethan noticed a group of pretty girls off to his left. They made eye contact with him and he immediately was smitten.

Two of the girls made their way over to where he and Skylar were standing near the temporary barriers.

"Hey, wanna burn one with us?" asked one of the girls, referring to smoking a marijuana cigarette.

"Yeah, but, um, I'm with my sister," replied Ethan, embarrassed that he was tasked with what amounted to babysitting in his mind.

"Man, we've got enough for everybody," said the other girl as she reached into her pocket and pulled out a small Ziploc bag full of pre-rolled joints.

Ethan vigorously shook his head and held up his hands. "Nah, she doesn't smoke and can't know that I do. I'll meet you back over there with your friends in a minute."

They giggled and swatted playfully at his long hair. The two left, glancing back over their shoulders to make sure Ethan was watching. He turned to Skylar.

"Hey, Sky, there are a couple of girls over there I wanna say hi to. You wait right here."

She immediately protested. "Ethan, no. You just said hello to them. Don't leave me alone."

"Come on, Skylar. Don't mess this up for me. You'll be fine. Just stay right here on this rail and I'll be back in a minute. You'll be fine."

Skylar thought for a moment and glanced to where the girls were standing. It was about thirty feet around the curved, temporary barriers. "Okay, but please hurry. When you're done, I wanna go back to our seats. Okay?"

"Yeah, sure, Sky. That's what we'll do." Ethan spun around and forced his way through the crowd as the tempo picked up onstage and the concertgoers increased their energy.

Skylar dutifully remained behind, clutching the steel barrier with both hands, an eleven-year-old girl in a light blue track suit amidst thousands of drunk and high people dancing to the hip-hop music of Mr. and Mrs. Shawn Carter, also known as Jay-Z and Beyoncé.

CHAPTER 23

Delta Flight 322

The two men continued making obnoxious jokes about the relative safety of flying compared to jogging, riding a bike, driving in a car, and swimming the English Channel. None of it was coherent and only served to frighten the women next to Cort even more.

One of the elderly women reached over and touched Cort's arm. "Sir, what does he mean by that?"

Cort, who was disgusted by the two men for many reasons, shook his head. "Ma'am, that's just an old tired joke muttered by a man who'd be well served to keep his mouth shut. Delta is a good airline with an excellent safety record."

"Really?"

"Yes, of course. Listen, Delta operates about fifteen thousand flights a day." Cort paused to do the math in order to make his point and soothe her flight jitters. "Think about it. That's five and a half million flights a year. Granted, all airplanes are susceptible to accidents, but to my knowledge, Delta's only had about a dozen in the last forty or fifty years. That's a pretty good track record."

She pursed her lips and then allowed a slight smile. She appeared relieved. "Okay, thank you, young man. I'm sorry for bothering you. It's just, well, my sister and I are returning home from burying a dear friend in Atlanta. She's younger than the two of us, and it just seems odd that someone could pass before we did."

"Ma'am, I think it's natural to think about our own mortality after burying a friend or loved one. I just left the bedside of my father-in-law and he's not well. Sadly, I have to figure out how to tell my wife and his granddaughter the bad news. While most people are enjoying

New Year's festivities, I have to tell my wife her father is very ill and possibly near death."

Cort closed his eyes and pictured his father-in-law, who despite the sudden onset of his debilitating illness, remained one of Washington, DC's top powerbrokers. At least, his words were still powerful.

The woman patted Cort on the arm again, somehow relieving her burdens and also comforting his own nerves, a troubled passenger who happened to sit by her side. They exchanged knowing smiles and turned their attention toward the aisle.

The attractive flight attendant approached the passengers and the exit row. She went through her FAA-mandated questioning of those passengers regarding their abilities to comply with exit-row requirements and their familiarity with the operation of the exit doors. After she asked each passenger whether they understood and were able to perform their duties, one of the men began flirting with her.

"You know, if I have to open this door, you'll be the first one I rescue."

"That's very nice of you, sir," she said as her face blushed.

She began walking to the back of the aircraft, prompting the men to gaze at her backside.

Cort, however, reached out for her arm and stopped her progress. "Miss, may I mention something to you?"

"Yes, of course."

He motioned for her to lean down as he lowered his voice. "Before I boarded, I saw those men in the bar drinking and talking loudly. I can't say whether they're drunk, but I am saying they might not be the best passengers suited to handle the exit-row duties."

Sometimes Cort came across as an attorney, which, of course, he was. He'd always been one to choose his words carefully, a trait he shared with his father-in-law.

"Sir, thank you, but it is New Year's Eve. Three-quarters of the passengers on this flight are most likely tipsy."

Cort shrugged and the flight attendant continued toward the rear of the aircraft, running her hands along the overhead bins to make sure they were adequately secured. She was probably right. The passengers appeared to be in high spirits. Perhaps it was the excitement of getting home, as he doubted anyone was traveling to Mobile to celebrate. Naturally, alcohol had been consumed, as was tradition on the last night of a year.

Cort finally settled in for the trip. He'd had logged many miles on airplanes, but this was his first New Year's flight, and his last.

CHAPTER 24

Metrorail System
Washington, DC

Hayden walked through a large crowd of people in the vicinity of Lafayette Park to enter the McPherson Square Station two blocks away. As she walked past them, she moved largely unnoticed despite her appearance. Most of the people were dressed in sweatpants or jeans, coupled with heavy jackets. They were equipped to endure the elements in order to stand up for their cause.

She was standing on the platform, waiting for the blue line train to arrive. She studied the people who surrounded her. In stark contrast to the protestors aboveground, the awaiting passengers looked more like her. Her building was located near K Street, known worldwide for its numerous think tanks, lobbying firms, and political advocacy groups.

Dressed in high-end trench coats and carrying expensive briefcases like she was, these people made a living from the influence they held with lawmakers and bureaucrats. By contrast, the protestors surrounding the White House felt it was their duty to influence the government through their voices.

Certainly, quite a few of the protestors were *astroturf*, an ostensibly grassroots movement that was actually funded by the types of political interests and advocacy groups that inhabited K Street. That didn't diminish their beliefs, but it did explain their ability to organize so quickly while lending the appearance they came together as a spontaneous uprising.

She rode the blue line to the transportation hub of the DC Metrorail system—L'Enfant Plaza Station. Located more than one hundred feet belowground just a block south of the Smithsonian Museum, L'Enfant Plaza was packed with New Year's revelers, protestors, and late-working professionals like Hayden.

Inside the station, the noise level was high, and the cold wind that blew through the tunnels did nothing to tamp down their spirits. The mix of people in the station was a microcosm of what was happening around DC on this holiday weekend. Some conversations were consumed with politics, discussing the fate of the president. Others were slightly inebriated as they talked about their plans for the evening. Some, like Hayden, stood quietly waiting for the green line train's arrival to carry them to their homes in Maryland or, in Hayden's case, Congress Heights on the DC-Maryland border.

Hayden was keenly aware, as always, to watch for signs of troublemakers. After she'd moved to DC from North Carolina, she'd learned to practice situational awareness. During her first month of working in the District, she learned that the city that held the leader of the free world was just as susceptible to crime as Chicago, Detroit, or Los Angeles. She'd witnessed purse snatchings, muggings, and even a knife attack in those early days. She vowed not to become a victim.

The first thing she did was research how to be aware of her surroundings, but without becoming paranoid. She studied numerous websites on the subject and then applied it to her experiences riding the subway.

She quickly learned that the vast majority of people were simply tuned out to the world around them. Most were engrossed in their smartphones, catching up on the local news or reviewing their social media accounts. Others were in a daydream state, focusing on a song or radio program rather than their surroundings. She often wondered if any of them remembered how they got from point A to point B.

Some people were more responsible, practicing what she considered to be a relaxed state of awareness. She equated it to defensive driving, constantly scanning her mirrors or looking ahead for possible hazards. In the city, it could be as simple as looking both ways before entering a crosswalk as opposed to following the herd with their nose in their phone's display.

After her early experiences in the city, Hayden learned to adopt a more focused level of awareness, one which she equated to driving on an icy road back in Tennessee. Sometimes, if she felt her mind wandering while she was taking the subway to and from work, she'd remind herself by thinking—*both hands on the wheel*, an admonishment her father used often when teaching her to drive.

Hayden considered her mental acuity while in public to be a form of managed paranoia. She practiced staying in the present when in vulnerable situations rather than thinking about the rigors that accompanied her career.

Managed paranoia. Both hands on the wheel.

Hayden smiled to herself as she stepped onto the train for her quick, ten-minute ride to Congress Heights and home for a quiet evening with Prowler.

CHAPTER 25

Delta Flight 322

"Ladies and gentlemen, from the flight deck, this is Captain Bowen. I'd like to thank you for joining us on this short flight to Mobile this evening. We've received an updated weather report from our folks on the ground, who've advised us that we'll be experiencing a little boost from those cold, northerly winds, which will place us in Mobile a few minutes early. However, the turbulence and shortened flight time requires me to suspend cabin service for the safety of our flight attendants. I know that you have a choice of airlines when you fly, and on behalf of Delta, let me say thank you, as well as wish you a happy New Year."

The men seated in the exit row in front of Cort moaned and lamented to one another how they were being prevented from keeping their buzz going with another drink. After some complaining back and forth, they finally quieted down, and within a few minutes, one of them was snoring loudly.

Cort checked his watch and made the adjustment from Eastern to Central time. Their scheduled arrival was 10:47 local time, an hour earlier than DC time.

The aircraft shook and wobbled slightly as a gust of wind grabbed the wings. Cort instinctively leaned toward the porthole window to look outside. Although it was pitch black, when something happens on an aircraft as a result of turbulence, most passengers believe they can catch a glimpse of the culprit, giving them a sense of relief that nothing further is going to occur.

Cort saw darkness, but a hint of frosty ice forming on the window. His dad used to say *bad weather always looks worse through a window*. Growing up on the Gulf Coast, the bad weather didn't ordinarily resemble ice on glass, but rather, pummeling rain and high winds brought by hurricanes. This past hurricane season had come in like a lamb and left like one as well, leaving many dumbfounded. For the second year in a row, a major hurricane had not made landfall in the United States.

Cort sighed as he considered that a storm of a different kind was coming. One that had been brewing for many years and was truly giving credence to the saying that history often repeats itself.

His melancholy mood carried him right back to Washington and the visit with his father-in-law. George Trowbridge came from a long line of New Haven, Connecticut, aristocrats dating to the early 1800s. The Trowbridge name was synonymous with shipping and the founding of the Wisconsin Territory before it achieved statehood.

Like many families, the Trowbridges had risen and fallen over the centuries as they made a living in America. George was a self-made man, parlaying his connections in New Haven with the Bush family into a career in politics, although not in public service. George Trowbridge had learned that true power was wielded with money, which bought influence, and that in turn provided him power.

Nothing happened on K Street—the major thoroughfare in Washington known for its lobbyists, political think tanks, and public advocacy groups—without Trowbridge's knowledge. Over many decades in Washington, Trowbridge established connections within, and outside of, government. Without a doubt, he had a pulse on everything that was happening in Washington, and was rarely surprised by an outcome.

Trowbridge was a Yale graduate, having attended undergraduate there with his friend, former President George W. Bush. While President Bush was floundering with a 2.35 grade point average, so low that the Texas School of Law rejected his application, Trowbridge excelled in his studies and rose to the top of his class. Over the next five decades, he epitomized the movers and shakers of Washington, establishing contacts on both sides of the aisle to benefit his clients.

Now he was withering way, suffering from failing kidneys, and forced to remain at home near his dialysis machine. His mind, however, was sharp. And while he was no longer an imposing, physical force, like he once was, George Trowbridge was still dialed into the secrets of K Street, Capitol Hill, and the White House.

Cort was a senior at Yale when he met Meredith Trowbridge. She was a stunningly beautiful girl, who, as a freshman, set the male population abuzz when she arrived that fall. She was not necessarily at Yale because of her desire to follow in her father's footsteps. She had little interest in politics and didn't intend to pursue a postgraduate degree. Her goals were to obtain an education degree and pursue her passion of teaching. If a nice young man came along during the process, then all the better.

Cort met Meredith at a fraternity event following an early-season basketball game, and the two hit it off immediately. They began dating and he eventually was offered the opportunity to meet her parents.

For a small-town Alabama kid, it would've been easy for Cort to be intimidated by his first visit to the Trowbridge home. An imposing house overlooking Long Island Sound, the Trowbridge home represented years of successes achieved in Washington by Meredith's father.

At first, his interaction with her parents was somewhat cold. She was a freshman, and Cort was a senior and four years older than she was. However, after a private conversation with her father, Cort was accepted with open arms. As it turned out, he and his would-be father-in-law had a lot more in common than one might surmise at first glance.

It was a commonality that sealed his fate.

CHAPTER 26

Delta Flight 322

After that fateful dinner party, Cort's life was never the same, nor did it belong to him. Prior to meeting George Trowbridge, he planned on returning to Mobile and getting a job. He was an above-average basketball player, but on an Ivy League team like Yale, he was never bound for the NBA. Cort had no interest in politics, unlike the vast majority of students at the university.

He was, however, a student of history, especially from a political perspective. Cort couldn't read enough about the founding of America. He studied historical accounts, and when he felt like the modern treatises were skewed to lead the reader to a particular conclusion, he sought antiquated books from the seventeenth and eighteenth century.

To Cort, in order to understand what the Founding Fathers had in mind when forming the United States, you had to read their words, not someone else's summation. He read *The Way to Wealth* and *Poor Richard's Almanac* by Benjamin Franklin. A constant source of reference was *The Federalist Papers* written by James Madison, Alexander Hamilton, and John Jay. He even read the *Two Treatises of Government*, written by John Locke, that was a major influence on Thomas Jefferson in his writing of the Declaration of Independence.

In short, Cort was a history nerd, intent on studying the past in order to make an impact on the future of America. His frame of mind suited him perfectly for the policy wonk positions he was inserted into by his father-in-law early in his career.

As his relationship with Meredith grew closer, it became apparent that Cort would be the Trowbridge son that George never had. As a result, he was taken under the patriarch's wing and was groomed in George's vision.

George Trowbridge viewed politicians with a jaded eye. He'd seen them bought and sold over the years. Some were swayed by emotional arguments, while others were directed through promises of future accommodations and power. All were interested in money, the universal means of gaining influence.

Cort's future was not as a politician. Instead, he was being groomed to be an *influencer*—the person the politician turned to for sage, unbiased advice. Cort's advice was, in fact, based upon good judgment and wisdom. Although he'd never admit this aloud to anyone except his mentor and father-in-law, his advice was biased. Anyone who claimed to be unbiased, in Cort's view, was lying. It was not possible.

To be sure, Cort gave excellent advice and had the best interests of the country in mind when he helped his boss, the senior senator from Alabama, who also happened to be the chairman of the Senate Intelligence Committee. As a senior aide on Senator McNeil's staff, Cort sat in on every policymaking meeting involving the intelligence apparatus of the United States. As a result, Cort held a very high security clearance.

The only meetings he was excluded from involved political matters. This would change at some point in his career as Trowbridge maneuvered Cort into a higher position, either within the White House or as chief of staff for another influential senator. With a potential power shift coming in Washington, it might be time for Cort to prepare for the future.

Despite the change in the political winds, his future was bright and financially secure. The hours were long and the travel schedule was tedious. Even though they'd lived apart more than they were together in recent years, he and Meredith agreed it was better to raise their daughter in Mobile than in Washington. Not only was the cost of living less, the schools were significantly better. That benefitted both daughter and wife, who pursued her dream to teach grade-school kids in Mobile.

Cort's mind eventually wandered to the other passenger on the flight who held a position of power and influence in Washington—Congressman Pratt. He was an anomaly in Alabama, a state dominated by republican voters. He was the lone democratic congressman in Alabama, representing the seventh congressional district.

Gerrymandered many years ago to cover a large swath of the rural areas of South Alabama, including Montgomery and Selma, Alabama-7 encompassed almost all of Birmingham and a sliver of the state along the Alabama River where Pratt Farms was located.

Congressman Pratt, a longtime democrat, was seen as a centrist who was willing to reach across the aisle to strike an accord when it was in the best interests of the country. But, like all politicians, sometimes a three-way tug-of-war existed between constituent interests, national party demands, and personal principles.

Of late, the demands of the Democratic National Convention, or the DNC, overshadowed what Congressman Pratt believed in his heart. However, after being in office for two dozen years and continuously winning reelection efforts with little or no opposition, Congressman Pratt found himself in a position that placed national party demands ahead of all other considerations.

Cort knew Congressman Pratt well enough to realize he was in an untenable position as chairman of the House Judiciary Committee. The stresses of Washington were beginning to take its toll on the man anyway, and the upcoming change in power would likely test his limits, especially in light of what he was tasked to do. That said, Cort knew Congressman Pratt was highly respected by all, making him nearly immune to partisan attacks.

Cort shook off the machinations of politics, and his thoughts turned to how much he missed his girls. He checked his watch again. It was 10:22. They were only twenty-five minutes from touchdown at Mobile Regional Airport.

He decided to use Delta's in-flight internet connection to FaceTime with them, even if it was only a couple of minutes. He was glad he did.

CHAPTER 27

Mercedes-Benz Stadium
Atlanta, Georgia

"Dammit!" Will had been walking behind the food-service vendors in the other direction when he heard an older woman yell out the profanity. Within the bowels of Mercedes-Benz Stadium, the noise from the concert was somewhat muted, allowing stadium personnel to carry on a conversation or utter a word in frustration.

Will turned to find the woman struggling with a garbage bag that she'd attempted to hoist into one of the roll-off dumpsters parked behind the restaurants. In her attempt to lift it over the edge, the bag had caught the sharp corner and torn, spilling its contents onto the concrete floor.

When Will approached her, she was on her hands and knees, picking up the garbage and throwing it into the dumpster. He knelt down to help her and glanced at the name tag of the distressed woman.

"Hi Esther, I'm Will Hightower. Let me give you a hand."

The woman stopped and noticed Will's uniform. "Thank you, officer. This bag was too heavy for me to carry, and the young man who's my partner on the 200 Concourse is more interested in watching Beyoncé jiggle than doing his job."

Will stifled a laugh at the older woman's description of the performer's dance moves. He continued to help her gather up the debris, which had fallen all around the dumpster. Fluids covered the floor from half-empty soda cups, mixed with ketchup and mustard left over from hot dogs or burgers.

He scooped the last of the trash and dropped the pile over the edge of the dumpster. As he did, Esther reached underneath and began mopping up the liquids using a large bundle of blue cotton material.

"Here, let me help you with that, Esther. Do you have access to a mop and a bucket of water?"

"Sure do," she replied. She fumbled through her pockets and produced a set of keys. "I'll be right back."

As she walked away, Will continued to use the material to clean up the spillage. He turned it over and used the drier side to swipe up some mustard and suddenly stopped. He unfolded the bundle and discovered it was a stadium maintenance uniform. He spread it out on the floor and searched its pockets. They were empty.

The sound of Esther rolling a mop bucket down the hallway grabbed Will's attention. He stood and ran to her side.

"Esther, where is this trash from? One of the restaurants? Or on the concourse?"

"It was in front of the ATL Grill, just in front of gate two-oh-eight."

Will looked frantically in both directions and grabbed his two-way radio from his utility belt. He turned to Esther.

"This is very important. You stay right here and don't touch anything, okay? Leave the uniform as it is and wait for my return. Esther, do you understand?"

"But what did I do wrong?"

"Nothing, but please wait here."

Will didn't wait for a response. He found the door that exited the maintenance hallway into the 200 Concourse. Without slowing his pace, he forced his way through the crowds of people amassed outside the entrance to Harrah's Cherokee Valley River Casino Club on the southernmost point of the concourse and searched for the trash cans at gate 208.

A tall young man wearing a food-service uniform like Esther's stood in the opening, watching the concert.

Will grabbed him by the arm. "Hey, do you work with Esther?"

"Yeah, man. I don't know where she went," he replied as he jerked his arm out of Will's grasp.

"Listen to me. We've got a problem. I need you to come with me. Now!"

"Man, I don't work for you."

Will was frustrated, but he kept his cool. "Please, it's important!"

"Yeah, always is. What do you want?"

"Help me look through these trash cans."

"For what, man? This crap's nasty."

"I'm looking for blue maintenance worker uniforms. You know, the coverall type. Come on!"

Will hustled to the first hard plastic, Rubbermaid trash receptacle and removed the lid. He began digging through the trash without regard to the mess he was making of himself. There was nothing there. He looked all around the concourse for anything out of the ordinary, such as abandoned packages, boxes, and bags.

While he moved on to the next one, Esther's partner slowly picked through a can, looking for a dark blue uniform. Neither found one.

Will abandoned the search and gave up on his helper, who'd wandered back into the gate opening to resume watching the concert. He pulled his radio out again and forced his way back through the crowd until he reached the maintenance hallway. Esther was dutifully standing guard over the uniform.

He called in the suspicious find to his superiors on the AMBSE Security Management Team. Within minutes, he was surrounded by men in suits and an armed member of Atlanta's SWAT team assigned to the stadium.

The group was doing an honest assessment regarding the importance of the uniform. They contacted food services and the maintenance department to determine if any of their staff had failed to show up for work tonight or had left early, claiming to be sick.

After several minutes, both departments reported nothing out of the ordinary other than the fact that service personnel were being reprimanded all evening for straying from their posted areas to watch the concert.

Will tried to make sense of this. Most likely, this was an employee who used his last night on the job as an opportunity to see the concert and decided to dump his uniform in order to wear his street clothes. Then he put himself in the mind of terrorists and other perpetrators of mass violence.

Regardless of motive, killers watch others in action to study their methods and law enforcement's reaction. If something works, they adopt it. Unfortunately, widespread media coverage, which was itself a main goal of any mass-casualty attack, brought public awareness to the methods and served to inform future attackers. Whether it be a teenage school shooter or a terrorist, successful attacks were studied, and their tactics used.

Suddenly, the cell phone of the lead member of the Security Management Team rang. He wandered away from the group, but his voice could be heard by the others.

"Are you absolutely certain?" He paused as he listened to the caller. "The feds have been alerted? They've made the decision?"

He looked over at the group and began to walk back toward the group. He concluded the conversation. "All right. All right. I concur. Let's clear the stage first, and then the stadium."

CHAPTER 28

Delta Flight 322

Delta Flight 322 banked to the right and took up a westerly course as it turned parallel to the beaches. The aircraft was over water and would remain so for the remainder of the flight until touchdown in Mobile. The copilot, along with passengers on the right side of the plane, had an unobstructed view of the sparsely populated coastline of Florida.

The pilot of the aircraft, Arlie Hasselbeck, was considered to be something of a whiz kid within Delta's ranks. He was the youngest pilot to be hired by Delta's subsidiary, Compass Airlines, a regional airline headquartered in Minneapolis.

In very short order, he'd graduated from the Brazilian-made Embraer narrow-body jet to the McDonnell Douglas MD 88 aircraft flown by another Delta subsidiary, Endeavor Air. The MD 88, nicknamed *Mad Dog* within the airline industry, had over a hundred seats but was much smaller than most of the Delta jets. It was ideal for regional travel and short flights, like the trip from Atlanta to Mobile.

It had also gained a reputation for being a training ground for new, unseasoned pilots. Part of an aging Delta fleet, the MD-88s, the oldest aircraft in service with any major U.S. airline, were being sold off to discount airlines like Allegiant Air, and foreign carriers like *Aeronaves* and Bulgarian Air.

Over the past several years, young pilots were given the opportunity to rise through Delta's ranks by flying routes in the Mad Dogs. Seasoned pilots who were relegated to fly the aircraft found themselves relearning checklist procedures and changing habits they'd grown accustomed to in newer planes.

For Hasselbeck, who was flying his third trip as the captain of an MD-88, everything was new and exciting. He'd logged plenty of hours in the flight simulators in Atlanta, as well as the requisite hours flying right seat as a copilot. He was willing to pay his dues despite the fact the Mad Dogs were being retired to the boneyard or sold off within three years. Hasselbeck had lofty goals for himself, and this was just one step in his ladder of success.

His copilot on this trip was a complainer. Hasselbeck loved flying and couldn't believe Delta paid him for the privilege of doing it. His first officer, on the other hand, needed a job and cared nothing about the experience. He was content flying right seat, checking essential items off his list, and talking about anything but the wonder of air travel.

"Flying on New Year's Eve just plain sucks," the first officer groaned as he stared out the *eyebrow windows* of the MD-88, so-called because of their shape. The window design was also antiquated because it tended to let light glare in the pilot's eyes and had been designed back in the days when many pilots navigated by the stars.

"Did you have a hot date in Hotlanta?" Hasselbeck asked jokingly as he checked his altitude. He was prepared to fly the aircraft without his copilot and would've preferred to do so if it wasn't against FAA regulations.

"Nah, but I mean, everybody else gets to pop the bubbly or throw down a beer. We can't even take a whiff of the good stuff because we have an early morning flight outta here."

"Yeah," said Hasselbeck, who glanced down at the digital clock in the cockpit. He was counting down the minutes to landing as well, primarily to get rid of his pissy first officer. The two had nearly nine hours of flying time that day, and a total of thirteen hours on this trip, which had sent them all over the Eastern United States.

The first officer continued to complain. "I mean, who wants a layover in Mobile freakin' Alabama on New Year's Eve. Say, do you think we can hit the lobby bar of the hotel tonight? Maybe a quick one will be out of our system by preflight check-in tomorrow morning."

"Nah, you go ahead. Besides, I think we're laying over at the Hampton Inn. I'm pretty sure they don't have a bar."

"Are you kidding me? I have no idea why I signed up for this trip. I would've been better off—"

Hasselbeck was fed up, but his good nature prevented him from blasting his first officer. He interrupted the man's negativity. "Well, here's the good news. I'll be making our final turn in a moment, so we need to prepare this bird for landing. This flight's almost over for you."

CHAPTER 29

Metrorail System
Washington, DC

The silhouette of the train emerged from the dark subway tunnel, slowing as it rounded the final bend into L'Enfant Plaza. The passengers-to-be crowded toward the edge of the inlaid brick marking the transition between platform and rails. Metallic squeaks could be heard as the silver nose of the green line train arrived, drifting to a stop in front of the crowd.

The crowd began to chatter in excitement, as if the famed Polar Express had arrived to take them to the North Pole. Shoes shuffled on the brick as people toward the front started to back up, allowing disembarking passengers room to leave.

Hayden had a routine when she rode the nine-car train home. It was designed to occupy her mind during the trip and to ensure her safety. She had not been approved to carry a handgun within the District. Handguns had been illegal to possess until a Supreme Court decision struck down the law in 2008. Following the Court's ruling, DC enacted a series of stringent rules and regulations for handgun possession, registration, and concealed carry. The regulations were challenged in the courts for many years as being tantamount to a gun prohibition.

Finally, in 2017, a set of standards was adopted that passed constitutional muster, so the District was forced to accept and issue permits. The process, however was intentionally tedious. The staff assigned to review the applications was considered bare minimum. In the first year, only a few dozen permits were issued. Hayden's application had been waiting for fifteen months.

For self-defense, she adopted a two-prong approach. One was to avoid conflict. She adopted a demeanor that let others know she was fully aware of her surroundings and was ready to fight back against any attacker. She never flashed her jewelry or pulled cash out of her wallet. She sat alone, in the middle of the railcar near an exit, not making eye contact with others, but constantly scanning for sudden or hostile movements.

She kept her distance from individuals who appeared unstable or dangerous. On occasion, she'd gotten off the train a stop early because she felt uncomfortable with the interactions between some aggressive young men and the female passengers on board. In her mind it was better to arrive later, on the next train, than pulling out her pepper spray or having a physical altercation with a bunch of thugs.

As for the ability to engage in self-defense, Hayden was extraordinarily fit, and part of her exercise regimen included regular Krav Maga classes. The self-defense fighting technique was built on simple principles, instinctive movements, and practical techniques developed by the Israel Defense Forces.

Initially, she undertook the training as part of her fitness training. After a few years of watching the news reports and seeing the gradual collapse of society, she immersed herself in the curriculum so that she felt comfortable taking on any form of attacker.

The ride that evening was uneventful until passengers boarded at the second stop of her trip home at the Navy Yard Metro Station. A group of drunk tourists boarded the train and immediately caused a ruckus in her car. Because they were gathering near the entrance, Hayden gave up her seat and moved toward the front of the train, which also gave her a clear view into the car in front of hers.

It was only a minute after the train pulled out of the Navy Yard that the first sign of trouble began. At the Navy Yard station, the train cars became packed with exuberant, inebriated concertgoers headed for the late-night New Year's gala at the Entertainment and Sports Arena near her stop at Congress Station. The concert featured the band Judah & The Lion and Grammy Award-winner Mary J. Blige.

The concert, and the crowd it would draw from the city, hadn't even crossed Hayden's mind until she saw the new passengers cram their way onto the train. Standing at the end of the car, she was able to see the scrolling advertising above the handrails, which included ticket sale posters for the event.

She took a deep breath and checked her watch. She was halfway home and had plenty of time to get home before the ball dropped. Catching an Uber to her home shouldn't be a problem at this hour, especially with all of the additional activity at Congress Station. The train pulled away and Hayden held on to her strap as it accelerated with a sudden jolt, propelling it downward and under the Anacostia River.

At its deepest point in the tunnel, the train lost power and abruptly came to a halt. When the lights went out, Hayden immediately thought of her earlier experience in the elevator. Logic took over, leading her to conclude that the periodic power outages in the District were due to the weather. Only, the snowfall had just begun, and it wasn't anywhere near the ice storms they'd experienced in the past.

"Great," she muttered in the dark, amidst the shrieks and laughter from the others in her train car.

"Hey! Watch where you're stepping!"

"Get your hands off me, jerk!"

The only ambient light in the car came from cell phone displays being illuminated in an attempt to place a call or text. The depth of the Anacostia was known as a dead zone to regular riders of the green line between the city and the southernmost end of the District. Hayden reached into her saddlebag-style briefcase, not to grab her phone, but rather, to search for her mace.

Her fingers closed around the pepper spray as a series of morbid screams emanated from the car in front of her. She turned and pressed her face against the glass door, her eyes searching blindly from side to side, searching for the cause of the distress.

Pushing and shoving was occurring behind her as people became frightened, and others became angry at the prospect of missing their concert. Hayden squeezed the pepper spray for reassurance, trying to fight back a second bout of claustrophobia while keeping her head together to protect herself.

A shot rang out in the rail car in front of her, followed by another, and then a third. The shrieks of surprise turned into chaotic screaming as people pushed and shoved to get closer to the exit door. Hayden held her position and allowed the others to dictate what happened next. She was certain that once the doors were forced opened, the train car would empty, leaving her alone. She didn't want to be wandering the tracks, in the dark, hoping for the power to come back on, while there were gunmen on the loose.

Her mind raced as she considered what had happened. The train had lost power completely, as had the inside of the tunnel. Were they connected to the same power source? Why weren't there emergency lights?

These questions occupied her for a moment until a loud snap sound was heard, and the doors were forced open. As predicted, the frightened and unruly passengers jumped to the floor of the tunnel, sometimes landing on top of one another. Within a minute, Hayden was left behind, in the dark. And alone, or so she thought.

CHAPTER 30

Mercedes-Benz Stadium
Atlanta, Georgia

The AMBSE Security Management Team had a detailed emergency action plan for scenarios like this one, but Will never imagined it would have to be implemented. A full evacuation of Mercedes-Benz Stadium created an operational nightmare that was potentially deadly in and of itself.

The plan covered designated responses for all levels of employees within the stadium, from security to ushers. Each person filled an important role to ensure their safety and the safety of the event's attendees. Like in life, people don't pay attention to their surroundings when it comes to an emergency. They need guidance.

While driving, the operator of any type of vehicle must consider the possibility that an oncoming car or truck might swerve onto their side of the road. However, they don't. They don't pay attention to the exits in a theater to avoid an active shooter or the safety instructions given by flight attendants as a flight takes off. For most, if they hadn't personally experienced a life-threatening event, they didn't bother to consider safety measures to protect themselves.

That can't happen to me.

Will knew better. First, he sent a text to his son.

9-1-1! Stay in your seat. I will come for you.

Then he entered the 200 Concourse and made his way to the handicapped seating along the rail of the balcony just as the performers were being removed from the stage without warning to the concertgoers.

The first reaction of the attendees was one of dismay. The harrowed look on Beyoncé's face could be seen on the gigantic monitors, which filled the entire stadium. Shocked at the sudden stoppage of the performance, the adoring fans stood primarily in silence until a few began to yell.

"Hey! What's going on?"

"Is it over? It's not New Year's yet!"

Others got angry and began to boo. Overall, the mood of the seventy thousand plus fans became surly. Will's first inclination was that crowd control would be challenging as the announcement finally came on the public address system that the concert was over, and the stadium needed to be evacuated immediately.

The crowd was instructed to leave the stadium in an orderly manner, to seek out clearly marked exit signs, and to move away from the building as quickly as possible.

Will stood at the top of gate 208 and helped direct the departing concertgoers toward the ramps that took them to the ground levels and the exits. Despite the grumbling and complaining of a few, the exodus was mostly controlled, so he made his way toward the elevators designated for security personnel.

He was a *rover*, as the Security Management Team called his position. He was not assigned a specific duty or area during an event or an emergency. This freed Will up to respond to specific calls and emergencies as needed.

The first thing on his mind was to get to his kids and ensure their safety. Just as he reached the elevator located in the maintenance hallway, the first explosion sent blast waves through the 200 Concourse. Will rushed out to investigate.

Panicked, the once subdued crowd forced themselves back toward their seats, colliding with those attempting to exit. Young people were knocked down and trampled. Some were forced backwards into the railing, crushed under the weight of the retreating mob.

Will frantically searched for the source of the explosion. The frenzied crowd was racing toward him from the entrance of Harrah's, so he pressed himself against the wall and pushed against the flow.

He was just about there when the ventilation system caught his eye.

He keyed the microphone on his two-way radio. "We've got smoke coming out of the ventilation system on two hundred. Possible fire. Repeat. Possible fire on two hundred."

Seconds later the high-pitched wail of the fire alarms sounded, causing everyone to cover their ears as the piercing noise filled the air.

Will pulled his cell phone out of his pocket and looked at the display. Ethan hadn't responded to his text from earlier. He texted his son again.

Are you in your seats? Please confirm.

Will stared at the phone's display for several agonizing seconds. The crowd was rushing past him, shoving bodies in his direction and bouncing him off the wall. He was oblivious to the madness as he nervously awaited a message from his son.

No response.

Now he was in a panic. He crashed into the crowd, knocking people to the side as he bulled past them to get to the nearest entrance to reach the maintenance hallway. He raced past food-service workers who were trying to cram into a service elevator. They were jockeying for position, knocking one another out of the way. Will opted instead for the stairwell, which led to the lower floors and the ground level.

Less than a minute later, he rushed onto the 100 Concourse and found the scene to be similar to the other level. Masses of people were pushing and shoving their way into the concourse in an effort to make their way to the exits. Screams of fear surrounded Will as he pushed his way through the sea of terrorized people.

He made his way to the gate where his kids were seated for the show. He prayed to himself that Ethan had heeded his instructions. He was concerned by the fact that his son hadn't responded, but seeing their faces, safe and secure, was all he needed at the moment.

Will got tripped up in another man's feet, causing them both to crash to the floor. Attempting to break his fall, he lost control of his radio, which was promptly kicked down the walkway leading to the seating in the 100 Concourse. Will crawled to the side of the entrance, getting kicked in the ribs and his hands stepped on in the process. He was finally able to regain his footing and forced his way toward the kids' assigned seats.

His eyes searched in all directions. Most of the seats were empty now, including the seats that his kids had occupied.

They were gone.

CHAPTER 31

Times Square
New York City

Like two teenagers, Tom and Donna had hustled back to their room and changed into their walking clothes, as Donna called them. Living in downtown Charleston, they had access to all of their doctors, favorite shopping spots and restaurants. They strapped on their sneakers, bundled up in warm, fleece-lined pants and bulky sweaters, and braved the cold air filled with snow flurries to join the madness in Times Square on New Year's Eve.

Unless you're a wide-eyed tourist, on a normal day, New Yorkers look at Times Square as the unhappiest place on earth, the polar opposite of Walt Disney World, the self-proclaimed happiest place on earth. The traffic creeps along, the tourists wander into the paths of those who have a purpose in their foot travels, and then there are the creepy people looking for handouts or wearing disheveled clown suits, performing for a few bucks.

To many New Yorkers, Times Square was the city's armpit. The capital of trickery. Nothing about it was real, at least to those who lived there. The glitter and glam portrayed on *Dick Clark's Rockin' New Year's Eve* was far from reality.

If there was one time of year that a New Yorker would rather be caught dead than visit Times Square, it was New Year's Eve. On that glorious night enjoyed by millions on television worldwide, New Yorkers would rather be anywhere but on the streets of New York. But to the visitors, it was nothing short of one of the Wonders of the World, right up there with the Great Pyramid of Giza or the Statue of Zeus at Olympia.

For Donna and Tom, who were hesitant at first to enter the throngs of people, it was an experience that took them into a potentially stressful, uncontrollable situation. However, within minutes, they embraced the year's biggest party as they bounced off other revelers and made their way through the crowd to the south end of Times Square, where the ball would drop.

They talked about catching a glimpse of Ryan Seacrest or Anderson Cooper, sans Kathy Griffin. They found their way near music stages featuring performers they'd never heard of—Antonique Smith, Chyno Miranda, and Camila Cabello.

None of that mattered as Donna beamed, her grin spreading from ear to ear at the spectacle. The smile on her face was priceless to Tom as he held her tight. She'd been through so much, fighting hard through the emotional and physical devastation of her breast cancer diagnosis. As the couple worked together to bring the cancer into remission, they felt they had a new lease on life. Their personal struggle, and forty years of marriage, had brought them to Times Square to ring in the new year.

And they were all ringing it in. There were people as far as the eye could see, dancing, singing, and waving their arms in the air. Tom swore the ground was shaking slightly, as if the Earth itself was pulsating from the energy generated by those above it. The noise levels were deafening, causing conversation between the two of them to be near impossible. Donna's normally soft voice couldn't be raised loud enough to overcome the constant roar of yelling and the occasional shriek in delight.

Tom had quickly determined they could approach One Time Square if they moved away from the middle of the crowd and hugged the Jersey barriers, the hard plastic modular walls that lined Seventh Avenue and Broadway as they came closer to merging together.

Tom and Donna felt the rush, transforming them from sixty-year-old retirees to partygoers. They were surrounded by more than a million people, with another hundred million or more watching at home. They began to live in the moment, one filled with confetti and snow flurries and heart-thumping music.

And the illusion. The illusion that New York's Time Square was, in fact, the center of the universe. In that moment, Times Square felt like the right place to be for Tom and Donna Shelton.

They finally stopped as their progress toward the front of the ball-drop stage appeared before them. They'd traveled several blocks to get the best view in the house through pushing and shoving of strangers, all of whom were experiencing the same excitement.

Midnight approached and the anticipation was building. That evening, Tom learned that despite the differences he and Donna had with all of the revelers, whether it be age, race, or culture, they were all sharing the adventure of New Year's Eve in Times Square together.

He'd opened his mind to the phenomenon and threw caution to the wind to please his wife, and he was glad he did. For when you were spending time with the one you love, even an outside-your-comfort-zone night could turn out to be magical.

Unless something went horribly wrong.

CHAPTER 32

Port Imperial
Weehawken, New Jersey

Just a few years prior, it would've been difficult to find a junior staffer in Washington who was interested in discussing the use of drones by terrorists. Then suddenly, the face of drone warfare changed. An entire division of experts was created at the National Counterterrorism Center after it was reported that Islamic fighters in Iraq and Syria had effectively deployed off-the-shelf quadcopters to drop grenades on unsuspecting targets below, including U.S. Special Operations forces. The experts opined that if terrorists could use the airborne devices in Raqqa, there was nothing to stop them from using drones on Americans' homeland.

The expectation was reached that the threat was both probable and imminent. Drones were easy to acquire and were virtually untraceable. With advanced technology, they were fairly simple to operate, nearly impossible to disrupt or monitor, and their range capabilities grew with each new product.

While most drones sold in the U.S. were small short-range devices aimed at hobbyists and unsuited to carry cargo, technological advances had created commercial models to be used by companies ranging from UPS to Pizza Hut. These commercial counterparts were heavier and more powerful, capable of delivering a small package weighing up to twelve pounds for miles.

Commercial quadcopter drones were nearly silent, easily maneuverable at low altitudes in all types of weather, and capable of bearing a small bomb or toxic material far above the metal detectors, police barricades, and SWAT teams that surrounded Times Square on New Year's Eve.

Drone technology had advanced with respect to their operation as well. For the average consumer, the drones were guided using a handheld device that resembled the Nintendo controllers of old. The antenna's range was limited and, therefore, the drone became increasingly unreliable at greater distances.

All of that changed as scientists adapted quadcopters with global positioning technology. Using GPS to identify package drop-off locations for UPS, for example, a commercial drone could be dispatched from a central warehouse facility with the exact coordinates of a home or business. With a small computer operating the drone autonomously, it could identify and survey terrain and potential obstacles, adjust accordingly, and steer itself between trees and power lines to its destination.

The device could then navigate on its own to a home's front porch, drop the package, and photograph it as it departed to create proof of delivery that was immediately emailed to the recipient.

Once again, the wonder of science was created for commercial use to make the consuming public's life better. And it created a new weapon for terrorists in the process.

As was true with any new weapon, it was difficult at first to guard against. Law enforcement and the military's best defense against the small low-flying quadcopters was radar detection, radio-jamming devices, and interrupting the GPS signal to the drone aircraft. The commercial advances took all of these security measures away. The only other option was to identify them in-flight and shoot them out of the sky—not one hundred percent accurate and certainly a potential danger to anyone caught in the line of fire.

The winds were growing stronger as the muscular young man made his way from One World Trade Center through the Lincoln Tunnel into New Jersey. The eight-mile trip took him over an hour, but he'd allowed himself plenty of time to rendezvous with his team. From their vantage point, they'd need less than fifteen minutes to implement their operation from start to a chaotic finish.

He arrived at the shuttered warehouse located in the heart of Port Imperial in Weehawken, New Jersey, a revitalized stretch of the Hudson River waterfront overlooking Manhattan across from Midtown.

The building had been on the market for years at an outrageous price. Despite its prime location directly on the water, no one had risked their capital on the slowly dilapidating structure, not that the owners cared. Their financial resources stretched around the globe, and on this night, the hundred-year-old warehouse would serve a greater purpose than some more zeroes added to their bank accounts.

He climbed the eight flights of stairs, working up a sweat despite the near-freezing temperatures. The precipitation had changed to mere snow flurries now, which lifted his spirits. He hadn't been completely truthful with his benefactor during their conversation. Weather could negatively impact the drones' operations if the precipitation changed to a heavy snow that caused it to stick to the quadcopters' rotor blades. Just like an airplane, if the snow accumulated on a drone, it could be weighed down, crashing before reaching its target.

"Ladies and gentlemen," he announced as he arrived on the rooftop of the warehouse.

Two dozen people huddled together near the edge of the flat roof's parapet overlooking the traffic on Port Imperial Boulevard. They turned around in unison and approached their boss.

He was still dressed in a short-sleeve shirt, considering the need for a coat as a sign of weakness. He continued. "First, I need a weather update."

A smallish woman stepped forward with an iPad opened to Wunderground, a weather website known for its accurate forecasts and variety of storm predictors, including radar. She responded, "Not much change, sir, although the precipitation has remained to our south toward Philly and Baltimore. The cold air has arrived as expected."

"What is our ice potential?"

A man in mechanic's coveralls stepped forward. He replied in his proper British accent, "Based on the temperature drop, we should be fine, but I've taken some measures to ensure our success."

"Such as?" the leader asked.

"Quite simple, actually. I anticipated this obstacle, so I created a mixture of glycol and water to simulate the deicing fluid used on airplanes."

One of the team interrupted. "I thought that only applies to preflight. What about while in the air?"

The Brit nodded and quickly responded, "Ice usually accumulates in flight when small droplets of precipitation freeze on the front surfaces—the leading edges like the wings of the aircraft. This changes the shape and texture of their wings and flaps, thus interfering with the flow of air."

"Quadcopters don't have wings," interjected another member of the team.

"True, but ice buildup on rotor blades will change the shape of the airfoil and, consequentially, the quadcopter's ability to produce lift. This is not unlike helicopters except our drones have the benefit of four rotors instead of one. Losing one or two rotors might slow the quads down and even reduce their altitude, but it won't stop them from advancing."

The team leader pushed through the group to admire the twenty-four quadcopters that rested silently on the rooftop awaiting their mission. Each carried a specific payload designed to unload its package at precise, strategic locations for maximum effect. He turned back to the group.

"What is our longest travel time?"

"Twenty-six minutes, sir. That's to reach the easternmost targets. Per your instructions, we've routed those quads around Times Square to avoid the sniper patrols on the hotel rooftops."

"What if we modified them for a more direct route?"

Several members of the group conferred until they arrived at a unanimous answer. "Sixteen minutes, sir. That's if we fly them right down the pipe along Seventh Avenue."

"I don't like it," the team leader said. "If detected, those few minutes saved could mean the difference between mere annoyance and our success."

"Sir, if I may?" the Brit interrupted.

"Go ahead."

"Sir, the glycol mixture is not just a deicing agent as it was originally intended for aircraft. I've also added a viscous fluid to bind the glycol ever so slightly to the rotor blades."

"Speak English, mate!" shouted one of the drone operators from the rear of the group. It drew a chuckle from everyone except the team leader.

The Brit continued. "A viscous fluid, or non-Newtonian fluid, does not follow Newton's law of viscosity."

He was interrupted again.

"Sir, I'm gonna knock this guy out if he doesn't explain what the hell he's talking about!"

"Hold on, and everyone calm down," replied the team leader. He walked over to the British man, who hung his head sheepishly, kicking at the gravel on the roof. "What was the solution you used? Salt?"

"No, sir. It would fall off at speed. I used shampoo. It will gently coat the rotor blades, together with the glycol mixture, to prevent icing."

The head of the operation smiled and patted him on the back. Every team needs a science nerd, and he was glad he had this one on board. The other two dozen people involved in this operation were expendable, as they'd soon learn.

"Okay, people!" he shouted. "Let's get this show on the road. By my watch, we've got about twenty minutes to liftoff."

It was 11:11 p.m.

CHAPTER 33

**Six Flags Great Adventure
Jackson, New Jersey**

Temperatures had dropped into the forties as darkness set in at Six Flags, but the Rankin family didn't notice. The vacation together was such a rare event due to the demands of their parents' jobs that the kids were thrilled to be chilled as they rode one heart-stopping roller coaster after another.

Many of the park's attendees that evening found their way to the Polar Point section of the park to listen to a rare outdoor show performed by Mannheim Steamroller together with the Blue Man Group.

The entire park was illuminated with Christmas lights, fresh-cut pine trees, and whiffs of peppermint spray delivered by their misting system, which was ordinarily used to keep attendees cool during the summer. Six Flags also had their snow machines turned on to ensure that a touch of winter filled the air as snowflakes fell throughout the park.

The family saved the best ride for last as they kept pace with Kaycee's regimented schedule. "The wait time for Kingda Ka is only forty-five minutes," she explained her approach to the final event. "We've got cookies and hot chocolate to keep us warm while we wait in line. The ride takes about a minute, and—"

"That's a short ride," interjected Tyler.

Kaycee was quick to correct him. "No, Dad. It's not short, just fast. You'll see. I've watched it on YouTube dozens of times."

"Okay, I see," said Tyler with a laugh as he took another sip of hot chocolate. He silently cursed the Founding Fathers for not doing all of their American Revolution stuff in sunny Florida, where it was warmer.

"Anyway," continued Kaycee, "after the ride, we'll have time to find a good spot for the New Year's Eve fireworks!"

"And champagne, too?" asked J.C.

"What do you know about champagne, young man?" asked Angela as she scruffed her son's hair.

"That's what they do on New Year's, Mom," he replied.

"Well, they, being the adults, can do champagne. Eight-year-olds cannot."

Kaycee chimed in, "Mom, can I since I'm in double digits?"

Angela laughed and rolled her eyes. "No, Peanut. Double digits, such as eleven-year-olds, don't qualify. You can wait until you're thirty."

"Thirty! No way!"

Tyler grabbed his daughter by the neck and pulled her close. He'd felt guilty for years after the near-death accident. As a lifeguard, he should've been more aware of the helicopter being in distress. He'd failed to react quickly enough, and it had almost killed Kaycee. It was a seminal event that gave him a completely different outlook on life—one that placed the safety of his family above all else. During her recovery, he'd prayed and made a promise that he'd never allow anyone, or anything, to take away or harm his family.

They made their way through the long queue and approached the front of the platform, where riders were boarding the coaster. The kids insisted in riding in the first car, so they stepped aside until the ride operator motioned them forward.

Tyler glanced up at the security cameras pointed at them. "Hey, check it out," he said as he put his arm around Angela. "Big brother is watching."

She laughed. "Isn't he always? Listen, if you're afraid, it's not too late to bail out."

Tyler laughed and slid her hand onto his butt. "Feel that? Still dry after the twenty-story drop on the Nitro ride. I can handle Kingda Ka."

Angela looked at the vertical lift rising to the apex of Kingda Ka. "This is over forty-five stories. That's taller than any building in Virginia."

Tyler leaned in to his wife's ear and whispered, "You want me to fill my pants, don't you?"

Angela started laughing. "No, I guess not, especially since we're sitting together. Say, are you gonna film it for the kids on your phone?"

"Does that mean I can only hold on with one hand?"

"Um, yeah," she replied.

"Oh, sure. Great idea. Ugh."

The next section of cars pulled up and the riders spilled out. Some of the faces were white from fear with bright red cheeks from riding at over a hundred miles an hour in the cold evening air. Others were laughing hysterically as the nervousness of the intense ride forced out their emotions.

The caravan of five cars carried eighteen passengers. The family loaded in the first car, which was a four-seater with a bright green hood in front. Angela and Tyler were seated immediately behind the kids in front of a car that contained two girls in their late teens. Tyler rolled his eyes as he saw them slide into their seats, knowing full well ear-piercing screams would be breaking his eardrums throughout the ride.

Once they were settled in, the cars moved forward to ease behind the two sets of cars in line in front of them. Tyler pointed to a sign that read:

Attention Riders. On occasion, Kingda Ka's train will not travel over the hill. This is a normal occurrence. The train is designed to safely roll back and reset to be launched again.

"Nice of them to let us know that *after* we're stuck on board this thing."

Angela laughed and squeezed his knee. "Just record and the whole thing will be over before you know it."

Tyler got his cell phone ready, and their section of cars moved forward until they were first in line. He was getting nervous. "The other car is barely at the top of the loop before they fire off another one."

Angela laughed and shook her head as she ignored Tyler's continued protestations. "Okay, kids. Who's ready?"

The mechanical announcer issued its final warning to the riders before the ride commenced.

Arms down. Head back. Hold on.

To which Kaycee replied, "Let's go!"

With the blast of a cannon firing, the ride took off on what was once the fastest roller coaster in North America. The upside-down U-shaped track bolted up forty-five stories, reaching one hundred forty five miles per hour in just three and a half seconds.

Tyler managed to film and hang on as the cars sped up ninety degrees into the first spiral before approaching the apex of Kingda Ka. At that speed, everything was a blur as his mind attempted to process something it had never experienced before.

When placed under such intense stress, the human mind doesn't count the seconds using the childhood way of saying *one Mississippi, two Mississippi*, and *three Mississippi*. The mind was far more advanced, acting like a high-speed computer capable of receiving and analyzing stimuli faster than any human could imagine.

Tyler's mind was in a heightened state of awareness when his vision transmitted his cell phone losing power just microseconds before it processed that everything around him disappeared into the darkness of the night.

CHAPTER 34

Delta Flight 322

Slowly descending as it passed Panama City Beach on the Florida Panhandle, Delta Flight 322 flew over the open water, just three miles above the Gulf of Mexico. The pilots were several minutes ahead of schedule as they made their gradual descent in preparation for landing in Mobile, Alabama. The white aircraft with the red and blue markings of Delta Air Lines could barely be seen on the moonless night. They were just twenty minutes from touchdown.

Eventually, the bumpy turbulence they'd encountered earlier gradually stopped as they cleared the cold front. The cabin continued to be filled with now-muted chatter, as the high created by preflight libations began to wear off. Fortunately for Cort, who was trying to relax from his stressful week, the inebriated men seated in front of him had dozed off, and the wailing infant three rows behind him had found solace in a milk bottle.

He input his credit card information into the empty fields of the Delta in-flight entertainment website, which was displayed on his iPad. While the connection was being made, he inserted his Bose earbud-microphone combination into his ears and turned off the external speaker. Curious passengers could see his wife and daughter appear on the screen, but they would only be able to hear his side of the conversation.

Colt's face lit up as his wife answered the FaceTime request, and his daughter, Hannah, leaned in so she could be seen too.

"Hi, baby!" Meredith genuinely greeted him with a smile. He missed her as much as she missed him.

"Hi, Daddy!" Hannah was chipper as usual. She was always an

upbeat, happy kid. But then again, she was only seven and hadn't been jaded by the world around her.

"Girls, I have really missed you. You have no idea."

"Oh, we believe you, don't we, Hannah?"

"Maybe a little," Hannah added with a giggle. "But we have big plans for our New Year's Eve party, Daddy."

His daughter was wide awake considering how late it was. He suspected Meredith had insisted she take a nap in exchange for staying up late, or Hannah was jacked up on sweet treats.

"Do tell," said Cort, who continued to beam during the conversation.

Hannah and Meredith commenced to reel off the finger foods and desserts they'd created throughout the day in anticipation of his arrival. Hannah proudly took credit for recording the New Year's festivities from Times Square on their Comcast DVR so that they could watch the ball drop together.

After the family bemoaned the concept of time zones and Cort added his two cents' worth about the media moguls of New York thinking the entire planet revolves around them, they talked about their long weekend together.

"Girls, whadya think about watching some football with me tomorrow?"

"Yale isn't playing, Daddy," Hannah complained. "I won't be able to wear my Handsome Dan sweatshirt Grandpa got me for Christmas."

Meredith's father had purchased Hannah a sweatshirt featuring the Yale mascot, an English bulldog, leaning up against a large Y. The tradition had been established in the late 1800s when a young Englishman who attended the university brought his bulldog to college with him. Yale became the first university in the United States to adopt a mascot, and now eighteen English bulldogs had proudly filled the position of *Handsome Dan*.

"I know, honey, this time of year, high-quality schools like Yale don't have to play football anymore. We're stuck with the other guys like 'Bama and Notre Dame and Ohio State."

"Daddy, why does 'Bama have an elephant as a mascot?"

Meredith laughed at the back-and-forth between her husband and daughter. "Yes, please enlighten us, Cort."

"Well, um, once upon a time Alabama was full of Republicans. So—"

Hannah was having none of it and scowled into the camera. "Daddy, I know when you're fibbin'. If you don't know, it's okay to say you don't know. Mommy told me that everybody can't know everything. Right, Mommy?"

Meredith pulled the phone closer to their faces. "That's right." She tilted her head and smiled at Cort as if to say, *the ball's in your court, Daddy-O.*

"Actually, I do know one thing. Your mommy knows everything. We made sure that was understood the day we got married."

"You betcha," said Meredith. "Okay, We're almost to the airport. Do you want us to park and come inside?"

"I don't have any bags, so why don't you guys just pick me up at departures."

"But, Daddy, you're an arrival."

Smart kid.

"I know, honey, but I think there'll be less traffic at departures at this time of night. I can just walk—"

Ding—ding—ding.

The flight attendant interrupted their conversation. "Ladies and gentlemen, the captain has turned on the fasten-seat-belt sign, indicating our approach into Mobile. As we start our descent, please make sure your seat backs and tray tables are in their full upright position. Make sure your seat belt is securely fastened and all carry-on luggage is stowed underneath the seat in front of you or in the overhead bins. Also, please discontinue the use of all electronic devices. Thank you."

Cort turned his attention back to his girls. "Ladies, I hope you two are ready to party. I can feel my second wind kickin' in, and there will be smooches covering your cheeks in just a few minutes."

"I'll take 'em!" exclaimed Hannah.

Meredith added to her daughter's sentiment. "Me too, darling. I've missed you more than—"

Then complete and utter darkness swept over Delta 322.

CHAPTER 35

Delta Flight 322

As Delta Flight 322 cruised toward an uneventful landing, a continuous supply of conditioned air kept the temperatures inside the cabin at a comfortable seventy-two degrees. Outside the aircraft, it was a different story. Temperatures at a plane's cruising altitude can drop to well below zero, especially when factoring in the windchill. Even in balmy climates like the Gulf Coast, the temperature differences were remarkable. The only thing separating the passengers of Delta 322 from this stark contrast in temperatures was a thin metal tube and a few inches of insulation that would soon prove to be no match for the fifty-degree waters of the Gulf of Mexico.

Mobile tower personnel reported the conditions as they advised Captain Hasselbeck on his final approach. "Delta 322, you've got winds at three to five knots. Ceiling is twenty-five hundred, scattered. Visibility is four to five nautical miles."

"Roger that," replied Hasselbeck. "Straight into runway 15-33?"

"Affirmative," replied the tower. "Delta 322 is clear on approach to runway 15-33."

Hasselbeck spoke aloud as he made his adjustments. "Altitude down to three-eight on approach. Wilco."

"I'll advise the flight attendants," said his first officer. He reached for the intercom switch and addressed the main cabin. "Flight attendants, prepare for landing."

The pilot continued. "Speed set, one-quarter flaps."

His first officer repeated the instructions as the two pilots worked in tandem to coordinate the routine landing. "Speed set, one-quarter flaps."

"Gear down."

"Gear down."

"Altitude two-eight."

"Confirmed."

The men rode the next sixty seconds in silence as the lights of Mobile came closer into their view. Hasselbeck pressed his face against the window and looked down to the hundreds of oil rigs that dotted the gulf waters to their left. The lights twinkled like thousands of Christmas trees floating on buoys. He turned his attention back to his instrument panel as the MD-88 continued its slow, gradual descent. Then the panel went dark.

"What the hell?" exclaimed the first officer.

"Where are the emergency lights?" asked Hasselbeck as he began to frantically flip switches, attempting to force a reaction on the instrument panel.

"We've got nothing! Absolutely no power!" The first officer became panicked.

Hasselbeck took a deep breath and recalled his training. Modern airplane engines were very robust pieces of engineering, and only rarely did a pilot encounter a *dual flameout*, the term given to the loss of both engines.

Hasselbeck's mind raced as he focused on trying to keep the aircraft in a glide while he ran through the emergency procedures to regain power.

"Pull the guides out," ordered Hasselbeck. "Now!"

The reference guides for an aircraft provide guidance and checklists for a wide variety of operational situations, including the loss of power on all engines. But this was different.

"I can't see!" exclaimed the copilot.

Hasselbeck kept his composure but was nonetheless firm with his frenzied copilot. "The flashlight is attached to the right side of your seat. Hurry!"

Hasselbeck leaned up in the seat and looked for landing options.

He recalled their altitude, which was now dropping rapidly. Mobile was still too far away. He began mentally preparing himself for putting the plane in the water.

Normally, if a ditching of the aircraft was imminent, it was preferable to be at a higher altitude, allowing for a smoother approach to the water below. The higher altitude would give the pilot the ability to force the plane into a pronounced nose-down attitude in order to maintain enough airspeed to prevent the aircraft from stalling. Their low altitude on approach did not allow for this emergency procedure.

There was an additional consideration to factor in. He had no instruments and no communications with the tower to tell him his precise altitude and speed. He was truly flying blind and unable to see the water. He only had the oil rig platforms below him to use to guide him.

He also had to consider whether to hit the surface with the gear locked in position or tucked inside. The recommended position was to ditch with the gear in the up position. However, Hasselbeck recalled from a conversation with a senior Boeing 777 captain that having the gear down might prevent the aircraft from skipping along the water, which leads to multiple impacts against the fuselage.

All of these things were running through his mind in those seconds before the aircraft began to lose airspeed and plummet toward the water. The chaos taking place behind him was beginning to enter his mind as a combination of flight attendants shouting and passengers screaming penetrated the security door.

Brace! Brace! Brace!

Hasselbeck couldn't advise them, as their communications were down. Everything was dark and unresponsive.

The first officer was holding the flashlight in his mouth, frantically thumbing through the pages of the manual. "Nothing works. There's nothing in here about a total blackout!"

Hasselbeck remained calm. "It doesn't matter. We're too low to initiate any engine restart procedure."

His copilot was not calm. "What are you gonna do?"

"I'm going to keep flying this plane and do whatever it takes to drop it safely in the water."

The first officer finally became helpful. "I'll get our life vests."

For the next twenty seconds, neither man spoke a word. The continuous chants of *Brace! Brace! Brace!* and the passengers' screams permeated the aircraft, barely drowning out the high-pitched whistle created by the plane dropping rapidly out of the sky.

Hasselbeck tried in vain to keep the nose of the aircraft up in an attempt to glide onto the surface of the Gulf. His eyes darted to his left. They were eye level to an oil rig. He took a deep breath.

"It's now. Hold on!"

The wing's flaps were the first thing to come in contact with the water. The left-wing tip caught the top of a wave first, and the plane yawed to the left. Then the fuselage slammed hard into the water. The first officer let out a bloodcurdling scream as they were slammed forward in their seats upon impact.

Likewise, the passengers let out primal expressions of emotion and pain as the sudden deceleration threw them forward in their seats. Hasselbeck could hear galley equipment being tossed around behind them and overhead bins dropping luggage on top of the passengers.

The MD-88 shook violently for several seconds; then it got eerily quiet. The vibration stopped and the plane seemed to be weightless as if it were floating in space.

Inside the cockpit, it was pitch black. Hasselbeck regained his composure and pressed his hands against the windows. Then he heard them. The sound was imperceptible at first. Yet unmistakable.

Bubbles.

Bubbles were rising upward around the windows of the aircraft, and the faint trickling of water could be heard. The plane was underwater.

Hasselbeck tried to get his bearings and orientation within the cockpit. His first officer had fainted and was dangling slightly above him in his protective harness. He surmised they were banking to the left because the left wing had caught the water first. Instinctively, he pulled the yoke to the right. Incredibly, the aircraft responded ever so slightly. The wings leveled, but they continued to sink.

A loud crack caught his attention, and he immediately assumed the cargo hold had been breached on impact. Suddenly, reassurance swept over his body as the nose of the aircraft seemed to make a slow ascent toward the surface.

Water began entering the cockpit. It dripped from the windows and rose around his feet from the floor panels. Hasselbeck studied the rise of the water. It wasn't pouring in, but it was rising fast enough to have an impact on the buoyancy of the aircraft.

He looked over to his first officer, who didn't appear to be physically injured, but only limp as a result of fainting. Hasselbeck used the rising water to revive his copilot.

"Hey! Wake up!" he shouted, scooping water out from around his feet and splashing the man in the face. The cold water worked to revive him.

"What? What?"

"Get out of your harnesses," ordered Hasselbeck as he flipped the toggle on his instrument panel to unlock the cockpit security door. "We need to help our passengers get out. Hurry!"

Hasselbeck was already unstrapped and making his way to the security door separating the cockpit from the galley. The rising water would make it difficult to open.

"Come on, help me!"

His copilot climbed around his seat and moved alongside Hasselbeck in the notoriously cramped cabin of the MD-88.

"Turn the handle while I get my fingers in the crack to pull it open."

"Okay, got it."

Hasselbeck prepared himself to pull the door inward against the weight of the water around his legs, which now rose to his knees. As the copilot released the latch, they were both surprised by what happened.

The door swung open violently and slammed into the head of the first officer, driving him backwards in a daze. Before Hasselbeck was struck by a wall of water rushing through the opening, he saw that the rest of the aircraft was gone.

CHAPTER 36

Delta Flight 322

Cort, like everyone else on board Delta 322, suddenly grew deathly quiet. While everyone's reaction to a traumatic situation is unique, there are certain common reactions innate to all humans. A trauma leaves its imprint on the human brain. The intense sense of fear causes the body to freeze as it processes the threat. Then it reacts. And the reaction aboard Delta 322 was almost uniform—panic, followed by crying, screaming, and praying.

Initially, Cort assumed, like others on the flight, that this was a temporary glitch and would be remedied within seconds. When the emergency light strips along the floors failed to illuminate and none of the overhead signs lit up, he knew they were destined to crash.

His mind raced as he tried to recall the preflight safety instructions given by the flight attendants. He silently cursed himself for not paying attention, and then he considered the fact that the two drunks sitting in the exit row in front of him certainly didn't know what to do.

The flight attendants tried to yell over the mayhem, but because they were all shouting instructions at the same time, the passengers became increasingly panicked. When the oxygen masks dropped from the ceiling, full-blown chaos ensued as passengers scrambled for oxygen.

"Hey, nothing is coming out!" shouted a man to his right.

"They're not working!" hollered a lady from the back of the plane.

"Neither is mine!"

The flight attendants stumbled through the aisles as the plane began to drop in altitude, looking for their seats. Cort reached for his oxygen mask, which also failed to function.

No power. At all. Not even emergency backup generators.

Finally, one voice took over for the entire crew, shouting over the mayhem, "Everyone, please fasten your seatbelts and tighten them around your waist. Think about your seat assignments. Remember where the exit rows are. They are located at the front of the aircraft where you boarded. Also, they are above the wings in exit rows twenty-four and twenty-five. At the right rear of the plane, there are exit rows at thirty-two and thirty-three."

Another flight attendant shouted from the rear of the aircraft, "We all need to prepare for an emergency landing. Please remove your life vest from the pouch beneath your seat. Slip the open end over your head, pull the straps around your waist, and adjust the tabs at the front. To inflate the vest, pull firmly on the red cord, but only—"

"Red cord! We can't see anything. Where are the lights?"

Cort shoved his iPad into the seat pocket in front of him and felt underneath his seat for the life vest.

The flight attendant continued. "Pull the cord to inflate your life vest after we land. If you can't find the cord, blow into the mouthpiece next to your shoulder. There is also a whistle that can be used to attract attention. Remember, don't inflate your vest before landing! It might puncture upon impact."

"Impact? Are we gonna crash, Dad?" A young boy clearly couldn't grasp the gravity of the catastrophe they were facing.

Cort found the pouch, but the strap holding it together was stuck. He quickly unbuckled his seat belt and dropped to his knees to wrestle with the straps. He retrieved it and then noticed the elderly women next to him were dazed and confused.

He tried to remain calm, for his sake and theirs. "Ladies, don't mind me, but I'm going to pull out your life vests. We'll figure them out together."

Cort could feel the plane take a sudden turn downwards, and the flight attendants began to yell, *"Brace! Brace! Brace!"*

Cort put on his life vest and assisted the women. He told them to tighten the strap, but not too tight. They didn't need to feel constrained while swimming.

He then positioned their arms to illustrate how to maintain the brace position.

"Lean forward like this," he began, bending at the waist as far as he could. He turned his head to the side, although he could barely make them out in the dim light provided by passengers who were using their phones to video the impending disaster. "Then clasp your hands behind your head, interlocking your fingers. Try to tuck your elbows against your thighs. Okay?"

He could barely hear their responses between their crying and the other panicked passengers.

Brace! Brace! Brace!

Cort closed his eyes and prayed to God to take care of his family in the event he didn't survive. He repeatedly told Meredith and Hannah that he loved them, hoping that somehow the universe, which had dealt him this bad set of cards, would deliver the message on his behalf.

While others prayed or screamed in panic, Cort's body relaxed and he smiled, allowing the memories of his family to fill his consciousness. He was at peace with his fate.

That was when the plane plowed into the water.

CHAPTER 37

Mercedes-Benz Stadium
Atlanta, Georgia

"Ethan! Ethan!" Skylar screamed for her brother as chaos engulfed the stadium. At first, the young girl was confused by the sudden turn of events. Three security personnel ran in front of her between the barriers and the stage and then quickly climbed the stairs to interrupt the performance. They ushered Beyoncé and Jay-Z off the stage first, and then the other dancers followed close behind.

Dumbfounded, Skylar looked around for her brother to see if he knew what was going on. That was when the announcement to evacuate came. At first, the people around her were quiet, and then they became angry. They started shouting at the stage despite the fact that nobody was on it.

The hostility began to frighten her. One moment, the crowd was cheering, swaying back and forth to the beat of the music. The next moment, the stage was emptied, the concert was cancelled, and the fans were told to leave.

Those on the floor in front of the stage, both high and drunk, immediately took exception.

"Come back out here!"

"Hey, I paid for a full concert!"

"I want my money back!"

The mob was pressing toward the stage, mashing those along the steel barriers to the point they were screaming in agony. Skylar was one of them. She was the youngest and smallest of anyone else around her. Most of those who were waving their fists in anger and inching forward didn't see her. Her attempts to scream for Ethan went unanswered.

Skylar didn't know what else to do, so she found a way to climb over the barrier. Using the back of a man who'd fallen over next to her in a vomiting fit, she stood on his back and hoisted herself onto the barrier and flopped over to the other side, landing on her back with a thud.

The impact knocked the breath out of her for a second, but then she recovered just as a huge push from the crowd shoved the barriers forward a foot or more. Skylar scrambled out of the way and crawled toward the black skirt that covered the underneath structure of the stage. She stood and looked in the direction of where she last saw Ethan.

Everyone was pushing and shoving as those at the front of the stage wanted to exit the building, but many others were pushing forward to voice their displeasure at the concert's cancellation. It was a massive scrum that was being won by the angry mob.

Skylar recognized one of the girls who had approached Ethan earlier by her purple hair. She ran toward the group of girls and then noticed Ethan's black locks. Skylar cautiously approached the rail and screamed his name again. This time he heard her.

"How did you get in there?" he shouted.

"I had to climb on top of a man and then jumped over. Can you jump over?"

Ethan looked around and started to wedge his way through a group of four young men when they got mad and pushed him back.

"Check yourself, man!" one of them yelled angrily.

"I need to get to my sister. Let me through." Ethan was determined.

"Let me help you, boss man," the man said threateningly. He grabbed Ethan by the shirt and pulled him forward, throwing him downward until his head struck the post of the steel barrier. Blood immediately gushed from his forehead and streamed down his face.

The gang of four burst out in drunken laughter. "Look at this freak show, man. This ain't a Megadeth concert. You've come to the wrong place, punk."

The men began to kick Ethan, who'd curled into a fetal position to avoid the onslaught.

"Leave him alone!" shouted Skylar, which only drew more laughter and ridicule.

"Oh, baby sister gotta take care of you?"

"Or maybe that's his girlfriend?"

"She's a little young for you, man!"

The men kicked Ethan again until they abruptly stopped—when the lights went out.

CHAPTER 38

Six Flags Great Adventure
Jackson, New Jersey

Many of the riders on Kingda Ka at that moment were unaware that the power had been lost to Six Flags and the surrounding area, as they had their eyes clenched shut from fear. They didn't realize anything was wrong until the forward momentum of the roller coaster cars designed to carry them up and over the curved top came to a sudden, bone-jarring stop before it entered the two-hundred-seventy-degree spiral to the bottom of the ride.

That was when the sincerely terrified screams filled the air, not the ones that were adrenaline-driven just seconds before. The eighteen-passenger coaster was stuck, pointed straight down, forty-five stories in the sky.

The sense of fear was as old as life on Earth. It was a fundamental, deeply wired reaction that evolved into a complex, existential anxiety in humans. There was a big difference between a high arousal state during a daring task, such as the rush of the passengers on Kingda Ka that New Year's Eve, and primal terror as one realistically fears their death.

The fear that overtook those eighteen passengers started in the brain and spread throughout their bodies in the blink of an eye. Their brains became hyperalert, and their breathing accelerated. Heart rates reached dangerous levels, and blood flow increased to the bodies' muscles. All of these physiological effects occurred much faster than the brain was able to communicate the ramifications of what caused the fear.

That fact had now hit the group of riders nearly simultaneously. Some continuously screamed at the top of their lungs while others broke down in fits of sobs and wails. Others went into shock, their bodies' response to the fear preventing them from rationally comprehending their fate.

Then there were two people who had lived through a traumatic experience already, and whose bodies understood catastrophic events as a result. Further, they had seen death in their jobs and were fully aware of when their lives were at risk.

Angela and Tyler, like the others, were frightened as the coaster came to a halt, but then their minds processed the situation, drawing from their past experiences. They were not falling, and they assumed safety measures were put into place that prevented them from detaching from the rails.

The worst case, in Tyler's mind, was that the coaster's brakes would fail, and they'd go sailing downward until it ran out of steam or ran into other parked coaster cars at the ride's station. Not good, but better than falling forty-five stories to their deaths.

First, he comforted his wife. "Angela, don't worry. We're gonna be all right. They have safety measures in place."

She nodded and managed a smile. "Let's help the kids."

Kaycee was already in the process of calming her brother down when both Tyler and Angela reached forward to touch their children's shoulders. The heavy restraints kept them pressed against the back of their seats for safety reasons, but the ability to make contact with their kids helped both parents and children cope with the danger.

"Kids," began Tyler in the calmest voice he could muster under the circumstances, "listen to me. It's going to be okay. We're secure in our seats, and the coaster is just temporarily stuck. They'll have the power back on soon."

Tyler had to raise his voice over the screaming passengers behind them and the people on the ground, too. The reality of the power outage was beginning to set in.

Angela continued to comfort the kids while Tyler looked around

Six Flags and beyond. The power was out as far as he could see. He then remembered his cell phone going blank. He looked down to the ground, where he could barely make out a crowd below them. At over four hundred feet above ground, they looked like ants, perhaps smaller.

What immediately struck him was the lack of illuminated cell phones recording the event for YouTube, Facebook, and Instagram. That was impossible, he thought to himself. Today, people recorded a dying man in the street before they thought to call 9-1-1 to get help.

"Angela, can you reach your cell phone?" he asked, interrupting her conversation with their children. Between her soothing tone and Kaycee's big-sister approach, J.C. had relaxed and was sitting calmly in their front-row seat.

"Yeah, hold on," she replied casually.

"Um, no problem there," Tyler quipped.

Angela reached into her hip pocket and pulled out her iPhone. She pressed her thumb to the screen to unlock the display.

Nothing.

She tried it again, this time attempting to press buttons on the side of the device to elicit a response.

It was still not turning on.

"Here, but it's not working. Tyler, it was fully charged when we left the truck, and I've barely used it except to FaceTime Brett."

Tyler tried to turn around and look to the coaster passengers behind him. Some had stopped screaming and turned their cries of despair to shouts of help. None, however, were using their cell phones to place calls.

"Dad, why aren't they helping us?" asked Kaycee.

"There's more to this, Peanut. Somehow, I think our ride isn't the only problem. The power is out everywhere."

Angela leaned over to Tyler and whispered, "EMP?"

"It has to be," he replied. "The first thing I look at in a power outage is my phone. It's not just ours. Plus, look around. Do you see any lights anywhere? I mean in the buildings, the cars, anything?"

"No," replied Angela despondently. "How the hell are we gonna get off this thing?"

Tyler closed his eyes and answered the question honestly, "I really have no idea."

CHAPTER 39

Six Flags Great Adventure
Jackson, New Jersey

"We have to get off here!" a man shouted from the back of the coaster. "This thing could fall off any minute!"

"Yeah, nobody is coming to help us. I think they forgot we're up here!" a younger man added to the panicked situation.

"Why aren't they helping us?" a woman wailed her question in response.

Tyler hesitated to respond at first, and then he felt the coaster cars begin to wiggle as the panicked passengers became agitated. He needed to calm them down.

"No, it won't fall off!" he yelled. "Everyone, please listen to me. I'm a firefighter and I've been trained for these situations. The roller coaster is safe, and the cars are firmly attached to the rails. They are not going to fall off."

"I don't believe you!" one of the men shouted back. "If it was safe, we would never have gotten stuck in the first place."

"I agree," said the other man. "Plus, the power is down everywhere. It's freezing cold up here. We can't wait forever!"

Tyler was growing frustrated because the other passengers were buying into their hysteria. "There's nothing we can do but wait." He paused and then asked sarcastically, "Do you see a ladder anywhere?"

One of the know-it-all men quickly responded, "Yeah, over there in the middle of the rails. If we could make it to the platforms, then we could climb down."

"You ain't Spiderman, mister," said one of the teenage girls behind Tyler.

"Well, I think I can make it. What about you, buddy?" the mouthy know-it-all said to the younger man who had agreed with him previously.

"Um, I can wait for a little while, I think," the young man responded after taking a look at the risky option.

The group quietened down for a moment, bringing a sense of relief to Tyler. The coaster was no longer being jostled, giving the other passengers and his children an opportunity to calm down as well.

Angela leaned in to him. "Do they make a ladder truck that will reach up here?"

Tyler grimaced and shook his head. "The longest I've heard about exists in New York City, and they're only ten stories. I saw a video of some passengers being rescued from a coaster in Japan once, but that was only ninety feet off the ground. We're four times that, at least."

"Chopper?" asked Angela.

"Most likely. Probably a Coast Guard rescue unit with a basket. They're equipped to handle two people—the rescuer and the rescued."

They paused their conversation for a moment as the men in the back continued to discuss their bail-out options.

"They're idiots," said Angela as they eavesdropped on the conversation. "They might be drunk too."

"It's New Year's, wouldn't surprise me at all," added Tyler.

"Ty, why wouldn't they have a means to release the emergency brake so we can just coast to the bottom?"

"I thought about that. First, there are probably additional braking mechanisms at the end of the ride to bring us slowly into the ride's station. They may not be working because of the power outage. If they're not, the other cars would be in the way. We'd come around the last bend and crash into them at Lord knows how fast. Fifty, sixty miles per hour? We'd be killed."

Angela nodded and gave his hand a squeeze. "Maybe they're in the process of moving the cars off the track. But there is still the matter of releasing the emergency brake. If it's electronic, it won't respond.

If it's manual, somebody's got to climb up here to do it. These rails are built like ladders, but that's a heckuva climb. I couldn't do it."

"Me either," agreed Tyler. "My guess is that the Coast Guard will be brought in at some point. Keep in mind, we're not the only people stranded on a ride in this park. And, depending on how widespread this outage is, they may have bigger problems."

"Agreed," said Angela. "What do you think we're looking at?"

"Several hours, maybe more," replied Tyler.

The words were barely out of his mouth when one of the teen girls behind him started yelling. "Hey, everybody! The fireman said it may take hours until they rescue us. We have to wait on a helicopter from the Navy or something."

"That's not what I said!" shouted Tyler. "We need to remain—"

"Well, that's all I need to hear," said one of the men at the rear of the coaster. "I'm not sitting up here all night. We're gonna use these pipes to make our way over to those platforms. It's like shimmying down a pole. No problem, right, mister firefighter? You guys do that in the firehall all the time."

"No!" shouted Tyler. "It's not like that at all. Just wait. We can sit here as long as it takes, right?"

The coaster started rocking back and forth, causing several of the passengers to scream. The man didn't respond to Tyler but instead began pushing against the U-shaped safety bar, which held his torso against the seat.

"Push, honey!" he shouted to his female companion.

Tyler couldn't turn to see what they were doing because of the restraints and the high-back seat.

"Stop it!" he shouted, to no avail. The man kept pushing the bar forward. As it snapped back, he'd push even harder, and eventually, it gave way, as did all four safety restraints in his car.

A bone-chilling scream filled the air as the two passengers in the car with the man panicked in terror. They were dropped forward toward the car in front of them until they crashed into the back of the seats.

"Hey, sorry about that," the man began to apologize. "I didn't know ..." His voice trailed off as the two college-age kids yelled for help. They were holding onto the restraints of the other car in an effort to avoid falling over the top of the inverted coaster.

"Jim! You have to help them get back in the car!" a woman hollered at the man.

"I can't reach them without crawling around the side," he immediately responded.

"Then I'll do it!" she yelled back at him.

That was when the weight of the coaster began to shift. The machine was designed to remain on a certain balance. The weight of the riders was not relevant so much as the distribution. If a passenger stepped outside the ride's protective compartment, it caused the ride to lean on the rails to one side or the other. The woman must have been heavyset, because the cars tilted slightly to the right on the rails.

"Stop! Now!" yelled Tyler. He was beginning to question his theory on whether the coaster could derail. "You can't exit the car like that. Just sit down!"

"We need help!" yelled one of the college kids.

"You'll be okay," said Tyler. "Just find a comfortable grip and hold on. Let the weight of your body push you against the back of the seats in front of you."

The cars started to sway again, and this time the lean was more pronounced to the right.

Now what?

"Jim, are you sure?" the woman asked her husband.

"Yeah, I'm sure," he replied defensively. "I wouldn't be doing this if I wasn't. Do you think I wanna die? Just follow my lead."

The coaster listed farther to the right as the man leaned over the side of the car and stepped onto the rail. Using the now broken safety bar to balance, he walked over to the blue pipes and support until he could reach them both at once. With a slight push off, he grasped the pipes and held on. For a moment, he stood there, maintaining his balance and gathering his courage. Then he addressed his wife. "See, baby? Piece of cake. Now, we bear-hug this support pipe and slide down toward that platform. It's only about thirty feet. Heck, we could drop the last fifteen feet and make it just fine."

"Um, okay," the woman replied.

Tyler desperately wanted to see what they were doing, but his view was obscured. Looking to his left, he could see the support pipes as they stretched toward the platform.

The man was growing more confident. "Okay! See. We can do this."

Tyler looked over the side of his car. The man was bear-hugging the pipe and inching downward.

"Look, it's working!" shouted the younger man from earlier.

"Yeah, come on!" shouted another.

Soon, the coaster was shaking again as some of the other passengers were trying to force their safety bars open.

"Mom!" screamed J.C. as he began to cry.

"Everybody, stop!" shouted Angela as she became instinctively protective of her frightened child.

"Push harder!" was the response she received.

Tyler saw the man in full view now, and the legs of his wife were slowly descending into his field of vision.

The shaking continued until a loud crack occurred.

"We're free!" shouted the young man. And then it happened.

The jostling of the cars caused him to lose his grip and fall over the top of the coaster. Instinctively, Tyler reached up to grab the young man's arm as his body tumbled past, but it would've been impossible to save him

Sixty feet below them, where the track began its two-hundred-seventy-degree turn, a blue support crossed the track, which momentarily broke his fall, and his back. By the time his body flattened onto the concrete amidst the onlookers below, he was already dead.

That was just the beginning.

All the passengers screamed. Angela tried to calm her children but could only do so much with the safety bar restraining her.

The woman who'd followed her husband onto the pipe panicked. "My hands are slippery, Jim. I can't hold on!"

"We're almost there!" This grabbed Tyler's attention as he looked over the side of the car.

The woman's nervousness caused her palms to moisten and she was unable to hold onto the slick steel pipe. She began to slide and scream.

"Jim, catch me! I can't—arrrggghhh!"

Her body suddenly twisted on the pipe and she sailed downward. Her husband grabbed for her leg, causing him to lose his grip, and he spun around on the pipe before dropping too.

The two bodies sailed helplessly through the air, periodically bouncing off the steel supports and platforms, breaking bones and rupturing internal organs. Unlike the first passenger, who fell already dead, these two were fully conscious when their faces met the pavement.

Everyone was crying now, including Tyler. It was so senseless. One man's ignorant, misguided attempt to be the big shot caused his death and took the lives of two others. Tyler wiped the tears off his face and closed his eyes.

There was a lesson to be learned in all of this. He just didn't know what it was.

CHAPTER 40

Metrorail System
Washington, DC

Hayden found herself in a vulnerable position. She moved toward the open doors and stood, somewhat shaky, in the center of the aisle. Listening in the pitch darkness. Outside the train, passengers were scurrying along the gravel bed that flanked the rails, some insisting it was quicker to return to the Navy Yard station while others were pushing forward toward the Anacostia station and Congress Heights beyond that.

A sigh escaped her as she held a metal pole in her left hand and the mace in her right. She switched the mace to her left hand as she sought her cell phone to provide some light inside the car. She powered up the display, revealing a picture of Prowler partially covered by her phone app icons. A slight smile came over her face as the familiarity of her best friend's steely gray eyes fixed on her, encouraging her to be strong.

Hayden looked up and turned her phone around to illuminate the dark rail car. That was when she saw the man staring at her from the car behind hers, looking through the glass doors. His eyes narrowed as he turned the latch to open the door to his train car.

She froze, assessing her options. She wished she'd dressed differently. She'd have given anything to be in her Nike running shoes and sweats. The high heels were now a burden to her because she couldn't jump out of the train with them on, nor could she run in the gravel with the heels digging into the rocks, or barefoot.

Hayden quickly turned and ran to the door that led to the next car.

She hoped to find an ally or, at the least, make her way to the front, where the operator of the train was. *Surely, he hadn't abandoned ship like the rest of them.*

She pulled the taut handle upward and the door slid to the side. Hayden glanced over her shoulder to see the man banging on the glass in an attempt to break it. Hayden knew better. During her many trips on the green line, she'd studied the operations of the train out of boredom. She knew there was a handle to the next car's door concealed behind a panel near the bottom of the door. She'd watched DC Metro personnel access it many times. Once she was on the coupling between the two trains, she studied whether dropping to the ground was an option. The slope was steep, and her footing would be nearly impossible, especially against an assailant who could catch her within seconds.

She stuck to the plan and reached downward, using her illuminated phone to locate the handle. She ran her fingers along the door and found the seam. She pushed the panel in, it gave way before popping out, and the handle was revealed.

The man had broken through the glass. Now he was removing the bits and pieces that remained, so he could reach the inside handle. He would be upon her in seconds.

Hayden jerked the handle with all her strength, breaking the seal in the door and allowing her to enter the next car. She closed it behind her as she pushed her way forward in the dark. She immediately tripped over a body on the floor of the train.

She let out a gasp and scrambled to regain her footing. She used the light of her phone to see what she'd tripped over. That was when she saw it.

Blood smothered the train's floor. The walls and ceiling were splattered in crimson. So were the seats. Everything and everywhere. And there were two more bodies on the floor, writhing in pain, incoherent but their pleas for help obvious.

Hayden tried not to be overwhelmed by the coppery smell of the victims' blood or the sight of the dead body, which lay at her feet. There was no time.

She raced ahead and efficiently opened the door to the exit of the train car. She heard a thump behind her as the man chasing her slipped and fell in the bloody mess. Quicker than before, she exited the car and searched for the handle of the next door.

"I'm comin' for you, baby! Make no mistake, we're gonna party!"

Hayden popped open the door, and then she came up with an idea. She quickly made her way into the next car, which was also empty. *Everybody left the train? Were they playing follow the leader or blind leading the blind?*

Either way, Hayden slammed the door shut again and closed the latch. She hoped to buy precious seconds to move forward toward the next car. This time, however, she planned to fight.

First, to trick her attacker, she opened the door at the far end to feign her escape. Then she quickly removed her heels, jacket and briefcase, and stowed them under a seat. Armed with her mace and her defensive skills, she vowed not to be a victim.

Just as before, the man decided to bust through the glass rather than find the exterior handle. This gave Hayden an opportunity to use the darkness, and surprise, to her advantage. He was using a large rock to crack the glass, and then he began to kick the window with the bottom of his boot. With the last final thrust, his boot and leg pushed through the glass.

Hayden was waiting for him. With her left hand, she grabbed the man's pants near his ankle and pulled him forward, causing him to lose his balance and fall against the door. When his face hit the corner of the window frame, she doused his eyes with the pepper spray.

He was screaming in agony as he recoiled from the blast and spun away from the car until he landed on the coupling with his legs spread apart. The pain to his groin only surpassed the burning impact of the direct hit of the pepper spray to his eyes for a moment.

Hayden didn't stop to admire her accomplishments. She swung around and gathered her belongings. Following the same procedure as before, she made her way to the front of the train until she reached the operator's cab.

There was no operator tonight, as the trains were running on their computer programming from the central station. Hayden quietly cursed herself for not remembering this, but she had to keep moving. The door to the cab was locked and she had no way of breaking in. She had no choice but to make her way to the tracks and the railbed.

The groans and obscenities she heard from the man she'd left in agony two cars back could be heard as she stepped down a steel ladder to the railbed. She gingerly found her footing and then thought about the best way to travel under the circumstances.

One by one, she took her Bruno Magli pumps and snapped off the three-inch heels, leaving awkwardly shaped flat shoes, but ones that were better equipped for her long walk home.

CHAPTER 41

Mercedes-Benz Stadium
Atlanta, Georgia

Will started toward the exit, hoping his kids were waiting for him outside the stadium. Then, suddenly, there was darkness except for the faint glow of battery-powered EXIT signs and emergency lighting inside the arena's concourse. The lights could barely be seen through the haze of smoke that filled the building.

Over a span of thirty seconds, the sights and sounds of cell phones coming to life resulted in phone calls being answered and placed as news of the stadium evacuation reached the outside world. In our interconnected society, the panicked mob just kicked it into overdrive.

"The news said it's terrorism!"

"The whole country is under attack!"

"Get out! They say it's a bomb threat!"

"Run!"

The voices rang through Will's head. An already volatile situation just erupted like a supervolcano. Thousands of people crushed each other as they fought their way toward the exits. Will joined in the exodus when he felt his phone vibrate. It was Ethan calling.

"Where are you?" he shouted so he could be heard over the mass panic.

Ethan tried to respond, but all Will could discern was the word *stage*. Frustrated, he pushed himself out of the way and leaned against the plate-glass windows outside the exit. At least now he could breathe.

"Ethan, I can't hear you. Watch for my text!"

Will disconnected the call and quickly sent a text to his son. *Did you say stage? Are you near the stage?*

Will rubbed his hands through his hair, nervously tapping the display of his iPhone. "Come on, son. Where are you?"

Ding! The phone announced a response.

Yes. Front of the stage. I got hit on the head. I'm bleeding.

Will didn't hesitate in his response. *Stay! Don't move!*

He caught his breath and glanced up at the entrance signs to get his bearings. He looked to his left to assess the obstacles in his way. He was at the south side of the stadium. In order to avoid the crowds on the floor, the most accessible access point to the stage at field level was from the east.

Will tucked away his phone and began to push his way along the perimeter of the stadium. His job was made easier by the fact that the crowd was running away from the exits as soon as they hit the open air. At each exit, he pushed through them and then was able to scamper to the next one.

He and his son texted each other one more time to confirm nothing had changed before Will forced his way back inside and into the dark, secured stairwell leading down to the field level. Using his SureFire tactical flashlight, he lit up the stairs and scurried down, being careful not to slip.

The smoke pouring out of the air vents had begun to dissipate. He cursed himself as he realized he'd not taken any precautions to cover his mouth and nose. As he reached the bottom, he shook his head, chastising himself for not warning the kids to cover their faces either. It was too late now.

He used his flashlight to find his way along the base of the stage.

"Dad, is that you?" He heard Ethan's voice.

Will rushed past a couple of stragglers, who seemed disoriented. He shouted at them as he passed, "Get out of here, now! What are you waiting for?"

"We're lost, man."

"And we can't see."

Will shouted back at them over his shoulder, "Just go behind the stage and look for the exit signs. Hurry!"

He turned back around and immediately crashed into Skylar, who'd run toward him. He lifted her up, and she wrapped herself around him, squeezing so hard that he asked her to loosen her grip so he could breathe.

"Baby girl, are you okay?"

Tears streamed down her face as she managed a smile and a nod. "Ethan's hurt, Daddy."

He set her down and walked over to his son, who was still bleeding from his forehead. Will removed his uniform shirt and turned it inside out to avoid the garbage stains from earlier. He used it to dab the blood off Ethan's cheeks and chin.

"Dad, I'm really sorry. I didn't know—"

His son looked downward in a gesture of genuine remorse. He smelled like marijuana smoke, but then again, so did Skylar, although not quite as strong. His son's demeanor was far different than what Will had seen in the airport and during the ride over to the stadium. Perhaps his son was high, not that it mattered at this particular moment. That was a conversation for later.

"Not now, son. Let me take a look." He turned to Skylar for assistance. "Honey, can you light up Ethan's face for me?"

"Okay, Daddy."

He handed Skylar his flashlight and patted her on the head. Will placed the palm of his left hand on Ethan's face and gently dabbed at the wound on his forehead. Ethan winced slightly.

"Well, son, I predict a gnarly bruise and maybe a slight scar. More than that, you'll have a heckuva headache."

"I can deal." His son seemed to feel better.

"Yeah, you can. Now, let me ask you a few quick questions so I can make sure you don't have a concussion, okay?"

"Okay."

"Did you pass out after hitting your head?"

"No."

"How about ringing in your ears?"

"Dad, it's hard to tell. The music was so loud that, um, I don't know."

Will wiped some more blood off his son's face and then folded it over. He applied gentle pressure to the wound and held it there. "Can you hold this firmly in place? You know, keep pressure on it?"

"Yeah," Ethan replied as he took over for his dad. Will took the flashlight back from Skylar and illuminated Ethan's face slightly. His eyes were already dilated, a possible sign of being under the influence of marijuana, or the lack of light might have caused it. Will was unsure and decided not to pursue it.

"Okay, do you feel nauseous, or have you vomited?"

"No."

"Dizzy, confused, or just generally in a daze?"

"Um, no," replied Ethan, and then he hung his head again. "Dad, I am very sorry. Um, I smoked a little weed."

Will sighed. He knew that already, but hearing Ethan admit it caused him to be conflicted. He couldn't decide whether he should be furious with his son for shirking the responsibility of protecting his sister. Or should he be angry that his fifteen-year-old was smoking marijuana in light of the difficulties he'd had at home with drug and alcohol use? Will adopted the third alternative.

He hugged his son and whispered in his ear, "It's okay, buddy. I love you."

CHAPTER 42

Delta Flight 322

Upon impact, the passengers were tossed violently around their seats. Most didn't have the strength or concentration to hold their brace position. Heads were slammed against seat backs and windows. Necks were thrown back and forth in a whiplash effect. And a few passengers who were caught off guard by the timing of the crash had their seatbelts unbuckled, which forced them out of their seats and into the aisle upon impact with the water.

The overhead bins, primarily designed for ease of passenger use, failed to remain latched and were all flung open. Heavy bags, hard aluminum briefcases, and laptop computers became dangerous projectiles, pummeling the passengers, including Cort.

The metal edge of a laptop came whizzing by like a frisbee, spinning just right so that the corner caught him above the right eye, immediately drawing blood. He felt for the warm substance, which partially obscured his vision. He pulled his right arm up to wipe the blood away.

Incredibly, the passengers became calm for a brief moment, except for the sound of a crying baby. It was if everyone waited to see if it was over, or just beginning.

The two men in front of Cort began to vomit. Their lurching was uncontrollable, and the awful stench filled the stale air within the cabin. The gross smell reminded him that the cabin had limited oxygen.

He leaned over to the two women next to him to see how they fared. Despite being banged around, they were not directly harmed like he was. Then he pushed the sliding window cover up to look outside. He expected to see something. Lights along the shore. Rescue boats. Oil rigs.

Nothing. Nothing but water.

Just as Cort came to the realization that the plane was submerged under the surface, several other passengers made the same determination.

"Oh, my god! We're sinking!"

"We're dropping to the bottom of the ocean!"

"Everybody, we have to get out!"

The hysterical passengers of Delta Flight 322 lost their collective minds. They flooded the aisles in a panicked search for the exits. In their frightened state, some had forgotten where the nearest exit row was and tried to force themselves toward the front of the aircraft. Others pushed toward the rear, thinking the exit rows over the plane's wings would be safest. The result was several immovable objects pushing against one another, resulting in a stalemate.

Several struggles were underway in which big, burly men lost all sense of decorum and chivalry as they shoved women and children back into their seats or onto the floor. An elderly man was being trampled as passengers forced their way toward rows twenty-four and twenty-five immediately in front of Cort.

Meanwhile, the plane was noticeably sinking, tail end first. Cort could sense that he was being pushed back against his seat by gravity. Then he heard shouts from the back of the plane.

"Water is coming in! Hurry. Get out. We're flooding back here!"

Everyone's sense of urgency came at once. One of the drunks fumbled with the emergency exit door. He shoved his large frame against the door while he opened the locking latch. Unaware of how the emergency exit door functioned, he undertook the task incorrectly.

The MD-88 had an escape slide built into the aircraft that automatically opened once the door was unlatched. The mechanism uses highly compressed air to inflate the slide, which doubles as a life raft.

Because the life raft was inside the aircraft, by inflating it, the door was forced open. But, when submerged, the process differed. The door was designed to act as a plug based on the highest pressure being inside the aircraft, which ordinarily forced the door outward in an emergency situation. Now, the greater pressure was outside, in the form of the Gulf of Mexico. The force was reversed, causing the emergency exit door to open inwards.

Much to the chagrin of the two drunks, as soon as the latch was released, the evacuation slide inflated and shot to the surface. The door, however, soared into the main cabin like an asteroid entering the Earth's atmosphere, crushing the two drunks together and cracking their skulls, rendering them unconscious.

Water was rushing in now and filling the aircraft when suddenly a groan of metal could be heard followed by a ripping sound. The plane was breaking apart.

All of a sudden, the aircraft's orientation in the water quickly shifted. The tail section began to rise until the plane was almost parallel. Then it broke away from the cockpit and the galley.

Water rushed to fill the opening, and the back of the plane shot upright, lifting the passengers backwards toward the surface. Cort, who had unbuckled his seatbelt with the intention of clearing the blockage created in the exit row, tumbled into the aisle and fell downward toward the front of the plane.

Gravity caused passengers to drop from the rear of the aircraft as the main cabin slowly rose to the surface. Cort struggled to hold on, using all of his strength to claw his way back toward his row. The front of the aircraft from first class to the exit rows was filling up with water as the open exit door provided a gaping hole for the Gulf to pour in.

The plane continued to rise, and when the tail section hit the surface, its ascent stopped, leaving rows ten through twenty-five, the exit row, full of water.

"This way! Come to the rear!"

A flight attendant began to shout instructions to the passengers from Cort's row to the tail section. A rush of air entered the back of the plane as the aft exit underneath the tail cone was opened. Some ambient light from the stars gave Cort the ability to see the carnage.

"Hurry!" shouted another flight attendant.

Passengers began using the seat backs as ladder rungs, climbing upward through the rear of the aircraft toward the opening. Cort assisted the ladies in getting unbuckled and pointed in the right direction. In the row across the aisle from Cort, a college-age boy was about to head up the seat ladder when Cort stopped him.

Speaking calmly, he placed his hand on the young man's shoulder. "Listen, will you help these ladies get out of here? I need to go help a friend."

The young man hesitated and responded, "Yeah, um, sure. Come on, y'all."

Behind Cort in the lower-numbered rows, passengers were swimming toward the tail-section exit. Some had the presence of mind to use their seat cushions as floatation devices, while others pushed their way toward Cort's location in search of air. Rather than wait to climb out the back, most of the passengers took a deep breath and swam through the doorways that were now open on both sides of the plane. One after another poured out into the fifty-seven-degree waters of the Gulf.

Cort didn't know if Congressman Pratt had already exited the wreckage. He was concerned that the sixty-something-year-old man, who was pushing three hundred pounds, might be in trouble. Cort did what he knew was right, setting aside any political differences the two men might've had, and the threat to his own life his decision meant.

After taking his life vest off, Cort shed his jacket and removed his tie. He kicked off his shoes and took a deep breath. Then Michael Cortland did something he almost didn't live to regret.

CHAPTER 43

Times Square
New York City

Tom and Donna stood arm in arm as the clock ticked a minute closer to midnight. In another three minutes, the twelve-foot-diameter geodesic sphere would begin its sixty-second descent to the bottom as millions of people prepared to count down the final seconds. Then they'd give their loved one a kiss for good luck, perhaps toast a glass of champagne, and belt out the words to "Auld Lang Syne."

The ball was covered with nearly three thousand Waterford crystal triangles in varied sizes ranging from four to five inches. Television cameras couldn't capture the enormity of the sphere that weighed in at twelve thousand pounds.

For this New Year's gala, the triangles included eight hundred eighty-eight special cuts representing the spirit of peace and kindness. The pattern resembled an Adonis blue butterfly, with its four brilliantly-colored blue wings that graced its body.

Of course, Tom and Donna couldn't see this design clearly, as the thousands of LED lights that illuminated the ball generated millions of vibrant colors and patterns, creating a spectacular kaleidoscope effect.

Mesmerized by the appearance, Donna hopped a little out of sheer excitement as her eyes were affixed to the ball perched nearly two hundred feet above them. Tom also stared upward, waiting for the ball to begin its descent.

That was when he caught a glimpse of something flying up Seventh Avenue directly toward them. He wiped the moisture away from his eyes, caused by the snow flurries that pelted his face. The object was getting closer, and then suddenly a second one appeared next to it, flying in formation about a hundred feet off the ground.

His mind raced to the many conversations he'd had with Willa about drone warfare. She'd told him that the United States might be the master of the remotely piloted aircraft, like the Reaper and Predator drones, as a tool of modern warfare, but terrorists were becoming adept at using commercial drones to level the playing field on a smaller, more localized scale.

Tom shouted to his wife, "Donna, we have to go!"

"No, why? It's just a couple more minutes."

"No! There's no time. Come on!"

Tom jerked her arm and began frantically forcing his way through the crowd toward the Jersey barriers. People shoved back, but not out of hostility. The entire evening, they'd been accustomed to being pushed and shoved.

Tom persisted and began issuing verbal commands. "Please move out of the way. We have an emergency!"

"Tom! Why? What's wrong?"

He heard the drone buzz over their heads. He ignored his wife's pleas, and when he reached the Jersey barriers, he straddled one and helped his wife climb over. He looked around for cover. Bubba Gump was closed, as was the Levi's clothing store adjacent to it.

He pulled Donna as close to the store's entrance as he could and tried to force himself through a packed group of people crowding the entrance to the Hard Rock Café. They wouldn't budge.

"This way!" he shouted, reversing course as he tried to shove through the masses to turn down Forty-Forth Street. They reached the corner just as the one-minute countdown was about to begin. The air around Times Square was filled with the sounds of shouting revelers eagerly anticipating the moment that people around the world had waited for. The noise was deafening, and the revelers distracted, so they never noticed the drones buzzing over their heads.

Two quadcopters carrying contact explosive devices raced toward their target. They were designed to detonate violently when exposed to a relatively small amount of energy created by sound or, in this case, pressure and friction.

As the quadcopters collided with the sphere, the nitroglycerin contained within their payload exploded, easily shattering the Waterford crystal that encapsulated the ball, sending millions of shards of glass fluttering downward upon the shocked crowd.

The sounds of explosions were heard in all directions, causing a chaotic stampede as over a million terrorized revelers sought protection.

Tom quickly assessed the situation. Blowing up the ball was most likely not the terrorists' goal. The visual of frightened Americans coupled with their dead bodies being trampled was.

"Dirty bombs," he mumbled to himself as he stared into the sky between the skyscrapers. "Come on, Donna, there's not much time!"

They were running with the crowd now, doing their best to hug the wall and avoid getting knocked over. None of the businesses were open. They needed to get back to the hotel, but the long city blocks prevented them from taking a direct route.

Tom led them under an awning and tucked into a doorway. He contemplated waiting there, but the wind was blowing too hard They kept moving as more explosions rocked the vicinity of Times Square, setting off car alarms, which joined the cacophony of sirens from police and fire vehicles.

Suddenly, Donna fell to the ground and screamed in agony. "My ankle!"

She'd turned her ankle on the edge of a sewer grate and crashed into the stampeding mob. Tom tried to help her up, but he was knocked over too. The collapse caused a chain reaction that looked like it was straight out of a Three Stooges movie, except it wasn't funny.

Those who were frantically chasing the rest of the crowd fleeing Times Square couldn't see what had happened in front of them. They all crashed into the pile of bodies strewn about the sidewalk in front of 1155 Avenue of the Americas, the Durst property remodeled after the turn of the century. The granite sidewalks proved to be much harder than concrete as people's heads struck the ground during their falls. Tom and Donna were now covered in a bloodied, panicked mass of injured revelers.

Donna moaned for assistance. "Tom, help me. I can't breathe!"

Hearing his wife in distress, Tom Shelton disregarded his age. He stood and began dragging bodies off his injured wife, slinging them about like they were rag dolls. This resulted in more people tripping into the bunch, but Donna was free of the pile. He helped her under the entrance to the massive office building, where they were able to catch their breath.

Tom found a scarf on the ground and gave it to his wife. "Wrap this around your mouth and nose. Do not breathe the air, okay?"

She did as he requested and then looked around. "What's happening?"

"I don't know, but from what I can see, this is what the apocalypse looks like."

CHAPTER 44

Near Anacostia Station
Washington, DC

Hayden's feet were screaming in pain from the unusual way she was walking along the Metrorail toward the south side of the Anacostia River. Her feet, however, were the least of her concerns at the moment. She was still alone, and now the tunnel was filling with smoke.

The DC Metrorail trains were powered by seven hundred fifty volts of electricity running through cable to third rails that run parallel to the two main rails. Insulators affixed to the concrete section that held the track kept this third rail off the ground. As the train traveled along the track, the train shoe extended outside the train itself, made contact with the third rail, and provided power.

When the power failure occurred, a surge shot through the third rail and created a stray current, a continuous flow of electricity beyond the third rail's normal capacity. This stray current instantly generated an enormous amount of heat and interacted with the insulators holding up the third rail, which resulted in a series of tiny fires up and down the tracks in the tunnel.

Hayden came across the fires as she made her way through the tunnel, but they were not a threat to her safety. The smoke, on the other hand, had become a real problem. Not only did it obscure her visibility, but it was stealing the oxygen from the confined space.

Hayden took her chances with the unsure footing and made her way to the bottom of the railbed next to the walls of the tunnel. The smoke was floating toward the ceiling, and traveling along the lowest possible point helped her breathing. She pulled her left arm out of her coat sleeve and used the cashmere material to cover her nose and mouth. Her eyes were still watering, but she was able to move faster now.

After fifteen minutes of walking up a slight incline toward the other side of the river, she heard voices ahead. Some people were talking excitedly while others were crying. The smoke began to dissipate, and she assumed she was nearing the Anacostia station.

Instead, she found a group of passengers huddled under a ladder affixed to the wall that led up through the smoke. The group huddled at the bottom consisted of Hispanic women and children.

Hayden wasn't sure how to approach the group. They didn't appear to be in danger but, rather, frightened. As she slowly closed the gap between them, she glanced upward. The ambient light from above ground allowed her to see the smoke pouring through the open space.

"What's going on?" she asked as she approached the group. One of the women was cradling a toddler while another one seemed to be tending to another child's leg.

"They all left us here," one of the women replied. "Some kept going and others climbed up the stairs. Nobody was willing to help us."

Hayden returned her arm inside her jacket, as the air had cleared thanks to the opening. She pointed up the ladder. "What's up there?"

"The ladder leads to a vent shaft," the woman replied. "The children are too weak to climb. This young one fell and sprained her ankle. I cannot carry the little one and go up the ladder. We fear it is too far to walk along the tracks; plus, we heard screams ahead."

Her added comment reminded Hayden there was a predator lurking around in the dark behind them. If they moved forward, they could be walking into trouble. If they stayed here too long, her assailant would be upon them, and he'd take out his furor on these innocent people, especially her.

Hayden raised her voice so she could get their attention. "Ladies, listen to me. Can you climb up?"

"Yes, but the children—"

"I understand. Now, please wait here and stay calm. Let me make sure it's safe, and I have an idea. Can you stay calm for me?"

"Yes, but please do not leave us. The men left us."

"Don't worry. Just wait until I return."

Hayden didn't hesitate. She looked back in the direction of the stalled train in the pitch-black tunnel, then adjusted her jacket and briefcase. She began her ascent up the ladder. With each rung, the smoke cleared, and fresh air hit her lungs. When she reached the top, the ability to breathe deeply was exhilarating and gave her a much-needed second wind to help those below her.

She climbed through the steel doors that had been flung open by other passengers. The vent shaft opened up into an empty field surrounded by dormant, tall grasses and leafless trees. Off in the distance, she could see a low-rise office building with a few lights burning.

She turned around and around, attempting to get her bearings. She could hear the roar of automobile traffic on the Suitland Parkway. She quickly spun around as a car alarm began to blare behind her. She then positioned herself so that the freeway was to her left and the car alarm was to her right. After taking into consideration the direction the track was following, she determined which direction was south, where Congress Station was located.

As her eyes adjusted from the smoke-filled tunnel to the outside, she was able to see lights off in the distance. A good sign. She assessed her options. The fact that the power was on both relieved and puzzled Hayden. What could cause the power to the trains to be cut off, but not the rest of the area?

She set aside her curiosity and looked up toward the light snow that continued to fall. She removed her coat and briefcase and set them to the side. A chill immediately came over her body, but she had no choice. She'd promised to help. Hayden immediately climbed back down the ladder, hoping that the women and children had not been joined by anyone else.

CHAPTER 45

Six Flags Great Adventure
Jackson, New Jersey

An hour after the coaster came to a screeching halt, rescue workers from the park had made their way to the uppermost platform of Kingda Ka. Inside the top-hat-designed structure on which the Rankin family was stuck with other passengers, there was another ride known as Zumanjaro, Drop of Doom. The drop tower featured three gondolas integrated into the Kingda Ka ride.

Zumanjaro was the world's tallest drop tower, featuring a floorless gondola with seating for eight. The cars were hoisted within the Kingda Ka loop, then dropped in three successive falls at ninety miles per hour.

At the moment the power was lost, Zumanjaro was being reloaded at the bottom, so no riders were stranded. Once park emergency personnel dealt with crowd control at the base of Kingda Ka and formulated a plan to extract the passengers, the rescue effort was underway.

Tyler was impressed when a fire chief as well as a firefighter arrived on the platform at eye level to their stuck coaster. Chiefs usually gave direction and certainly didn't climb forty-five-story ladders.

They climbed up the enclosed safety ladder, which rose from the ground to the top of the ride, utilizing ten interconnected platforms in between. The chief addressed the group first, with the firefighter illuminating his face and upper body with a flashlight.

"Everyone, can you hear me all right?"

"Yes," the group responded in unison.

"Good. My name is Chief Simpson with Jackson Township Fire and Rescue. First, let me ask if anyone is injured or needs priority medical assistance."

Nobody answered.

"Okay, I'll take that as a no. Let me make one thing perfectly clear to you. The coaster cars will not derail. Let me repeat this. It is physically impossible to derail under these circumstances. The only danger you will face is forcibly removing your restraints. Sadly, that wasn't understood clearly enough by some."

"How are you gonna get us out of here?" a woman shouted her question.

"We have a couple of options, and park engineers are coming up with the best possible solution. We have removed the other coasters from the track at the bottom of the ride, so your car is the only one that's left."

"Does that mean we can just ride to the bottom?" asked a man toward the rear of the coaster.

"Not necessarily," replied Chief Simpson. "The engineers are doing their calculations now. You see, without any electricity, the ride is unable to apply brakes before you round the last ninety-degree curve to enter the ride's loading station. Without a way to slow your descent, a whiplash effect could cause permanent injury as the coaster speeds through the final series of S curves before slowing on its own."

"Chief, my name is Tyler Rankin, a firefighter and EMT from Richmond. Are there Coast Guard rescue choppers available? Their baskets could handle an extraction."

"Hello, Mr. Rankin. Yes, and we're working on that. Without going into unnecessary details right now, but a lot has happened on the East Coast this evening, and it's all hands on deck for first responders and our Coast Guard."

The questions rained down on the chief.

"What happened?"

"Were we attacked again? Like 9/11?"

The chief held his hands up in an attempt to calm the passengers down. "I understand you have a lot of questions, and so do we. But for now, I hope you'd agree nothing is more important than getting you to the ground safely, right?"

"Yes, of course," said Angela.

Other passengers voiced their agreement.

"Good. Now, let me tell you what we have in mind. We have a team of specialists headed over here from Fort Dix. The Coast Guard Atlantic Strike Team has personnel specifically trained for rescue operations with specialized equipment to handle situations like this one."

"Great!"

"When will they be here?"

"Like I said, they are en route, but there are some things we can do to get ready to work with them."

"I think we can handle it, right, everyone?" asked Tyler enthusiastically.

The flashlight left the chief's face for a moment as three more firefighters joined them on the platform. Each was carrying a long stretch of nylon rope and was toting a large stuffed duffle bag.

Once the three firefighters unloaded their gear onto the platform, they caught their breath and listened to the chief assess their options.

Tyler leaned in to Angela and whispered, "The choppers aren't coming, and we don't want them to release the brake."

"I thought he was a little too optimistic about the coaster staying on the rails. But even if it does, he's right about our bodies being unable to handle the speed through those sharp turns. Every one of us will suffer whiplash or worse."

"Agreed. I think they're going to extract us up here and get us over to the platforms."

"How?" she asked hesitantly.

"My guess is the chief is about to add a new ride to the scariest theme park on earth."

CHAPTER 46

Six Flags Great Adventure
Jackson, New Jersey

Two of the firefighters left the group and began climbing higher to the top of Kingda Ka, carrying one of the duffle bags with them. They were wearing headgear, which included a flashlight to illuminate the way, leaving their hands free to climb. Tyler watched them ascend the ladder until he was unable to turn further in his seat.

The chief began to explain his rescue plan. "The key to your rescue is to remain calm at all times. Now, let me say this. You're much braver than I am to get on this crazy roller coaster to begin with. The fact that you've remained calm is a remarkable testament to your mental willpower in the face of danger."

"Too bad the others didn't sit still," mumbled one of the female passengers behind Tyler.

"That said, I'm going to ask you to have trust in me and these brave men who will be helping you. While we wait for the team from Fort Dix, we're going to outfit each of you with safety harnesses and suspension belts. In a perfect world, we'd measure you for size and weight to fit your body type. We don't have that luxury, so we have to come as close as we can without putting you in danger."

"What do you think, Tyler?" asked Angela.

"My guess is they want to hook us up to a safety line to keep us from falling when the restraints are lifted. Then I'm assuming the squad from Fort Dix are experts at the kind of high-wire rescues you only see on television."

"Is it safe?" she asked.

"Yeah, if the equipment is correct and we don't panic. The last thing the rescue workers need is us flailing around and out of control. That puts us, and them, in danger."

The chief continued. He used his flashlight to illuminate the entire coaster. He and the firefighter were counting heads and assessing body types. J.C. and Kaycee were the only children of their age on board. The rest were older teens and young adults. Ironically, the heaviest man riding on that evening had been the first to depart—to his death.

"Okay, young lady. The single rider outside your restraints. We'll have a full-body harness for you. You'll be the first extraction."

"Why does she go first? I'm at the back. Take us off first!"

"Ma'am, I need you to relax," the chief said in a calm, but firm tone. "This young lady has no protection at the moment. Besides, our teams will be able to use her vacated car as a base to stage this rescue operation. We will get to you as time and balance allows."

Angela whispered to Tyler and asked, "Balance?"

He shrugged and squeezed her hand. Then he looked at the orientation of the coaster to the track. They'd just entered the two-hundred-seventy-degree twist.

"I would want to keep the weight forward, just in the event the brakes malfunction. The whiplash effect at the bottom will be less for us."

Angela thought for a moment, then agreed. "Yeah, you're right. The back end gets the worst of it. But, Tyler, that means the kids will be the last ones off the ride. Whatever happened to women and children first?"

"Let's wait and see, okay?"

Angela's palms were sweaty, a rare show of stress for her. She had nerves of steel, and although she was a genuinely loving person, showing her emotions through crying never happened except when happy. Tyler had never seen her cry from fear, stress, or out of anger.

The chief hollered up to his men, "Take the full-body harness first. Let's remove the young lady in the middle car using the ropes and pulleys. The rest we'll outfit with their harnesses and wait for the team from Fort Dix."

A Class III full-body harness was designed to wrap over a person's shoulders, around the waist, and around the upper legs for full-body support. They had multiple heavy-duty D-rings attached to them so they could be secured to a line at various angles to transport a person in a prone position or upright, as required. Class III industrial harnesses, like the ones available to workers at Six Flags, had one main connection point, as they were designed for fall protection. Rescue teams often had a more advanced design with multiple D-ring attachments.

"Young lady! Our men are in the process of climbing down the rail system of the ride. The steel supports are designed very much like a ladder. They are wearing body harnesses like the one you're about to receive. My men will help you put it on, and we'll go from there, okay?"

"Yes, sir."

"Now, I want you to listen to one more thing," continued the chief. "There will be one point of connection with our safety rope system. This type of harness is designed for maximum fall protection by offering even support throughout your body. If you become inverted, um, upside down, please do not panic. This is very important. The harness is designed so there is no risk of you sliding out. Okay?"

There was no answer at first, so Tyler offered a few encouraging words. "Hey, my name is Tyler. I'm a fire and rescue worker too. Can you hear me?"

"Yeah. I'm scared."

Tyler could hear her sniffling and the fear in her voice. The man she came to the park with had flown forty-five stories to his death, and she was suffering from the trauma as well.

"I know, and that's okay. The chief knows what he's doing. I wouldn't risk my family if I didn't think it was safe. Follow the firefighter's instructions, and above all, don't panic, even if you turn upside down. They will control the rescue rope and get you to safety while the rest of us wait."

"Um, thanks," she said to Tyler before addressing the chief. "I'll be okay. Tell them to come on."

All the passengers sat patiently as the firefighters arrived at the back of the coaster. There were several gasps and screams as they climbed their way down the cars toward the one where the single rider remained cowered on the floor. With each movement, the coaster shook side to side as the weight distribution shifted, but thus far, there was no downward slippage, which suited Tyler just fine.

After the full-body harness was attached to the young woman, the rest of the passengers caught a glimpse of the rescue plan. With two heavy safety lines and hooks attached to the single D-ring on her harness, they slowly allowed her to swing away from the car and into the center of the Kingda Ka structure.

Initially, the woman screamed and then she vomited. But she never swung her arms and legs, as the chief had instructed. After the initial shock of floating forty-some stories above ground tethered to a rope wore off, she calmed down as the firefighters gently lowered her onto the platform next to the chief. He quickly assisted in removing her harness and gave her a bottle of water. Their conversation could be overheard by the remaining riders.

"Oh, god, thank you. I'm sorry I threw up on you."

The chief laughed. "That's okay, miss. It's not the first time. I missed most of it. You did a great job."

She then addressed the others who awaited their turn. She raised her voice so she could be heard. "You can do this, everybody. I threw up because that's what I always do when I get scared. I really shouldn't be riding roller coasters anyway."

This drew a chuckle from the other passengers, the first time they'd had a light-hearted moment since they had become suspended, face down, on Kingda Ka.

CHAPTER 47

Six Flags Great Adventure
Jackson, New Jersey

"Who's Rankin, the firefighter?"

"First car!"

"You understand the harness options, right?"

"Yeah," replied Tyler. "We're not going to be able to go full harness because of the safety bar restraining us. The same applies to Class II seat harnesses. I just don't know how we'd have the ability to maneuver in these cramped spaces."

The Class II seat harnesses were designed similar to the full-body harness used on the other passenger except there were no shoulder straps. The smaller belts that wrapped around the wearer's thighs worked to keep the wearer in an upright seated position.

"Understood," replied the firefighter. "Here's our situation. All of this safety equipment is designed for workers here at the park. Ideally, we would have Class I body belts that could adjust to fit your children. Instead, we'll have to try to work with suspension belts."

Tyler took a deep breath and exhaled. He immediately recognized the issue. The Class I body belts could be easily adjusted to fit the smallest of bodies, even children. They also had D-rings at the front and back that could be attached to carabiners. The Class IV suspension belts were designed to be worn by workers who needed to create a work seat. They were typically not used as a fall-arrest system. Tyler was about to raise this point to the firefighter when the man spoke first.

He seemed to anticipate Tyler's concerns. "This is not a long ride, and therefore the Class I isn't necessarily needed. It's important, however, for the passenger to hold on to the safety rope. Can your kids do that?"

Tyler leaned toward Angela and whispered, "Babe, if the kids freak out during the process, they could begin spinning and become inverted. Plus, the belts are designed for adult rescue personnel and construction workers."

Angela thought for a moment. "Kaycee isn't a problem. She'll love it. J.C., however, is another story. Don't they have another option?"

Tyler turned his body to speak with the firefighter. "Do you have a chest harness? We can tie my son off at two points of attachment. That will take the pressure off him to hold his body weight."

The firefighters were silent for a moment, and then the firefighter responded, "No, we don't. There is another option. I can retrieve the full-body harness from the first passenger, but we'll have to release your safety bars before you can put him in it."

The man's words weighed heavily on Tyler's mind. That meant for a brief period of time, J.C. would be tied off, but not totally secured until the transition could be made to the full-body harness. Plus, affixing his harness would have to be done by Kaycee with Tyler's assistance from the side.

"What do you think?" asked Angela.

"It's risky, and it puts a lot of responsibility on Kaycee. She's tough, but there's not much margin for error. The kids are in the front with no seat backs or raised safety bars to block their fall or give them a sense of comfort."

"Agreed. Why don't we just wait until—"

"Coleman!" shouted the chief from the platform below. "We're 10-85. 10-77 unknown."

"Dammit," muttered Tyler, quickly deciphering their use of ten-codes. "The team from Fort Dix is delayed for some reason. He used the old ten-code system to communicate to the firefighter that they were standing down for now. Nowadays, we all use plain speak when communicating."

"Why?"

"He doesn't want to panic anyone. The rescue team from Fort

Dix isn't coming."

Angela sighed and turned her body toward him. "Do you think they can take everyone off the way they did with that girl?"

Tyler shrugged. "Yeah, if none of them freak out."

"I know it's risky, but the longer this goes on, the worse it will be on the kids."

Tyler chuckled. "Honestly, it's the adults I'm worried about. They're losing it more than our two warriors up there."

"Tell the chief," said Angela with conviction.

"Chief, it's Rankin again. I think we have a pretty strong-willed group up here who are ready to set their feet on the ground. Am I right?"

Several of the stuck passengers chimed in.

"You bet!"

"Hell yeah!"

"There you have it, Chief. We have confidence in your people. And I'm here to help any way I can. Let's do this!"

The chief and his men were discussing the logistics, and then he hollered up to the two firefighters who now occupied the empty coaster car.

"Okay, gentlemen. Get everyone outfitted and strapped in tight. We'll send the full harness and a suspension belt to the young man in the front row. First thing we'll do is make sure everybody's equipment is properly outfitted and secured. Then we'll tether you with safety ropes to the coaster for added security. After that, one at a time, we'll get you down."

"Yessir, chief," responded one of the firefighters.

They quickly sprang into action. Once again, the coaster wobbled on Kingda Ka's rails, causing a few gasps, but after the first time that happened, nobody screamed. The firefighters moved systematically through the cars until everyone had their gear. It was checked for both safety and comfort to allow for an extended period of suspension without the risk of cutting off circulation during the drop.

As Tyler predicted, the process started at the rear of the coaster. One car at a time, the safety bar was manually released, a task that required the firefighter to climb down the coaster's rail and crank a lever on the undercarriage of the car. As the safety bars opened with a loud pop, gravity immediately pulled the riders forward within the car. They were instructed to use the seat in front of them to support their weight while the firefighters affixed the safety rope and swung them to safety.

The deliberate process took ten to fifteen minutes per passenger, raising the anxiety levels of the remaining passengers in the first two cars. In addition, the temperatures began to plummet as a cold front moved through the east coast. The combination of the colder temps, a slight breeze, and the inability to move in the cramped space caused the children to begin shaking.

Angela noticed it first. "Are you guys all right up there?"

"It's cold, Mom. We're tough, right, kiddo?" Kaycee genuinely loved her younger brother although, as was typical, she had a tendency to pick on him because she could. It was never mean-spirited. Eventually, she assumed J.C. would turn the tables on her.

"Yeah, I'm tough," added J.C. "I'm really cold, but I'm not scared."

The firefighters began to assist the passengers in the car behind them. Tyler came to admire the young girls, who had screamed louder during the ride than when their lives were truly in danger. Somehow, the death of the other passengers reminded them they still had a chance to escape this nightmare.

The firefighter who had conversed with Tyler earlier finally appeared next to Tyler and J.C.'s side of the car. He tried to insert some humor into the tense situation. "Rankin, party of four?"

Angela and Tyler got a chuckle from his lighthearted attempt to calm their nerves. Angela replied on behalf of the family, "Yes, that would be us. We had reservations to eat down there somewhere."

"I take it you're ready to get out of here?"

"Yeah! Let's go!" shouted Kaycee.

CHAPTER 48

Six Flags Great Adventure
Jackson, New Jersey

Kaycee Rankin lived for this adrenaline rush, her younger brother, J.C., not so much. He was a feet-firmly-planted-on-the-ground kinda kid. Tyler and Angela would lay in bed on those rare occasions when their schedules permitted, and talked about what their kids would be doing when they grew up.

Tyler was firmly convinced Kaycee would grow up to play football. The first time he suggested she could get a scholarship to a Southeastern Conference school like South Carolina, Angela slugged him. He recalled the conversation they'd had.

"My daughter is not gonna be one of those bikini babes during the Super Bowl halftime show on some crappy cable network."

Tyler always thought that was ironic because his wife previously made a living as a fitness model, which required her to wear swimwear for photo shoots. But it was natural for a mother to hope for something different for her daughter. Just the same, playing football wasn't what she had in mind.

As for J.C., he was still too young to have a plan set for his life. One thing for certain, he had the ability to be witty and a real charmer—even to the point of being manipulative. He could convince anyone of anything, eventually convincing himself in the process.

After Kaycee's accident, Tyler and Angela didn't realize how much love was showered upon their daughter to the detriment of J.C. During those formative years, it had somewhat of an impact on J.C.'s mental wellness. As a result, Tyler and Angela tried to focus on doing

196

things that were of interest to him, including this trip.

They often referred to their son as the president-in-training. He loved the theatrics of political campaigns in particular. While Kaycee would be in one room watching sporting events, J.C. would be in the other, watching replays of powerful political speeches. If the truth were known, the youngster knew more about politics than Tyler did.

When he began to show a strong interest in history, especially as it related to America's founding, Tyler and Angela promised a trip to historic places related to the War for Independence and the creation of the United States.

He was truly in his element during the trip, pointing out certain factoids to the family as they visited Boston. He told the story of Paul Revere to his sister and the importance of the Liberty Tree. Much to Tyler's surprise, J.C. was well versed in the history of the Loyal Nine and the subsequent Sons of Liberty.

As J.C. was explaining the backstory during the family's stroll through Boston Common, the two adoring parents asked each other twice how old their son was.

"He's like a history book in a child's body," Angela had remarked as J.C. went on and on about the Boston Tea Party and other major events that had occurred in Boston.

The firefighter finished attaching everyone's harnesses, and then he turned his attention to Tyler.

"I need you guys to brace yourself and be prepared when the safety bar lifts. For hours, you've grown accustomed to it holding you back. Your body is not used to the gravity pull that you'll feel at this altitude."

"Won't the ropes help?" asked Angela.

"Yes, but everyone needs to be ready to hold themselves in place. Understand?"

Angela and Tyler looked at one another and nodded.

Tyler addressed their children. "Okay, guys. It's time to get out of here. We need you both to brace yourselves against the front of the car until the firefighter can get into position to put the other harness on J.C. It will just take a minute, right?" Tyler looked to the firefighter with hopeful eyes.

"That's right. I'll be just underneath for a moment to release the safety bar. The extra harness is sitting in the car at your feet. As soon as you're loose, I'll scramble up there and get you squared away."

"Okay," said J.C. sheepishly, still seemingly unsure about the whole operation. He felt for the single safety belt strapped loosely around his waist.

Kaycee gave the belt one final tug to tighten it and then tried to encourage her brother. "I'll help you, buddy."

J.C. nodded and prepared himself. The firefighter crawled under the car and began to crank the release mechanism. At first, the safety bar opened smoothly, and then it stopped suddenly.

"It's okay," the firefighter began. "My hand slipped on the lever."

J.C. looked over at Kaycee for reassurance, and then without warning them, the firefighter cranked the lever the rest of the way, abruptly opening the safety bar before the children were prepared for it.

"Oh no!" exclaimed the firefighter as he lost his balance and swung wildly toward the center of the Kingda Ka structure.

"Ahhhhh," screamed J.C. as his small body crashed into the edge of the coaster compartment in front of him. He toppled over the hood and began sliding downward, desperately trying to hold on.

"Grab him!"

Kaycee was trying to hold onto his jeans, but J.C. kept sliding downward, slipping through her grasp. She grabbed one ankle, causing him to spin sideways until all she had was his shoe.

"Daaad!" plead Kaycee as she struggled to brace herself and hold onto her brother.

"Help!" screamed J.C.

Tyler hooked his right arm through the lifted safety bar and swung outside the car like an acrobat performing a high-wire act. He reached for J.C.'s leg with his left arm, but it was too late. His foot slipped out of his sneaker, leaving J.C. and his shoe careening toward the ground.

CHAPTER 49

Delta Flight 322

Using the seat backs, Cort pulled himself deeper into the water, quickly moving past several dead bodies that were stuck in their seatbelts or who'd been knocked unconscious from the overhead luggage. He'd lost count of the number of rows he'd passed, but when the curtains separating the first-class seating from the main cabin floated in front of his face, he knew he was there.

Cort wrestled with the curtains, which fluttered around his body. He grabbed the partition wall and heaved himself forward into first class. He quickly became disoriented, unable to remember where Congressman Pratt was seated. At first, he looked to his right, not realizing that the aircraft was upside down. The seats were empty.

Relieved, he turned his body around and planned to swim straight up the aisle to the aft exit. As he grasped the headrests to use them as a catapult, he felt hair. Cort reached into the dark water, grasping the seats on the other side of the aircraft for leverage.

He felt the unmistakable portly, bloated corpse of Congressman Pratt. The man was still strapped into his seat with his life vest around his neck. It had been inflated and wedged his body between the seat back in front of him, which had been fully reclined. The congressman had drowned having never had the opportunity to leave his seat.

Cort shook his head and closed his eyes. There was nothing he could do, so he focused on his own survival. Propelling himself upward using his arms like oars against the seat backs, Cort floated toward his row, where much-needed oxygen awaited.

However, upon reaching the exit rows and his original seat 26-C, there was no oxygen. Only water. The plane must have slipped deeper toward the bottom of the Gulf.

Cort kept swimming. Row after row, he expected the water to end and the much-needed oxygen to appear. It didn't. He looked upward toward the tail section. The faint glow of starlight was gone.

He stopped. *Did the plane shift? Am I swimming down now? Deeper into the water?* Panic set in. He didn't want to drown.

Cort tried to relax his body and mind. He had to decide. Go back to the exit row, or continue toward the tail section?

He thought quickly and then removed a seat cushion next to him. The buoyant effect would answer the question. He released it and it gradually floated toward the aft exit door. Cort didn't hesitate and chased it up the aisle, grabbing another seat cushion as he went. His legs kicked at the water, forcing his body past the lavatories and out of the plane through the exit door.

But it still wasn't over.

Using the seat cushion to aid him toward the surface, he kicked as hard as he could, mustering all of his energy and will to reach the surface. But he was fading.

The average person can hold their breath for thirty to sixty seconds. Cort, who remained in excellent physical condition by playing basketball at the congressional gym, was in better shape than most.

The instinct not to breathe underwater was so strong that it overcame the agony and feeling of helplessness when a person was running out of air. No matter how desperate a drowning person became, the body's innate desire to inhale didn't occur until it was on the edge of losing consciousness.

At that point, the body's bloodstream became filled with carbon dioxide, and the amount of oxygen diminished. The chemical sensors in the brain triggered an involuntary breath, one that cannot be suppressed willfully, whether the body was underwater or not.

Neurologists call this the *break point*. It usually happens after eighty-seven seconds. Some physicians refer to the brain's reaction as *neurological optimism.* It was as if the brain had made an irrational determination—*holding my breath is killing me, and breathing in might not, so I might as well breathe in.*

When the first involuntary breath was taken, most people were still conscious. In a way, it was unfortunate because there weren't many things more unpleasant than gasping for air only to have water forced into your lungs instead. Drowning was a horrible way to die.

Cort had entered a state of voluntary apnea when he took that last deep breath and descended into the plane in search of Congressman Pratt. That was two minutes ago. He had reached his *break point* when voluntary apnea becomes involuntary. A point where his next spasmodic breath would drag water into his mouth and down his windpipe. A point where the Gulf of Mexico would flood his lungs and end any transfer of oxygen to the blood.

His final breath.

The process of drowning made it harder and harder not to drown. The body became akin to a sinking boat, with its destiny the bottom of the ocean.

For Michael Cortland, former basketball player at Yale, as well as loving husband and father, the clock was running out. He was half-conscious and weakened by oxygen depletion. He was in no position to fight his way back to the surface. Fate had caught up with him.

His destiny.

CHAPTER 50

Times Square
New York City

A dirty bomb looked no different than any other conventional explosive, but it was wrapped in radioactive materials. Bundles of cobalt-60 or strontium-90 could take the most common ordnance and create radioactive dust clouds capable of causing severe sickness or death in millions who came in contact with the material. The cleanup costs associated with the widely dispersed radioactive particles could cost trillions of dollars, not to mention the fact the affected areas might have to be abandoned for many years or even decades.

As the quadcopter drones buzzed through the skies of Manhattan, dropping their payloads around Times Square, as well as near Grand Central Station, the island's transportation hub, widely dispersed particles of radioactive material blanketed Midtown New York. The dust was inhaled or absorbed into the body, but it didn't necessarily kill immediately. It could potentially hasten the demise of those whose immune systems were weak due to a previous cancer or other diseases.

Those who justify the use of dirty bombs as a humane form of warfare argue that, like an electromagnetic pulse attack, it's not a weapon of mass destruction but, rather, a weapon of mass disruption. In the attackers' minds, immediate body count was the standard by which the use of a weapon should be judged. Not fear.

The quadcopters delivered a deadly blow to New York City, one that wouldn't be fully understood for days or weeks. In addition to the panic, and the deaths that resulted therefrom, the financial center of the world would suffer an unimaginable economic calamity.

Tom knew about the threat, as he'd studied the subject extensively after a Thanksgiving Day conversation with Willa. She'd warned him that drone warfare would be used by terrorists in the years to come. He just didn't imagine it would happen so soon. He pushed the conversation into the back of his mind. For now, his focus needed to be on their survival.

"Donna, this is very important," he said calmly to his gimpy wife. "You have to keep this scarf wrapped around your face as tight as possible. I'm gonna keep my sweatshirt pulled over my nose and mouth."

"Tom, is there poison in the air?"

"Sort of. Maybe. I mean, possible radioactive material. Listen, you won't smell it and nobody will know they're ingesting it. But, trust me, it's there."

"I don't know if I can walk and hold this in place too." She looked down at her right leg, which was bent at the knee to keep pressure off her ankle.

"You're not gonna have to worry about that because I'm gonna carry you."

"Really?"

"Yes, ma'am. Really, just like I did the day we got married."

Tom couldn't see his bride's grin, but he could see her eyes smiling at him. "Okay, but I'm a little chubbier than back in the day."

"Well, I'm not that skinny kid from Beaufort, South Carolina, anymore either." Tom stretched out the name of his hometown, pronounced BYOO-fert, out of habit. The town's pronunciation was often confused with the coastal town of Beaufort, North Carolina, which was pronounced BOH-fert. Residents of both these Southern towns were quick to correct Yankees who got it wrong.

Donna, who was a Charlestonian through and through, mocked him from time to time and couldn't resist in this tense moment. "Okay, my BYOO-tiful husband, carry me up to your lair and have your way with me."

Tom rolled his eyes and laughed. "Okay, Miz Shelton, here we go."

With a grunt he swept her up in his arms, and the two momentarily touched their foreheads to one another. Tom moved along the Avenue of the Americas under the canopy-designed entrance to the block-wide office building until he made his way to the corner of West Forty-Fifth Street.

They were only a couple of blocks away from Times Square, and in the fifteen minutes since the bombs had begun to detonate, the crowd had thinned somewhat, scattering throughout Midtown Manhattan like millions of mice fleeing a giant cat.

He turned against the flow of people who were pushing and shoving their way down Forty-Fifth Street. Using the canopy as cover down the left side of the street, he noticed that Connolly's Pub across the street had been broken into, and people were stepping over the broken plate glass to get inside. Ignoring the melee as people fought to seek cover, he pushed forward until he saw the orange flags marking the entrance to the Hyatt Centric. Now his challenge was to cross the street.

Donna turned her head and saw the problem. "Should we wait until they pass?"

"It's a steady stream of people, and the longer we're in the open, the more dangerous it is. Hold me tight, Donna. I'm gonna need my arms to push people out of the way as we go across."

Donna gripped her husband's neck and shoulders so that her arms supported her own weight. Tom studied the flow of people. There were too many. Then he noticed the temporary sawhorse barricades put into place by the city. Most were toppled over, but one was pushed to the side next to a FreshDirect delivery van parked in front of Bobby Van's restaurant to their left.

"Here we go!" exclaimed Tom as he made his way alongside the delivery truck and tucked the barricade under his arm. It was heavy, as was Donna, but adrenaline and love fueled him.

Using the barricade as a battering ram at first, and then a method of diverting the crowd as he turned it sideways, the masses slowed and began to divide in the center of the street as he moved across. When he was close enough to reach the sidewalk in front of the Hyatt, he dropped the barricade, which allowed him to run the final ten feet to avoid the stubbornly approaching mass of people.

Tom's breathing became laborious and his chest was heaving from the extraordinary effort he'd given to get them across the street. Relieved, he took a moment to catch his breath and gently set Donna on the ground. With him leading the way and Donna hopping close behind, they kept their bodies pressed against the granite wall as they inched closer to the revolving glass doors of the hotel.

When they reached the overhang to the Hyatt hotel entrance, a new challenge presented itself. Getting inside.

CHAPTER 51

Will Hightower's Home
Atlantic Station
Midtown Atlanta, Georgia

They made their way to Will's truck and drove in silence as they traveled up Northside Drive toward Midtown. Will didn't bother to check in with the stadium's headquarters or the Security Management Team. Following the evacuation order, the entire stadium had emptied to make way for Atlanta's bomb squad and the SWAT team. FBI vans were pulling up to the stadium exits as Will led his kids in the direction of their car.

The kids were somewhat in a state of shock. Neither spoke as they fought traffic, which was also fleeing the area surrounding the stadium. Besides the frightening event's impact upon their emotions, it was late and several hours past Skylar's bedtime. Ethan's injury likely caused his body to be exhausted as well.

He glanced at the clock on his truck's radio. It was just after midnight. He shook his head and closed his eyes for a second while he waited for the traffic signal to change. He angrily tapped the steering wheel with his fingers, berating himself for the decision to take the kids to the concert and agreeing to work that night.

The fact of the matter was that he needed to earn the double-time pay to cover his upcoming credit card bill, which included the Christmas gifts he'd bought for the kids. For a paycheck-to-paycheck guy like Will, just because Christmas came along and gifts were purchased didn't mean he got an instant raise to cover the out-of-the-ordinary expense.

He'd learned that lesson the first year of divorce when, out of a sense of guilt, he'd overspent on the children's presents. Their joy and appreciation meant nothing in January when he tried to juggle his credit card bills with his child-support obligations. Karen certainly didn't give him a pass due to his Christmas generosity. The squabble with her resulted in a six-month hiatus during which he wasn't allowed to see his children, and his phone contacts were limited by their mother.

Now another holiday had resulted in him stepping in a pile of crap again.

Way to go, dad of the year. This was a New Year's my kids will never forget. Nor will their mother. Nor will I. Their mother will make sure of that.

As he turned off Northside Drive toward his home in the Atlantic Station neighborhood of Midtown, Will turned on the radio to listen to the local news reports of what had happened at Mercedes-Benz Stadium that night. He reached for his phone to see if his ex-wife had called, freaking out over the safety of her children with the *unfit parent*, a term she often threw in his face when he underpaid his monthly support.

There was no call or message from Karen. There also wasn't any news of the evacuation of the stadium. There were bigger, more deadly events taking place around the country.

Will quickly turned off the radio so his kids couldn't hear.

What was happening? Was this a coordinated attack? Terrorists?

Will's mind raced until he pulled into the driveway of the small turn-of-the-century craftsman-style home located near the shopping and restaurant district of Atlantic Station. The home suited his needs perfectly. He was in walking distance to the MARTA station, shopping, and entertainment, although he never indulged himself. Also, it was intended to provide the kids a sense of normalcy when they visited him, rather than staying in a condo or apartment somewhere.

"Hey, kids, here we are. Ethan, do you need some help inside?"

"No, I'm good," he responded sleepily.

"Sky, are you awake?"

"Yes, Daddy. Is it time for happy New Year?"

Will smiled and chuckled. From what he'd just heard on the radio, he wondered.

"It sure is, baby girl. Happy New Year to you both. Son, you keep that compress on your head and I'll get the luggage. Can you unlock the door with your free hand?"

"Yeah," he responded. He pulled the shirt away from the gash and touched it with his fingers. "It stopped bleeding. Do you want your shirt?"

Will laughed. "Nah, I probably won't need it anymore. Who knows? Come on, it's kinda chilly out here. Let's get you both cleaned up and settled in bed. I'm pretty sure we'll all sleep in tomorrow."

Ethan led the way up the sloped sidewalk to the front door and entered the foyer. Skylar sleepily followed him inside while Will carried all the bags. He dropped them just inside the door and closed it behind him.

"Let's get some lights on," he said as he walked into the darkened home and flipped on as many switches as he could reach quickly. The downstairs of the two-story home consisted of a living room together with a kitchen/dining area. Three bedrooms and two baths were upstairs. "Why don't you guys take a seat on the couch while I get some wet towels and bandages to take care of Ethan's busted noggin'."

"Daddy, can we turn on the New Year's party in New York?"

Will's face turned ashen and he quickly responded. His children had seen enough excitement for one night. "No, baby girl. We missed it anyway, and it's late for you both. Let's get your brother fixed up and you guys settled in bed."

He led them to the couch, and to ensure they followed his instructions, he slyly retrieved the cable box remote off the sofa table and slid it into his pocket.

Will gathered up what he needed to attend to Ethan's wound together with one of his Philadelphia Phillies sweatshirts to replace his son's bloodstained shirt. When he returned to the living room,

Ethan was standing in front of a painting on the wall above the fireplace.

"Hey, Dad, what's this? I don't remember it from the first time we were here."

Will hesitated and then responded, "Oh, that. It's a painting."

"Of a triangle, Daddy?" asked Skylar.

"Well, not exactly a triangle, baby girl, although it looks like one. It's a Greek symbol or, in this case, a letter."

Will helped Ethan remove his bloody shirt and then gently pulled the Phillies sweatshirt over his head, avoiding the wound in the process. He used a warm, wet cloth to wipe the dried blood off his face and then used alcohol wipes to cleanse the wound.

Finally, he applied Polysporin ointment rather than the more commonly used Neosporin. They both had the same active ingredients except Neosporin also contained neomycin, which had been associated with allergic reactions and contact dermatitis.

"Daddy, why do you have a Greek letter on your wall?" his daughter innocently persisted out of curiosity.

Will thought about his answer. "Well, it's sort of, um, part of a club that I'm involved with. You know, like a second job."

"What's it stand for?" asked Ethan.

"Delta."

CHAPTER 52

Six Flags Great Adventure
Jackson, New Jersey

J.C. plummeted in a free fall for nearly thirty feet before the safety rope halted his descent. The belt harness around his waist knocked the breath out of him, and he began to gasp for air. Bent over at the waist, his arms and legs dangled toward the ground.

The rope, which was now stretched between the safety bars, was swinging back and forth slightly, but at that height, it moved J.C.'s body ten to fifteen feet with each swing.

"Hold on, honey!" yelled Angela.

Tyler swung around and positioned himself in the car where J.C. had been sitting. "Grab the rope, everyone. Angela, grab the rope and pull!"

Tyler wedged his legs into the hood of the coaster car to gain leverage. Kaycee crawled behind him and straddled his back to get into a tug-of-war position. Behind them, Angela wedged herself into a crouched position so she could use her legs to pull the safety rope too.

"Hang on, buddy, we'll get you!" shouted Tyler.

Although they couldn't see J.C. because he was hanging out of view, they could hear and feel him struggling.

"Can't breathe," they could hear J.C. whisper in between gasps.

Tyler had dealt with this before, both as a lifeguard and as an emergency medical technician. When a sudden force is applied to the abdomen, it puts pressure on a group of nerves at the pit of the stomach. This causes a spasm of the body's diaphragm. Instead of

210

functioning to pull air into the lungs when the body breathes, it stops functioning temporarily, which results in a lack of air to the lungs.

He knew he had to keep J.C. calm and encouraged him to take deep breaths. His body would recover shortly as long as there weren't other internal injuries.

"Keep cool, J.C. You've got this!" shouted Kaycee.

"Try to take deep breaths, son. You're almost here."

The three of them continued to tug at the rope, hand over hand, until J.C. was rising a foot at a time. Their frantic tugs were working, and the slack in the rope began to pool around Tyler's feet.

He could hear J.C. heaving, his young chest inhaling air too fast. Tyler didn't need him to hyperventilate now. With his head below his body, it would be easy for him to become unconscious.

"We have to hurry," he growled as he urged Angela and Kaycee on. They continued to pull the safety rope until J.C.'s back appeared at the sloped hood of the coaster.

"There he is!" shouted Angela. "There he is!"

The three of them kept pulling until the youngest Rankin was in easy grasp of Tyler. He grabbed his safety belt and pulled him into the coaster until he was cradled in his lap.

"We've got you, son," said Tyler as tears streamed down his face.

Angela was leaning against the back of the seat and stretched her arm through so she could touch J.C.'s arm. The family continued to cry tears of joy until Kaycee finally spoke up.

"Dad, you're squishing me."

Tyler had been forcing his legs against the front of the car and pressing his back into Kaycee to get leverage. During the tugging process to retrieve J.C., Kaycee didn't notice the pain as she worked with her parents to save her brother. Now she realized her dad had forgotten about her being behind him.

"Oh, sorry, honey," said Tyler as he relaxed his body somewhat. This allowed Kaycee to squirm in the seat and get more comfortable.

J.C. turned his head upward and wiped the snot running out of his nose and onto his dad's shirt. His tone was sincere. "I'm never riding a roller coaster again. Never. Got it?"

The family erupted in laughter just as two firefighters arrived on both sides of their car to assist.

CHAPTER 53

Congress Heights
Washington, DC

Hayden reached the bottom of the ladder and was immediately hugged by one of the women. Tears streamed from her eyes as she thanked Hayden over and over for returning.

"I told you I'd return," started Hayden before the woman interrupted.

"Shhh. You must speak softly. The man might hear you."

"What man?"

"He was just here, and he was very angry. His eyes were wild and red, like a demon. He asked about a tall woman in a long coat, and I knew he was searching for you. He looked evil and smelled like liquor."

Hayden cowered somewhat and immediately looked around the tunnel for her attacker. "What did you do?"

"I told him you went farther into the tunnel along the tracks. He believed me and left. But he might come back, so we must hurry."

Hayden exhaled and began passing out instructions. She sent the mother of the toddler up the stairs first, followed by a young boy of seven or eight years old. Hayden picked up the toddler and held her tight against her chest. The young child wrapped her arms and legs around Hayden.

With her hands free, she immediately climbed the ladder behind the first two to escape the hellish conditions in the tunnel. Once topside, she breathed in the fresh air and prepared herself for the next, more difficult task.

She shook her arms to relax and then descended the rungs once again. At the bottom, she sent the remaining women and children up the ladder one by one until she was last, along with the young girl and her badly sprained ankle.

Hayden helped the girl to her feet and placed her hands on both her shoulders. "Okay, are you ready to do this?"

The young girl nodded her head.

"Good. Now, how much do you weigh?"

"Forty-two pounds."

Hayden allowed herself a chuckle. "Well, you are a very pretty forty-two-pounder."

"I'm afraid," the young girl began to whimper and then added, "but I want to be brave too."

Hayden knelt in front of her and smiled. "Honey, being brave doesn't mean not being afraid. It means being afraid and doing it anyway."

The little girl wiped away her tears and nodded, acknowledging that she was ready to go.

Hayden turned around in her crouch and faced the ladder. She instructed the child to wrap her arms around Hayden's neck and her legs around her waist. The child groaned slightly as she tucked her heels tight into Hayden's midsection, but she'd developed a newfound form of bravery thanks to Hayden's encouraging words.

With a deep breath to gather all of her strength, Hayden began to slowly climb upward, focusing on one rung at a time while offering reassuring words to the child, who held her in a death grip. Minutes later, they safely arrived to reunite with everyone.

After several minutes of muted celebration, Hayden led the group away from the freeway and toward the west of the air vent. As they walked through the empty field, more buildings came into view, and when she saw a Lifeflight helicopter soar over their heads, she knew they were heading in the direction of Unity Healthcare hospital near the intersection of Martin Luther King Jr. Avenue and Malcolm X Avenue.

"Follow me," she instructed as the group continued toward the lighted buildings. The young girl with the sprained ankle hobbled along with the assistance of her mother and the other woman. Hayden carried the youngest child and did her best to keep control of the three other children, who were now enjoying the adventure.

The group reached MLK Avenue and began walking down the sidewalk. Cars sped past in both directions, ignoring the group, which was obviously hobbling along. Hayden didn't want to flag down a car and lend the appearance they were in distress. Instead, she powered up her phone and navigated to her Uber app.

She summoned two cars, one for the group of women and children to pile into for further delivery to the hospital. The other for her to get home. This had been a New Year's Eve to remember.

She rode in silence as the driver made his way to her condominium overlooking the Potomac River. The Jamaican-born woman was playing reggae music that Hayden enjoyed, so rather than immediately turning to her smartphone to determine the cause of the power outage, she chose to relax, allowing her two worlds to meet, and think about what she would do first when she got home. Pop a bottle of Cabernet or take a shower. Or both.

After paying the driver a handsome tip in cash, she made her way through the secured entrance and was pleased that the lobby of her building was devoid of neighbors. She looked like a hot mess and smelled even worse. After steeling her nerves for yet another elevator ride, she found her way to the top floor of the building. Her body was flooded with emotion and relief as she entered her home.

Hayden, who lived alone, didn't hesitate to strip all of her grimy clothes off and left them in a pile by the front door. She looked around for a moment and considered turning on the lights but allowed the glow from the city to serve as the minimal light she needed to find her way to the shower.

"Prowler, where are you? You are an insubordinate, ungrateful cat. I know your mommy stinks like, um, subway, sewer, and dumpster combined. But I could really use a friend right now."

It was not unusual for her Maine coon cat to punish Hayden when he'd been left alone all day. He was stubbornly independent and smarter than any dog she'd ever had. She suspected the long separation of the day and the stench, which had filled the usually clean-smelling condo, kept Prowler hidden somewhere, which was hard to do considering his size. He weighed more than the toddler she'd carried up the ladder earlier.

When she walked past the kitchen, she noticed it was almost midnight, but that didn't matter anymore. Hayden found the shower and spent the first five minutes allowing the hot water to wash away the memories of the evening. Refreshed, she prepared to celebrate with her best friend, assuming they were on speaking terms again.

Hayden dried off the excess water, brushed out her hair, and cuddled up in her favorite plush robe. As soon as she arrived in the kitchen and flicked on the lights, Prowler emerged from a darkened corner of the open loft and immediately began walking figure eights through her legs.

"Oh, I see how it is. In my time of need, you pretend to be sleeping. Now that I'm all cleaned up, we're besties again."

Hayden quickly fed Prowler a plastic tub of Purina Beneful real beef dog food—his favorite. He was mostly a dog anyway.

After the day she'd had, a glass of Cabernet was much preferred to her Perrier. She poured a glass and immediately took a sip, allowing the warmth to ease down her throat. She made her way into the living area and retrieved the remote off her coffee table.

Without looking, she powered on her television and moseyed over to the floor-to-ceiling windows of her condo to admire the views of the Potomac and the city beyond. The news anchor interrupted her thoughts and quickly grabbed her attention.

"We have breaking news from New York."

Hayden tilted her head and said, "New York? Don't you mean Washington?"

She spun around, and the chaotic scene that filled the screen was unfathomable.

CHAPTER 54

Hyatt Centric Times Square
New York City

With the presence of the Clintons in the hotel, Secret Service protection was extraordinary. Now that New York City was under attack, the Hyatt had been placed on lockdown. They were refusing to grant access to anyone except registered guests. Tom had their room key card in his pocket and was also able to use his phone to show the email confirming their reservation. He was certain he could get inside except for the crowd of people in his way, cramming themselves against the glass entry.

Most of the crowd was not staying at the hotel. They were only panicked revelers seeking a safe haven. The security personnel at the single entrance door next to the revolving doors, which had been locked, were growing increasingly frustrated with the interlopers. He threatened to close the hotel to everyone, causing an immediate uproar from those guests like the Sheltons who were trying to gain entry.

"Out of my way!" shouted a man from the rear of the pack on the far side of the entrance.

"If you're not staying here, go somewhere else," yelled another.

"Screw you! We need help!" a woman near the front responded.

"Screw me? No, screw you!" the second man bellowed before grabbing the woman by the back of the coat and pulling her onto the ground. The pack immediately inched forward to fill the void left by her flailing body, which was getting kicked and stepped on.

People began pushing and shoving. The security personnel started screaming at them to calm down. Tom looked back and forth to assess his options. All he needed was an opening, just enough to push his way to the front so he could show the security guards his key card and identification.

They say you should never shout fire in a crowded theater to avoid causing an unnecessary panic. In this day and age, fire didn't frighten anybody, but yelling *gun* did. Tom took a risk that might backfire, but it was all he had.

He turned to Donna and whispered, "Dear, be ready to follow me. We'll only have a few seconds."

Donna stared in his eyes and nodded. "I'm ready."

"Keep your hands on my shoulder for support. Here we go."

Tom took a deep breath, studied the people blocking their access to the door one more time, and then he shouted as loud as he could to be heard over the scrum gathered around the entrance.

"Gun! Everybody run! He's got a gun!"

His gamble paid off. Shrieks of fear filled the air as those at the back of the pack immediately ran into the oncoming masses of people still fleeing Times Square.

As some of the people gathered around the door repeated the word *gun*, those close to the door followed their lead, assuming that the gunman was in close proximity to Tom's voice. They created an opening, and Tom and Donna shot the gap, slipping between the wall and the group trying to escape his voice.

Within seconds, he'd reached the plate-glass door and pressed his room key card together with his driver's license against the glass door.

The security guard scrolled through an iPad and found Tom's name on the guest list. He shouted above the fracas, "Room number?"

"Twenty-six twenty-six!" Tom shouted back.

The security guard turned the key in the lock, opening it slightly. He grabbed Tom by the arm to pull him inside. Donna hopped along behind her husband just as the security guard forced the door shut on a man who tried to force himself inside.

Donna groaned in pain as her injured ankle got caught in the door, but she quickly shook it off. They were safe, for now.

Tom helped his wife through the lobby filled with suddenly sober hotel guests discussing the evening's events. Many were speculating the nation was under attack based upon the news reports. Tom glanced at the monitors in the lobby bar and noticed CNN was broadcasting from several locations around the country.

He decided there would be time to catch up on what had happened after he and Donna were safely in their room. They stopped by the front desk and requested an ACE bandage out of the hotel's medical supplies. The staff also provided him a bottle of ibuprofen. After the assistant manager reminded Tom and Donna about the RICE method of dealing with sprains—rest, ice, compression, and elevation—they made their way to the room and quickly found the bed, where the two collapsed in exhaustion.

After several minutes of relative silence in which the only noise they heard was the sound of screaming coming from twenty-six floors below, Tom suggested they get out of their clothes. He didn't want any radioactive particles on their other belongings.

Once they'd changed, he bundled the clothes up in the duvet cover and stuffed it into the closet. Then he wrapped Donna's ankle and slipped out of the room to retrieve a couple of buckets of ice—one for the ankle and the other for the champagne they'd intended to drink at midnight.

"Tom, are we gonna talk about what's going on? How could terrorists miss detection by Tommie and the government?"

Tom walked to the window to look down at the chaotic scene. A gust of cold wind rattled the window, some of which penetrated the window jamb to blow the sheer curtain panel to his right. Alarmed, he grabbed the plastic rods and hurriedly closed the sheers and the heavy drapes. Then he leaned over and turned off the ventilation to the room.

"Tom?"

"I'm sorry," he replied. "Just a precaution."

He sighed and sat on the bed next to her, staring at the television monitor mounted on the wall above the dresser. He'd hesitated to turn it on. In a way, he wanted them to decompress for a minute before taking on any more bad news. Tom chuckled to himself as he wondered if sometimes the *ostrich's head in the sand concept* was a good one.

Donna persisted. "Tell me what you think, honey."

He was about to answer when he heard his iPhone vibrate on the round table sitting in a corner near the window. With a slight grunt, Tom lifted himself off the sofa and retrieved his phone. He stared down at the display, using his thumb to scroll through several messages he'd received from their daughters. But those were not the text messages that grabbed his attention.

Tom read it to himself. It wasn't designated *eyes only,* a phrase he'd grown accustomed to seeing while at Joint Base Charleston. This came from another source, one that he'd avoided contact with for years.

The real danger on the ocean, as well as the land, is people.

Fare thee well and Godspeed, Patriot!

MM

CHAPTER 55

USA Health University Trauma Center

"What do we have?" asked a male surgeon as he pushed through the curtain in the emergency room at the USA Health University Trauma Center in downtown Mobile.

The trauma nurse was quick to reply, "Doctor, we've cleared the airway and the patient is experiencing mildly labored breathing. We've trialed him with oxygen by face mask at a rate of fifteen liters of oh-two per minute. Initially, our goal of SaPO2 will be ninety-two to ninety-six percent." Monitoring the SaPO2 levels allowed trauma personnel to check a drowning patient's pulmonary functions and blood-oxygen saturation levels.

"Has he regained consciousness?"

"No, sir."

"Okay, continue monitoring him. If you detect a decline in his ventilatory status or SaPO2, find me stat. We'll move on to endotracheal intubation if necessary."

"Yes, Doctor."

"Oh, one more thing. If he comes to and is able to increase his breathing efforts without requiring extraordinary support, we'll need to move him out of the ER. We are seeing patients on gurneys in the waiting room."

"Yes, sir."

Cort was alive, but unconscious. He was unable to breathe without the assistance of the face mask and mechanical ventilator. Oblivious to what was going on around him, he lay in the emergency room for more than an hour on the respirator. And nobody knew his identity.

When he first regained consciousness, he had been moved to a recovery room on the second floor. Although he was still breathing through a face mask, he had awakened long enough for the trauma team to determine that he was going to fully recover.

He recalled nothing of what had happened after he'd blacked out somewhere near the sunken aircraft. Sore and exhausted, Cort tried to open his eyes to observe his surroundings. He couldn't.

He tried to raise his arm and then he attempted to wiggle his feet. Although he had feelings in his extremities, he felt like he was wrapped in a cocoon.

Cort's conscious mind was returning. He recalled the plane crash and being underwater. He'd swum for an eternity until he couldn't. He couldn't remember if he gave up or if he was helped. It was all pushed to a dark corner in the back of his brain.

He heard voices and tried to open his eyes again. Suddenly, his eyelid was opened and a flashlight rudely blasted his retina. The sudden intrusion of light triggered nerve impulses that passed through the optic nerve to his brain, resulting in a knee-jerk reaction.

Cort simply squirmed. But that was all it took to bring smiles to the three health care providers huddled around his bed.

"Well, sir, welcome back to the land of the living. I am Dr. Kenny Wayne."

Cort tried to talk, but his throat hurt. He subconsciously tried to reach for his throat and relieve the pain, but couldn't.

"Hang on, sir. Let us help you. Nurse, go ahead and remove his face mask."

Cort's eyes were fully open, and he glanced around the room, searching for his wife and daughter. He mouthed the word *wife*. Enough air passed over his larynx that one of the nurse's smiled and nodded her head.

"Wife?" she asked.

Cort nodded.

She continued. "Sir, do you also have a lovely daughter? Around six to eight years old."

Cort managed a smile and nodded. Tears began to flow from his eyes. He blinked rapidly as the salty fluid flooded his eye sockets. He'd had enough salt water for one day. Or a lifetime, for that matter.

The nurse took a tissue off the table next to Cort's bed and dabbed his eyes. Cort smiled and nodded in appreciation.

"Are you Michael?"

He nodded again.

She dabbed his eyes again and whispered to him, "I know exactly where to find them. Now, you listen to the doctor while I go downstairs and fetch them for you."

For the next five minutes, the doctor explained the ins and outs of Cort's near-drowning experience. He was told about how he had popped up out of the water unexpectedly near the life raft full of people. Nobody knew how to perform CPR, but the rescue boats from both Mobile and Pensacola had surrounded the area within minutes of the airplane crashing into the water. Cort was lucky. It was not his time.

"Of course, we'll keep you overnight for observation to see how you do now that you've been removed from oxygen. If your vitals continue to stabilize, your lungs hold up as they appear to be, and your mentation remains normal, we should be able to get you out of here tomorrow."

He tried to focus on the doctor's words and instructions regarding his care, but his mind was elsewhere. His eyes kept darting toward the door, hoping that each set of footsteps he heard were Meredith and Hannah.

The doctor sensed that Cort wasn't paying attention and finally congratulated him on surviving. He promised to check back in on him, and Cort smiled and mouthed the words *thank you*.

The room was empty again, and Cort became somewhat depressed, as the nurse had not yet returned with his family. Cort wiggled around under the blanket and pulled his arms loose. He hated being confined, and his body was nice and toasty, too much so, in fact.

He reached around the side of the bed until he found the wired remote, which allowed him to adjust his bed positioning and operate the television mounted in the corner of the room. Cort pushed the button that raised him up to a more seated position. Then he turned on the television.

CNN filled the screen, and images of emergency rescue vehicles with their lights on and first responders scrambling about depicted a chaotic event. Cort expected to see the plane crash on the news. Instead, the scene was in New York's Times Square.

The chyron read *Dirty bomb attacks in NYC.*

Then the screen switched to Atlanta. The scene there was similar. *Possible terrorist attack at Atlanta concert.*

A split screen then appeared showing Philadelphia, Pennsylvania, in complete darkness without power. Cort turned up the volume.

"As midnight approached, residents along the New Jersey and Pennsylvania border reported seeing a bright streak of light followed by the power grid collapsing. Local and state authorities have not issued any formal statements although we've learned through the Department of Homeland Security that this collapse of the grid was caused by some type of electromagnetic pulse."

Cort heard footsteps running down the hallway, and he quickly turned down the volume. He focused his attention on the doorway. Hannah rushed through first and raced to his bedside. Her smile stretched across her face and drew his attention away from her red, bloodshot eyes caused by her crying. He hugged her and then looked over her shoulder to his darling wife.

Meredith stood in the doorway with one arm folded in front of her, and the other dabbing at her wet eyes. She looked down shyly and then the waterworks opened up. She couldn't contain her exuberance as she rushed to Cort's side.

The three of them held each other, transferring their love to one another without speaking.

After a moment, Hannah broke their embrace and spoke first. "Happy New Year's, Daddy. I brought you some champagne gummy bears. Mom said they were your favorite."

Cort grinned and looked at Meredith. He motioned for Hannah to come closer to him so he could whisper, "Mom was fibbin'. Those are her favorites."

Hannah bent over and kissed her father on the cheek. "I know, Daddy. I knew it would make her smile if I said that. She was very worried. I wasn't. I knew God would protect you."

Cort touched her sweet cheek and smiled. He then motioned for Hannah to lean over and speak to him. As she came closer, he took another glance at the television, which showed cameras and reporters gathering in the White House briefing room.

Meredith followed his eyes and then frowned at him. "You shouldn't be seeing this, Cort. Let's turn it off."

Cort shook his head side to side. He motioned her closer and whispered, "New York, Philly, Atlanta."

Meredith closed her eyes and sighed. "Can't we talk about this—"

Cort squeezed her hand and pulled her closer. "No. What happened?"

"It's much worse, Cort. DC got hit. Detroit. Chicago. LA."

Cort raised his eyebrows. "Who?" he asked in a barely audible whisper.

"They don't know. It's obviously coordinated," she replied.

Cort leaned back on the bed and closed his eyes. He thought about the timing of his flight and the limited information he had from the newscast. The total power loss on an aircraft, completely obliterating all backup systems, was unprecedented in his recollection. He immediately wondered if there was a connection to these other events.

His mind wandered to Congressman Pratt. A powerful, influential leader in Congress, now dead from some unexplainable airline catastrophe. Then he thought of himself. He had almost been killed too.

Cort's eyes grew wide and he glanced around the room before looking at the television coverage again. He didn't believe in coincidences.

Meredith noticed that he was becoming agitated. "Cort, please calm down. You have to get your rest. Please."

Cort grimaced and pulled her close to his face. He whispered again so only she could hear him.

"I have to tell you about the Haven."

CHAPTER 56

Six Flags Great Adventure
Jackson, New Jersey

It took another hour to get the family out of the coaster and down to safety. Medical personnel were on the ground to check on J.C.'s injuries and also counsel the family on the emotional trauma he might sustain. Angela, being polite, allowed the local EMTs to advise them, rather than disclose that she was fully capable of helping her son through this. Nonetheless, it did help to have J.C.'s bruises checked out by other experienced medical personnel.

The next challenge the family faced was finding their car. The only lighting in the theme park was held by park security in the form of a flashlight. They were guiding visitors to the exits and onward to their vehicles. As they walked through Six Flags, there was evidence of looting within the park.

Stores and restaurants had been trashed. J.C. picked up a Superman cape, and Kaycee found a miniature basketball with the Batman logo on it.

"Look at this place," whispered Angela. "It looks like Hurricane Michael blew through here."

Two teenage girls rushed past them, holding bundles of tee shirts under their arms. One of the security personnel flashed his light on them and began blowing a whistle, but they took off undeterred.

"Looters already," added Tyler. "You'd think people would have more important things to be concerned with."

They made their way around the turnstiles at the front and continued to walk toward the parking lot. Tyler held Kaycee's hand,

and Angela kept her arm draped around J.C.'s shoulder as they walked.

As they pushed through a crowd of people standing in front of them, they overheard some of the conversation.

"One dude said we were attacked with missiles."

"Yeah, I heard the same thing."

"Nah, man, that's stupid. Ain't nobody gonna take on the good ole U.S. of A. I think it was one of them solar flares."

"No, dude. It wasn't a solar flare. If it was, the sky would've gotten really bright. I think it was a nuke."

"Then where's the dang mushroom cloud, huh?"

Tyler pulled Kaycee a little closer and picked up the pace.

Once they were clear of the scientist wannabes, Kaycee looked up to him and asked about what she'd heard. "Dad, are we in a war?"

"Honey, I don't know and neither do those morons. They're all just guessing."

J.C. chimed in, a good sign. "I hope they didn't hit Washington." He sincerely wanted to see the sights, although Tyler knew that was impossible under the circumstances.

"Son, the good news is Washington didn't lose power, or at least that's what the police officer told me back there. But places like Philadelphia and Baltimore and, of course, New Jersey did. That makes me think it could be just one big power outage."

They continued to walk in silence as Tyler tried to remember how to get to the car without the benefit of lighting to see the lot signage. They approached another group commiserating over the circumstances.

"New York, too. Did you hear? Just as the ball was about to drop, explosions went off everywhere. People freaked out."

"Did they lose power like us?"

"No, but folks were trampled to death and poisoned, too."

"Poison?"

"Yeah, that's what I heard."

Tyler put his right hand over Kaycee's ear and pulled her head next to his side. Angela noticed and did the same to J.C. The group continued to speculate, but eventually the Rankins were out of earshot.

"I think we're down this row, Ty," said Angela as she took the lead.

"You're right, Mom," said J.C., who had suddenly perked up. "Come on, I'll race you. I can beat you with one shoe on!"

J.C. took off, sporting just one sneaker, and the rest of the family chased behind.

"Good grief," said Angela with a huff in her voice. Then Dr. Mom hollered at him, "Joseph Charles Rankin, slow down! You're supposed to be traumatized, remember?"

"Not anymore," he yelled back over his shoulder. "Now I'm a survivor like Peanut!"

Within a minute, they were huddled around the orange-and-white Ford Bronco, waiting for Tyler to open the door. Kaycee encouraged her dad to pick up the pace.

"Come on, Dad. We're freezing."

Tyler retrieved the keys from his jeans pocket and was about to unlock the door when he suddenly stopped. He stood up and looked around. There were no lights on anywhere. Including vehicles. No interior lights. No headlights. No engines could be heard.

Nothing except the slight hint of dawn beginning to arrive on a new year.

"Kids, stay here. I need to talk to your mom."

"Tyler, what's wrong?" asked Angela.

He held his index finger to his lips and motioned for her to follow him to the back of the truck. He looked around nervously and, satisfied they weren't being watched, dropped to the ground and crawled under the truck.

Angela walked around his legs and looked in all directions until Tyler rose off the ground holding a black hard-plastic gun case.

"Do you think we need that?" she asked.

"Yeah, maybe. I had to keep it hidden in the chassis because New York and Jersey frown upon the larger-capacity magazines I have."

"Tyler, we don't know anything about what's happened for sure.

After we hit the ground, the firefighters got tight-lipped and the EMTs focused on their jobs. All we've heard is from those idiots back there."

"I know, Angela, but think about it for a minute. We've got a widespread power outage, which included killing our phones. We've talked about this. It has to be some kind of EMP."

"A solar flare? Or a nuke?"

"Same result, mostly. All I know is that this place isn't safe, nor will our trip home be. The minute I fire up this truck, they'll be all over us, looking for a ride or trying to steal it."

He held out the gun case to remind her of its contents.

"Do you think we're gonna have to shoot our way out of here?"

"I hope not. But I'm sure going to be ready."

Angela ran her fingers through her hair and walked a few paces away. She looked around the parking lot and then toward the east, where the sun began to peek over the horizon. She returned to Tyler's side. "Tyler, you know what we have to do."

"Babe, I may be wrong about this. What if there's nothing wrong?"

"If you thought nothing was wrong, why did you crawl under the truck and get this." She reached forward and rapped the case twice with her knuckles.

"Well, um, I'm just—"

Angela cut her husband off. "Listen, why take chances? If we're wrong, we can always drive back home. But if we sit around Richmond, waiting on the news to tell us what's happening, it could be too late."

Tyler nodded. "It may be too late already, depending on what caused this."

"So do you agree?" she asked.

"Agreed. We have to get to the Haven."

CHAPTER 57

I-26 North of Spartanburg, South Carolina

Will fought sleep as he drove past the Landrum, South Carolina, exit. He glanced down at his fuel gauge. He had a quarter tank left in the truck and quickly did some mental calculations. He'd have to stop in an hour, but he wanted to get away from the interstate before he did. He gripped the steering wheel a little tighter and sat taller in his seat, adjusting himself as he'd done frequently since he had hastily loaded the kids back into his truck along with a dozen duffle bags stored in his pantry closet.

He stared down at the text message he'd received for what was probably the fortieth time since it came through right before he turned in several hours ago. The words were simple but meant so much.

Time to come home. H.

The decision to leave Atlanta behind was not difficult. His original choice to run away from Philadelphia was, on the surface, for the good of his children, but in reality was for Will to keep his own feeling of self-worth. He was a good man, a loving father, and, he thought, a considerate husband. Every aspect of his life was under attack and he simply needed to escape. Atlanta was the solution, and it served its purpose, until tonight. Now he'd been summoned *home*.

He'd resisted the urge to turn on the satellite radio and pick up the news from the cable news networks. The kids were confused enough already, but they were too tired to protest when he woke them after they'd been asleep for less than an hour.

Will glanced into the rearview mirror and saw each of them leaning against opposite sides of the truck, propped against pillows and covered with the comforters off their beds. To be sure, they were zonked out, but Will didn't want them to hear what was going on around them.

Hungry for information, he scrolled through his Google news feed and frequently monitored the online news sources he frequented. The events of the evening astonished him, but in a way, he'd expected them to occur at some point.

It was a matter of time.

Will drove for another hour and stopped for fuel. The sun was just beginning to rise, and he picked up two large cups of black coffee as well as some breakfast sandwiches and orange juice for all of them. It wasn't until he fired up his diesel Chevy Silverado that Ethan stirred in the back seat.

"Where are we?" he asked sleepily as he sat up in the back seat. He glanced toward the convenience store. "Hey, I really need to pee."

Will thought about the television playing inside and the chatter among the attendant and some of the locals. "Um, it's out of order. We have to rough it."

He pulled around the side of the station and allowed Ethan to jump out to relieve himself. Will checked on Skylar, who was still asleep. A moment later, Ethan piled back into the truck. Will offered him a sandwich and Ethan declined, opting instead to sleep some more.

That was fine by Will. It was not the time for explanations.

He drove another hour and a half along Old Highway 64, running parallel to the South Mountains of North Carolina, until he picked up Interstate 40. A light dusting of snow had fallen New Year's Eve, but the roads remained clear. As the sun was shining brightly, Will smiled as he admired the North Carolina landscape. It was incredibly beautiful, especially under the circumstances.

He pulled off the interstate and made his way along narrow, two-lane country roads toward his destination. The kids had awakened, and after a brief pit stop for Skylar, during which she thoroughly enjoyed making yellow snow, they arrived at the end of their journey.

Will slowed the truck and approached the entrance slowly. Stone and brick columns flanked two wrought-iron steel gates. In the center of the gates, the letter *H* stood out prominently. Will stopped the truck and lowered the window as two armed men approached.

"Dad, where are we?" asked Ethan.

Will ignored his son for now.

The man dressed in khakis and a black hooded sweatshirt leaned into the window and spoke to Will.

"Welcome home, Delta."

CHAPTER 58

Monocacy Farm
South of Frederick, Maryland
New Year's Eve

Once again, they convened. They'd come from Langley and Fort Meade, Washington and Arlington. They weren't politicians or elected officials. They were spooks, spies, and soldiers. Government officials and bureaucrats—accountable to no one but themselves.

As before, their host greeted them at the front door, braving the cold wind, which swept across the snow-covered grounds, land that had witnessed one of the bloodiest battles of the Civil War—the Battle of Monocacy. As he waited for his compatriots to arrive, he recalled the history of Monocacy Farm.

In 1864, with General Robert E. Lee's army under siege at Petersburg, Virginia, to the south, Confederate forces led by General Jubal Early conducted raids into Frederick, Maryland and the Monocacy River area. The forces of Union General Lew Wallace were overwhelmed by the Confederates and beat a hasty retreat to Baltimore.

Emboldened by their successes, General Early rallied his troops and advanced to the outskirts of Washington, a surprise move that threatened to end the war with a decisive victory by the South.

Fortunately for the Union, General Wallace was able to delay the Confederate's advance long enough to allow General Ulysses S. Grant to send a portion of his Sixth Corps to defend Washington. The veteran soldiers, rested and more capable than the tired Confederates, successfully repelled the advance and saved Washington from the clutches of the Southerners. From that point forward, the Battle of Monocacy became known as the Battle that Saved Washington.

Now there was a different battle occurring in Washington. One that involved high stakes for both sides and threatened to tear the nation apart much like it did in the 1860s. The men and women arriving at Monocacy Farm on New Year's Eve were very much aware of the consequences of the fuse that had been lit. But they considered it necessary to save a nation they believed was founded on their ideals and principles.

As the evening wore on, they weren't celebrating, although they were sharing a traditional glass of champagne. As the clock ticked closer to midnight and the new year was upon them, solemn demeanors filled the grand ballroom.

Conversations were had in the simplest terms, and some were more philosophical.

"Newton's Law of Motion posited that all forces occur in pairs such that if one object exerts a force on another object, then the second object exerts an equal and opposite reactive force on the first." One young man with a British accent could be heard speaking above the others.

An older woman responded, summarizing the theory, "For every action, there is an equal and opposite reaction."

"Exactly," replied the Brit. "That is why this evening's events will be met with resistance, but not necessarily from Washington's reaction. There will necessarily be a force that rises in opposition to us, one that is formidable in ideology, if not will."

Their host interrupted the conversation and now had the attention of everyone in the room. A hush came over the gathering as he spoke. A ray of daylight began to peek through the heavy velour drapes.

Comfortable with his command over his peers, he raised his voice so all could hear him. "The dawn of a New Year has arrived; let me be the first to propose a toast. As our friend just said, for every action, there is an equal and opposite reaction. That's to be expected. Well, the same theory applies to the concept of luck.

"One man's luck is often generated by another man's misfortunes. I, for one, believe that we can make our own luck. It will be necessary to achieve our goals as laid out in our carefully crafted plans.

"With this New Year's toast, I urge all of you to trust the plan. Know that a storm is coming. It will be a storm upon which the blood of patriots and tyrants will spill."

He raised his champagne glass into the air, and everyone in the room followed suit.

"Godspeed, Patriots!"

And so it began …

THANK YOU FOR READING
DOOMSDAY: APOCALYPSE!

If you enjoyed it, I'd be grateful if you'd take a moment to write a short review (just a few words are needed) and post it on Amazon. Amazon uses complicated algorithms to determine what books are recommended to readers. Sales are, of course, a factor, but so are the quantities of reviews my books get. By taking a few seconds to leave a review, you help me out and also help new readers learn about my work.

And before you go …

SIGN UP for Bobby Akart's mailing list to receive special offers, bonus content, and you'll be the first to receive news about new releases in the Doomsday series. Visit: www.BobbyAkart.com

VISIT Amazon.com/BobbyAkart for more information on the Doomsday series, the Yellowstone series, the Lone Star series, the Pandemic series, the Blackout series, the Boston Brahmin series and the Prepping for Tomorrow series totaling thirty-plus novels, including over twenty Amazon #1 Bestsellers in forty-plus fiction and nonfiction genres. Visit Bobby Akart's website for informative blog entries on preparedness, writing, and a behind-the-scenes look into his novels.

Made in the USA
Lexington, KY
22 January 2019